CHECKMATE

ROWAN BOWMAN

SNOWBOOKS

Proudly Published by Snowbooks in 2015

Snowbooks Ltd.
email: info@snowbooks.com

www.snowbooks.com

Printed by Nørhaven, Denmark

British Library Cataloguing in Publication Data
A catalogue record for this book is available from the
British Library.

Paperback ISBN 9781909679467
Ebook ISBN 9781909679474

For John, Will, Henry and Charlotte

1. WEDNESDAY

I look up through a tall tree at the summer sky with clouds scudding across my line of vision. Nothing happens. It's just the tree and clouds. But when I stand next to the wall of a high building, or at the foot of a monument and look up at the same clouds, the movement seems to be in the artefact, not the sky. The human intervention makes one dizzy, makes one lose the ape's perspective. Our eyes cling to the manufactured. What we make is what we are.

I make mortar, proper lime mortar. It shields masonry from rain. It flexes with the seasons and lets water pass through its matrix so that the stonework can breathe. It's caustic, of course. Get the lime in your eyes and you're blind. The mortar takes the skin off your hands. Even when you're careful your fingertips become so rough they catch on cloth. I wear a sheep's worth of lanolin rubbed into my hands each night.

Then there's him, down there, Jason Holden. He doesn't really make anything. He is standing below me, shielding his eyes from the sun as he looks up for me in the scaffolding. I see him sway with the inversed vertigo of the fleeting clouds behind me. I am quite safe; he has no head for heights.

'Hey, Malcolm,' he calls up.

'Hello. Nice afternoon.'

'Can you come down for a minute?'

It takes three and a half minutes to descend the scaffolding safely, nearly the same to get back up, and a damned sight longer for Jason to make a point. By the time he has finished whatever he has to say my mix will have gone off. I wanted to get this side of the wall mended today.

'Can't you come up?' I ask.

I can hear the irritation from forty feet away. 'Not in this suit, I can't. No.'

He means that I am his employee, and why should he come to my bidding. That, and we both know how he shakes when he leaves the ground without a business-class airline seat behind him.

The employee bit is the deciding factor. I scrape out my bucket, pushing a gallon of mortar into a fissure between the inner and outer wall. At least it's not wasted.

He's all sulks when I get down to him five minutes later.

'Sorry to keep you waiting. I didn't want to waste my mix.'

'Yes, yes. I'm in a hurry, that's all.'

I stand long enough to demonstrate my attention.

'This repair to the north turret, how much longer do you think it's going to take?'

'Another two days at least,' I guess.

'Two *days*?'

'It's a big job.'

He sighs.

'Was that all you needed?' I ask.

His eyes are drawn up the tower. He shudders a little and brings himself back down to earth.

'The building programme may have to be deferred –'

He has my full attention now.

' – the committee has just received a letter from the Jacobite Society, making a claim on the building.'

'The Castle?' I thought it belonged to the Trust. No-one tells me anything.

'There is a ninety-nine year lease on it, but apparently Lord Muck may not have had the right to sell the lease in the first place.'

Lord Muck now – it was 'sir' last week.

'That, and the vandalism,' he adds.

'Kids.'

'Health and Safety issues. If we can't secure the site, we can't have the scaffolding up.'

'I could camp here.'

'We'll see how it goes over the weekend. You may have to if it continues. Anyway, if it turns out the lease is invalid, the Trust won't want to waste any more money on the restoration.'

I must look upset. He turns away to watch a couple reading the information board.

'So, do you want me to continue today?' I ask.

'Yes, yes. You're on a rolling weekly contract?'

I'm not, so I shrug. I didn't bother asking for a written contract.

'I'll speak to the Committee. Just thought I'd better let you know what's going on. Keep you in the loop. Stop the Chinese Whispers.'

Has he finished?

'Keep the troops informed.'

Apparently not.

'Flag up the problem…'

For all he thought he was in a hurry, he's still talking platitudes into space as I reach the first level. On my mixing platform one of the polythene-lined sacks has ripped open, spilling twelve kilos of lime onto the boards. White dust eddies in the brisk breeze. I rummage in my tool bag for goggles so that I can clear it up.

♜

It's 2.00am. I have woken all chewed up with worry. I can't help it, no matter how I try to get it in proportion. I don't need the job, or the hassle. I can always get work easily enough. I think it's the Castle. I like working there, being here. It feels like I belong, I can't explain it.

There is a beam of light coming straight into my room. Now I realise what has woken me. Bloody hell, someone's standing with a flashlight pointed right at my window. The light is dazzling as I pull back the curtains. Twin circles of reflection and refraction from the double glazing dance on my retina as I throw open the window onto – nothing. The garden is black, still and silent. I only know I'm scared now that I hear my own voice.

'Who's there? What d'you want?'

Silence. Deep, rural silence. The stillness between midnight and four. It is so quiet I can hear my knee joints creak. I ought to go down, even if I don't go outside, I should check the doors and windows. I'm not sure it would help. I fix the window so that it's only open a crack and climb back into bed, listening to the absence of noise. As I sink into sleep I remember that the beam of light was level with my window, not angled from below.

2.THURSDAY

I'm up a tree when Clara, older sister to Lord Muck, spots me. She is smiling, but we both know what she means when she asks, 'Having fun up there, Mack?'

There is no reply, so I don't make one. I haven't found anywhere that someone could stand to send a beam of light straight through my bedroom window. Even from up in the ash tree the line of sight is into the very corner of my room, not directly above my pillow. The lichen on the bark puts grey stripes on my jeans as I slide down the last eight feet.

Clara holds the gate open for me as I cross to the boundary. She is seeing me off her property in the most polite way. I wish I did not rent my cottage from Muck's estate. I manage to return her look of faint amusement.

'You still haven't mended the cracked slab on the water-table above the tearooms.'

She still hasn't paid me for the pier caps on the drive gates. No point mentioning this – we both know she has no intention of doing so.

'You would be better off getting a slater. You complained when I spoiled the flower beds underneath last time, and I only have scaffolding, not long ladders.'

She makes a face of annoyance. Masculine, but so close to a snarl a man could never get away with it without a fight. You can see the family temper, never far off, whenever any of them let their guard down.

'The estate doesn't have a slater,' she says.

No, but she could always find one in the directory and pay them the going rate.

My mobile phone rings. I make excuses so that she leaves me to answer it. It's Melissa.

Clara starts the Range Rover, so I miss what Mel is saying. Maybe I'll see her tonight.

'I miss you.' I mean it.

'For pity's sake, Mack—'

'I must have misheard—'

She rings off.

✗

The sun has come out by the time I have changed my dew-soaked trainers for work boots in the porch. I return Melissa's call at the foot of the stairs; it's not good when she's angry, phone calls day and night. I leave a wheedle rather than an apology. I am not a doormat.

The kitchen is cold – the window is open. Sudden wariness gives way to relief when Robin emerges from the pantry with a milk carton. The relief makes me babble.

'You gave me a turn, there, Father. Did you fly in through the window?'

'A bit stuffy. You don't mind me making myself at home?'

The morning sunshine makes his eyelashes look white. I'd not noticed before. Does he dye his hair? Is he allowed vanity like that in his profession? Surely he didn't really climb in through the window? But then I'd have heard him come in through the front door. It annoys me, I curb it. He's a friend.

He passes me a mug of coffee. Should I tell him about last night?

'Thought I'd drop in. There's a spot of trouble at the Castle, have you heard anything yet?' he asks.

'The Jacobites?'

'You can laugh, but I assure you they are serious.'

'Yes? Look, they don't really have a claim, do they?'

He shifts, looks me in the eye. Dilated pupils, skin drawn tight across his nose, displeasure.

'They may, Mack. Watch yourself.'

He turns abruptly. I follow him through to my sitting room. He pauses by our game. Damn, he's spotted my exposed knight. I shouldn't have moved my bishop last time. He snatches up the little horse and turns to smile.

'Mate in under ten moves,' he says.

'Hardly worth your while coming round tomorrow, then, is it?'

'Usual time? Thanks for the coffee.'

When he's gone I check the back door. It is locked.

♜

The Castle car park is full as I walk past it. It's too early for tourists, and there are never enough of them at once to take up all the spaces anyway. The cars are too new and expensive for the archaeologists, though there is Jason's shiny Land Rover, parked on top of the pansies the Trust volunteers planted a month ago.

Past the ancient Chapel, I hear raised voices from inside the Castle. No way to avoid meeting the meeting, whatever it is. A cloud passes across the sun.

The Great Hall is filled with men. The breeze is cold in here, blowing through the empty stone mullions. Their voices echo up to the high wooden beams, twelve inches square. Pine was stupid, already bowing, but oak was eight times the price.

Jason is standing next to Lord Muck in front of the huge stone fireplace. Peter, the Trust's custodian, stands by Muck's right side. The only women are the Ladies from the Trust committee, flushed and upset. I don't recognise any of the others. I count twenty-eight of them.

Jason actually looks pleased to see me and beckons to me across their shoulders. Hostile eyes turn towards me as I thread my way through the throng. The bluff of confidence makes them give way. That, or they fear close contact between my work-clothes and their smart bespoke suits.

Jason ignores my question before I can even ask it, frowning at me to listen. I stand beside Juliet, the most diminutive of the three Committee Ladies. Her cheeks are red and she is trembling.

'This is our stone-mason, Mack,' Lord Muck graciously acknowledges my existence, even claiming first-name acquaintance. Things must be bad.

'We don't hold him responsible for the vandalism and desecration.'

I should bloody well think not.

Another suit joins in, 'That is entirely your responsibility.'

His Lordship bristles. 'Look here, all works have been done under the direction of the Trust. My estate –'

'With respect, sir, all works have been done because you sold a leasehold to which you had no legal title.'

'My family has owned this castle and its land for a hundred and fifty years.'

'It was never your family's property. It was illegally requisitioned by the Crown and passed between parties who had no right to it. It was stolen goods when you bought it.' There is a general baying of agreement here, with falsetto disclaimers from the ladies of the committee and, embarrassingly enough, from Peter also.

Lord Muck's bellow for silence seems to make the whole structure shudder. In the quiet I think I hear an answering clunk of stone shifting against stone somewhere high above us. It is his face that keeps the peace. His skin has turned a mottled purple and his eyes are bulging. Temper and drink. He looks like he will either collapse or explode. Either way it will be messy.

Into this I realise another man has appeared, short and stocky, inferior in every way to the men around him. He weaves his way through the men and approaches Lord Muck. He passes him a letter. His Lordship is too astonished to ask what it is. I guess it is a summons, that the man is a Clerk of the Courts. Excellent dramatic timing. His Lordship deflates, colour drains form his skin. Without further fuss the men exchange glances and begin to file out of the door. They have seen what they came to witness.

I walk Juliet back to the car park. First time she has ever been this quiet. There is a notice on the Chapel door, a Court Order, forbidding us to trespass on private property. I wonder if Robin has seen this.

♜

It's easy enough to extricate myself from the general hubris. Once I start to shovel sand into the mixer even Jason gets the message. He has stopped trying to express his distress by the time I turn it on. The grinding covers his farewell and drowns out the return one I don't bother with. I feel sorry for him, but sorrier for me. Sorry for the Castle, too. There's a spirit about the place, an atmosphere. It's special. I don't want to have to leave it.

Up in the wind, lodged between the scaffolding and the wall, bracing my knee against a water spout, I run my hands over the masonry. I feel the cool face of a stone worked hundreds of years ago, check it's sound. I know the position will give me cramp in a few minutes, but I have to know the stone's good, so I work fast. Sulphur in the rain turns to acid, pollution rots stonework. It's no good pointing between rocks that are crumbling like Muscovado sugar. I finish my bucket before the pins and needles start and set off for the next load. When the Castle was built they would have had a team, with a lad to haul up fresh mortar. It is false economy, like the cheap pine beams, to have me working on my own. I have no say in the matter. I should have joined the Trust, maybe, got onto the committee, but I'm not a joiner-in. The exercise does me good.

I

Jason is back by the afternoon. Had he ever been away? I am aware of him stalking round the Castle. Is he looking for me? It becomes a sort of game for the next hour, getting down to the second floor where the mixer is and back up to the turret without him seeing me between the pillars of masonry. The only place I have to be careful is crossing diagonally from the scaffolding to the turret. I have a plank wedged from my tower of steel across to the battlement, only six feet apart, but with a good drop, and it's on a slope, too. Crossing this I know already Jason will call to me, before he does.

'Hey, Malcolm! You're not answering your phone.'

I stop, balance, and continue to the wall before I comment. 'I don't keep it up here in case it goes off when I'm crossing the plank and distracts me.'

'What?'

He heard me.

'Tosser,' I say at the same volume. He's fast enough to let it pass.

'Can you come down?'

'If you really want me to.'

I'll rinse out my water brush, so it's not a totally wasted journey. It's in my hand, then I drop it.

The difference between a steeplejack and the rest of the population is that when I drop something up a height, I let it fall. When someone who is not by nature a steeplejack drops something they somehow forget to let go, and inevitably descend with the item.

I watch it go.

13

I was having unfriendly thoughts towards Jason, it's true, but I hadn't meant to drop the brush on him. I bet he wouldn't use those words in front of Lord Muck. I trust he wouldn't use them in front of the Ladies from the committee, either. Two pairs of jackdaws soar out of the sycamore, screeching.

I get down as fast as I can. No point apologising. He claims the brush has hurt him, which I doubt. The watery mortar and sand grains have spattered down his suit. Couldn't have happened to nicer chap.

'No harm done,' I say.

'Shouldn't you be wearing some sort of safety harness?'

'It wouldn't have stopped me dropping the brush.'

'We need nets to protect the public,' he says.

'You were beyond the barriers. No-one should be in this area.'

He looks round. The barriers have gone.

'OK. Nets. That's your department. I'm only doing the actual work. I made it plain that I wasn't able to do the Health and Safety stuff. You have to provide me with a safe environment.'

'Safe?' he asks.

'It's OK – I won't sue you, and my brush has come to no hurt.'

It is so easy to wind him up it's almost rude not to. I don't think he is used to people standing up to him.

He takes a deep breath, pinches the bridge of his bony nose between thumb and forefinger. 'I came to tell you that we need you take down a wall beneath the Chapel tomorrow.'

'Ah, that may be difficult. Have you read the notice?'

'The notice isn't meant for you. I'll take full responsibility.'

'Can I have that in writing?' I'm not altogether joking.

'I'll speak to you tomorrow morning.'

There is no point making another mix; it's too close to four. He walks back to where the brush hit him and stares up at my work. He'd have to have excellent sight to distinguish the day's progress from the rest, so I watch the pantomime of critical overseeing with as much as patience as I can.

'Everything in order?' I ask.

He turns, his face stiff with dislike. He doesn't hear the soft rasp of sand on stone. As the stone falls I launch myself, land on top of him, feel the thud of a block of stone as it half buries itself in the turf beside our heads. The sharp smell of chlorophyll fills the air as I push myself off.

He lies there on his back, shaking. I reach down and help him up. He still can't speak.

'Lucky.'

I watch him try to swear at me. When he finally manages he's like someone with Tourette's. It's worse when he starts to laugh. I move away a little.

One thing I know from my job, it does you good to almost die every day. He'll get over it. He has run out of steam by the time Juliet rounds the corner with the other Ladies close on her heels. He is bending over, bracing himself against his knees, trying not to be sick.

'What happened, Mack? You've not been fighting?'

'A stone fell, nearly brained Mr. Holden.'

She looks at my jeans. I have torn them at the knees, and grazed my skin enough to bleed.

'I knocked him out of the way, not that he's realised it yet.'

I walk back to the stairway while the women fuss. A couple of archaeologists join in, an excuse to finish early. I wouldn't stand there if I was them.

I

I can still hear them now while I examine the stone. It's a block I had already looked at. There had been no fault, I swear it. The slanting sheer face shows red veins like a map through the yellow sandstone, as bright as the day it was quarried. I have become careless.

♟

I let the scalding water run down my skin for another minute. A decade ago I took three minutes in the shower. Now it takes ten, and the water has to be so hot it hurts. I turn the faucet off and step out of the shower, stretching while I rub myself dry, clicking the joints in my back. I can hear someone in my sitting room. I hope it's not Jason, bent on revenge for my seeing him unmanned this afternoon.

I am fastening my shirt with the pretence of casual preoccupation as I walk into the room.

Empty. Still.

No cars in the lane. The front door is still locked. Stupid, I must have imagined it. All the same, I'll turn the radio on for the reassurance of a human voice across the ether.

God, it's so cold. I can't light a fire in May. That's Mum, her voice in my head, Scottish when the rest of us sounded so English, gently advocating perpetual thrift. I catch myself humming one of her songs under my breath. No, I'll put the cap back on. I don't need a drink.

Will Mel reply, was my apology enough? Will it ever be enough? Bloody Archers, turn it off. Better ring her.

She's cagey, can't wait to get off the phone. Girls' voices in the background. People passing near her. Am I jealous or just lonely?

Bread and cheese again. I need to shop. I need to get out of this bloody house, not spend another evening on my own.

♟

So I find myself at the Castle again, as if I don't spend enough time here through the day. Friendly wave to David, doing his rounds. Some security guard, not noticing the kids messing around on the walls last weekend. Still, he has to walk all the grounds of the Hall, too, as well as the Castle.

This lock's been oiled. I don't like the thought of Jason Holden coming round here, tinkering with things. Now that really is jealousy.

Up past my mixer on the second floor, past the window that gives access to the scaffolding on the third floor, up past the iron gate that stops the visitors from going any higher. My privilege. Up the narrow stone stair, into the remains of the pepper-pot tower. It is a lovely evening.

It gets me every time, my breath catches in my throat and my mind clears. I stand where the stone is most worn next to the arched window which has framed the same view for centuries and feel the evening air on my face.

The guide book says that the First Baronet used to blow his hunting horn to gain the attention of his cousin in the castle two miles across the valley. That was in the days when the loudest man-made noise on the planet was a church bell.

The traffic is still roaring on the by-pass over the Tyne; it must be after eight now. Do these people have no homes to go to? The sun has sunk behind the hill so I can no longer make out the face of the stonework on the square tower I am busy with. David is whistling out of sight. He must be behind the Chapel. I watch the gloaming swallow the little valley below me. The tributary stream, low after a dry spring, is lost amongst the trees below but I can hear it trickling down to join the Tyne. Someone is walking up the steep footpath from the pack-horse bridge we restored last summer. She is dressed in some sort of wrap, far too heavy for an evening like this.

I am surrounded now by bat-squeaks as the pipistrelles from the Castle flit through the air, diving for insects across the fading sky.

I was lucky to get a job in a place like this.

The way Mum taught me to pray, it was just to remember to say thank you. I want to do that now for the first time in years, but does it count? Does it matter that I don't feel anything, if there is something out there? A beneficent being perhaps, independent of my need or belief, pleased to receive my gratitude. I quite like that. If there's anyone out there listening, then thank you.

Shit, I said that out loud. Loudly out loud.

The walker has stopped and is staring up at the tower. She must have come up the path at a fair pace, she's level with the Castle wall already. The wall is intact on the stream side so I doubt that she can see me up here. I pull back, just in case. I can hear David's heavy tread below. He's coming over, I'd better get down. Maybe he can't see me either, thinks it's someone else in the Castle.

The colour is draining fast, the stairs are shades of grey on grey, the voids of the doorways off the main stairs are patches of black. I know the stones like I know the teeth in my head, but I think I've missed a storey; I get down sooner than I expected. David is waiting for me in the barrel vault beneath the Great Hall. He is not impressed.

'You shouldn't be up there in the dark.'

'I didn't mean to startle you.'

'What'd you come in here for anyway at this hour?'

'I wanted to look over the west face of the tower.'

I don't sound convincing. He already treats me like a harmless eccentric. He's looking at me now like he's reconsidering the adjective.

'I don't want to have to come in here after dark again. Next time I hear you scream, I'll just let you get on with it.'

I didn't scream. He's making a mountain out of a molehill.

A bat swoops past my ear. He shines his torch onto the poor thing as it clings to the stone wall, clumsy and vulnerable as soon as it lands.

'I hate those bloody things. Filth. The mess in the Chapel,' he says.

There are no bats in the Chapel. I herd him out of the Castle and lock the heavy door behind us. We part at the gate by the notice board. David crunches off up the gravel path towards his round. As I reach down for the padlock and chain a movement catches my eye, a dim silhouette against the vast shade of the Castle door. God, I'd forgotten the walker. What is she doing? I stop several feet away, not wanting to alarm her.

'Can I help you?'

She lets go of the iron ring on the door. Stands there staring back at me, and I can't move. My heart hammers. I think I might scream for David now, if I can.

It passes. She is walking away without a word, back down the path towards the bridge.

I need to pull myself together. I'm not sure I really believe what I just saw.

Her face –

♟

Not surprising that I can't sleep.

The pillows are all wrong. My neck hurts.

I hope I am asleep now, though. One of those dreams where I can wake myself up when it gets too bad. A light drifts across my room. Dim, not like last night. It spins round the foot of my bed, very slowly. It's fading; the more I stare, the less I see.

Maybe I'll mention this to Robin tomorrow.

3. FRIDAY

I had forgotten about the crypt. Jason is there at the Chapel door waiting for me, wearing chinos and a hard hat and holding a briefcase.

It's quarter past eight. I slept late.

I knew it; instead of complaining he looks at his watch ostentatiously. A classic move from chapter one of *How to be a Dick*.

'Have I kept you waiting long?' I ask.

'I want to get down there before we are interrupted.'

What's he up to?

The Court Notice is still pinned up. He unlocks the door, and I follow him in. We use the door that the Family used when the Chapel was built in the early sixteen-hundreds, with the lime-washed spiral stairs up to the gallery and the bell tower above. The gallery is a small museum now, the hearth is empty, the bell silent.

The Chapel is still used for services. Robin takes communion here twice a month. The walls are lined with mounted displays about the Baronet, the would-be kingmaker, and his ill-fated descendants. But the Castle's history goes back far further than that. There was a stronghold here when the Romans invaded. No-one ever seems to prosper here. Dynasties come and go.

A comforting thought, given how unpleasant the current Lord is.

'Lift those boards for me,' he says.

The way down to the crypt is usually concealed under the pews. Today these have been moved to one side. Four eight-by-two wooden trap-doors are fitted over the stairway down to the crypt, each with two brass rings set into them to lift them up. I don't think they are the originals, but they are well made out of thick pitch pine. I will struggle to lift them on my own. He ignores my hesitation. I struggle.

Whenever I have been down into the crypt before I have only taken off the first two trap-doors. This allows access to the stone steps, but not sufficient headroom to walk down them, so that one has to crawl under the third door. When all four are lifted off it allows a procession to carry a coffin straight down into the room beneath the Chapel. I don't bother to ask if he wants all four boards taking up. He won't want to get his trousers dirty. I lean each one awkwardly against the wall, taking care not to damage the displays.

'I haven't got all day.'

'What exactly do you want me to do down there?' I ask.

'I'll show you when we get there.'

He takes a torch out of his briefcase. He won't need it; there's plenty of light coming down the stairs. Even with only two doors lifted it's not too bad as there's a tiny window in the eastern wall of the crypt directly underneath the altar. Now all four are off it just looks like a normal stairway. He's faffing. He's scared.

I was scared yesterday. I can do friendly. 'Have you been down there before?'

He shakes his head.

'The Family coffins have been taken out. There are four more burials under the floor, but they are very old, thirteenth century at the latest. Older than the Chapel. You can see where the archaeologists excavated them, but they're filled in again. Just earth over lead coffins, with nothing much left inside.'

'I read that on the information board.'

'OK. Some people don't like crypts, that's all.'

'You've been down there before. Show me the way.'

It's hard to get lost. A straight flight of well-made, broad stone steps leads eastward down to a square room with a stone arched ceiling. The room is about twenty feet across and maybe ten feet high at its tallest point. It is mostly subterranean, but at the top of the arch on the exterior wall there is that small window. It is in the shape of an upside-down cross. You can see it at ground level outside amongst the grass. The crypt is always quite warm, and there is only one patch of damp. Moisture glistens in the western corner furthest from the stairs above a small pit. He swings the superfluous torch over the wetness.

'The archaeologists found a medieval pot in that corner with the remains of a little girl in it. The pot was five centuries older than the bones.'

'I read that, too.'

Snappy for someone who's whispering.

Jason passes me the torch and takes a sheath of papers out of his briefcase. He flips through them for a diagram, then takes the torch back and shines it on the paper, completely unnecessarily.

'Are we looking for buried treasure?' I keep the sarcasm out of my voice.

'We are looking for evidence of an opening into this west wall next to the stairs'

'It's in the archaeologists' report. Look, you can see where the stonework changes from the well-tooled stuff to that rubbish.'

'I want you to unblock the opening.'

'I can't.'

'I want you to take that down. It shouldn't take long.'

'This is a job for the archaeologists, not me. I'm not qualified, I might spoil something, lose valuable evidence.'

'The owners of this Chapel have asked me to have this wall removed.'

'The owners being those friendly gentlemen yesterday?'

'The owners being your current employers.'

'The Committee wouldn't sanction this.'

'Who do you think is paying your salary, Malcolm?'

We argue, but I'm on a losing wicket. He has the facts; I have Juliet handing me an envelope of money every Friday with an anonymous payslip for the Inland Revenue. My accountant always says I need to look after my paperwork better. Juliet could have told me it wasn't the Trust paying me. Lord Muck clearly didn't know I was working for the Jacobites either. I doubt I'd still have a cottage to rent if he did.

'I'll need my tools. If it's been sealed because the roof has come down then I'll also need a structural engineer, or the owners won't have much of a Chapel left to argue over.'

♟

Back in the Castle I gather what I need, crashing the tools into my barrow with as much noise as I can. No-one comes to ask what the matter is. No opportunity to talk this over with anyone.

Jason is not in the Chapel when I return. He has left a note for me, pinned to one of the trap-doors:

> Malcolm. Remove the obstruction and resultant debris from the crypt.
> I'll organise a skip and have it put by the southern door. You are not authorised to proceed beyond the blockage. Any artefacts or documents beyond the wall are the property of the owners and must not be disturbed.
> Back at 4 o' clock for progress report.

♟

There is the skip, being unloaded now, outside the southern door. I pull my barrow into the Chapel and leave it by the foot of the gallery stairs. I shall have to carry out the rubble in a bucket.

It will take days.

I assemble a makeshift platform, two piles of three breezeblocks on their sides with a plank across the top from my scaffolding. I brought a couple of spars down too, just in case I have to prop the roof in a hurry. It's probably easiest to start right in the centre, at the highest point.

I have never spent time on my own in the crypt. I am looking forward to this. I want to know what's behind this wall as much as anyone else who's ever been down here.

Now I'm here alone the atmosphere is of a quiet country graveyard. Peaceful. A place to be laid to rest. They took away the Family's bodies in the Nineteenth century. They are buried with other Jacobites down south somewhere. It's just me and four anonymous corpses down here. And whatever is on the other side of this wall.

♟

The dust gets everywhere. The mortar is crumbling away, doesn't need to be hacked out. My clothes are sticking to me. I hadn't realised how much I enjoy working outdoors until now. The air is so thick I can barely see the empty coffin benches three yards away. The work has dulled my curiosity. I am less than a metre down from the roof and I'm not even down to the full width yet. It's very thick for a badly-made wall. I have never needed a break so much.

♟

It's quiet outside. I'm cold in the Chapel's shadow. The sky is pale blue and the sunlight is hazy.

Peter isn't in his hut. I watch a middle-aged couple walk up to the honesty box, read the tariff, and then walk on towards the Castle knowing how much they have saved.

Peter certainly hasn't been around enough to clean the toilets this morning. I have to stand on sodden paper towels. I can't wash properly, there's no hot water. I try to shift the dust up my nostrils. That's better. Now I can breathe through my nose I can smell death on me. Very faint, probably my imagination, but all burials taint the air. The mortar itself has been steeped in that atmosphere for centuries. I have nothing to get the dirt out from under my fingernails. I sniff my fingers. Soap and corpse. I am being stupid.

♟

I can still smell the grave as I lift the coffee to my lips. It turns my stomach. I never knew I was this squeamish. I have been here for ten minutes, all alone in the information booth. Peter didn't lock up, wherever he's got to. I guess leaflets and souvenir pens aren't much of a security risk. I help myself to a block of plasticky fudge and put a couple of pound coins next to the till. The paranormal-activity log is on the counter. It works – the tourists like it, and the Trust gets a substantial amount of revenue from the ghost-walks. A pile of fliers advertising the next 'paranormal-investigation evening' have been thoughtfully placed next to the ledger. The gimmick appals Robin even though it's his job to promote the supernatural.

There have been a lot of entries recently. Has anyone else seen the woman that I saw last night? No. The usual: footsteps, funny feelings, shadows. There must be a new series of that ghost-hunting programme – nothing like TV to heighten the psychic awareness.

I don't know why I am writing down what happened last night. What I thought happened. I'll make a mess if I cross it out. No-one will recognise my writing if I don't put my name down.

Time to get back. Better pull the hut door shut.

God, even the fudge smells of the crypt. There are wasps crawling over sticky wrappers in the bin by the picnic tables. I miss one by a split second as I ditch the fudge.

One of the kids from the Hall is sitting alone. You can always tell, even if you don't see their faces. A thousand little signals we're hardwired to pick up on, to detect the abnormal. Poor little blighters. Still, it's a nice school, they are good with the children.

'Why are you throwing that away?' she asks.

'It didn't taste nice. Shouldn't you be in a lesson?'

'What's your name?'

'I'm Mack.'

'I know you.' Too loud. She laughs and repeats herself, several times.

'Yes, I'm the builder. You need to get back to your class.'

She gets up clumsily and hitches up her baggy tracksuit bottoms. It's not an accident that she barges into me as she passes. 'I know you,' she says again, but she's not laughing anymore.

I don't know how the teachers cope, how the parents cope. She's whistling Mum's song as she walks away. I won't be able to get it out of my head now.

❚

An hour later and I'm still tapping out mortar to that bloody song.

> *Cam ye o'er frae France?*
> *Cam ye doon by Lunnon?*
> *Saw ye Geordie Whelps*
> *and his bonnie woman?*

This dust is wrecking my voice. Ah, the Fifteen. The tedium of all Dad's lectures. All the same, I wish I'd studied history instead of going to Aberdeen.

Oh, weren't ye at the place
called the Kittle Housie?
Saw ye Geordie's grace
a-ridin' on a goosie?
Geordie, he's a man,
there is little doot o't,
And he's done a' he can,
all can dae wi'oot it,
Doon there cam' a blade,
linkin' like ma lordie -
'Malcolm!'

Juliet. She patters down the steps, ducking to avoid imaginary cobwebs.

'I've been calling for the past five minutes. You're away with the fairies.'

Hell's teeth.

'You've got a good voice. We can hear you outside.'

'Ah.'

'So this is what Jason's got you doing,' she says.

'Why didn't you tell me I was working for him?'

'I thought you knew. The Trust has to get funds from somewhere.'

'So I was just on loan until he got the authority to put me on this job?'

'Well, we contributed towards your pay. As much as we could afford, but if we really haven't got the lease –' she trails off.

'Jason's stitched you up, then.'

'I don't think it's like that.' She looks miserable. This place is her life.

'So I'm not working on the restoration anymore?'

'It's not up to us now. I just don't know. We've been in a meeting all morning.'

That will have helped. No, I mustn't be sarcastic, she's too upset. She's sniffing, I don't know if it's tears or dust, probably both. She sneezes.

'I thought Jason was working for the Trust.' God knows I don't want to tip her over, but I need to get this straight.

She's soaking a tiny floral hankie. 'We can't even afford the archaeologists, let alone a manager. He seemed like a gift. We assumed he was a volunteer, even when he started ordering us around. You get people like that.'

'I know. I work here.'

'Do I boss you around?' She brightens as she comes back on to familiar territory, flirting with the builder thirty years her junior.

'I coped.'

She smiles through the sniffles. Shit. This is a ritual. She wants me to comfort her, but I find I can't. I'm too angry. I want to yell at her and all the rest of the sodding Trust Committee for being so feeble.

Make an effort and let it go. They did their best.

I take a deep breath and draw in enough dust to make me choke.

'You should wear a mask.'

'They're uncomfortable. It's lunchtime, anyway.'

She has laid a path of sacking for me from the top of the stairs to the southern door. I shall have to start taking the rubble out this afternoon, or it will get in my way.

♟

I am past singing now. I have rarely been so tired, and the wall is still seven foot high. I have no torch so I can't see anything beyond it.

Jason's here. I expected he would be trying to look into the void beyond the wall, but he wants to avoid the heaps of dust and rubble and is beckoning me up from the bottom step. He doesn't say anything, just waits for me to follow him back up.

The Court Notice has been replaced with a new bolt with a padlock on it, screwed above the old keyhole. That is to keep out the Trust members who have keys. Does he really think they'd trespass?

⚑

Resisting the temptation to flop down when I get in is harder than I've ever known it. I need to shower. The water runs grey with the dust as I rinse it out of my hair. I still don't feel clean.

Hell's teeth, that's Robin's car. I forgot what day it was. I usually cook, but I've nothing in the fridge. I sniff my hands as I dress. It must be my imagination.

He comes through the front door without knocking, nearly bumps into me at the foot of the stairs. He's carrying a basket like Little Red Riding Hood.

'Supper,' he says.

'Thanks. I didn't have time.'

'You look awful.'

'Thank you.'

He knows my kitchen surprisingly well. So well I forget I'm the host and let him get on with it. Clams and linguini with a crusty loaf. I must have dozed off.

'We'll eat in the other room,' he says.

He lit the fire while I snoozed. Just as well, it takes the chill off the room.

I don't like seafood, especially shellfish, but this is Friday, and the Father is cooking. Old habits die hard, even for the lapsed. The wine Robin brought doesn't quite take the smell of my work out of my nostrils. I'll have another glass.

⚑

The dishes can wait for the morning. Robin's fetched over the chessboard, careful not to spill the pieces. I learnt to play on this set. Granddad's lessons aren't a match for Robin's though.

There's a whisky I didn't ask for at my elbow. I must look bad for him to be cosseting me like this.

We walk through the moves. I know them already, it's just a formality. I know I cannot win.

We shake hands, then Robin's setting out the board for a new game. His hands move like a conjurer's, swift and practiced. I could watch them all night.

I am drunk. I know it in the warmth where my muscles ached and the thickness of my tongue. I cannot be as eloquent and erudite as I think I sound, but I babble on. Robin listens. I have told him about worse than this before. He is my confessor, though we've never bothered with absolution. I should stop. He should stop me. He is pouring me another whisky.

♟

'Let's get you up to bed.'

'Leggo o' me.'

I know I'll fall if he does let go.

4. SATURDAY

It's dark. There is a terrible pain in my back, shooting up my spine, drilling into my brain. I am lying across the two coffin benches in the crypt, supporting my weight on the back of my head and my heels. I can't bear this for much longer, but I know something much worse will happen shortly. Chains of light start to spin in front of my eyes. I can't hold on.

I'm screaming. *Jesus.*

It's over. The day is dawning through the curtains. My sheets are soaked and tangled round my legs. I drag them with me to the bathroom. Once I start to throw up I can't stop. I can't breathe at times, choke and cough, slumped over the pan, holding onto it like I might fall through. Stomach acid burns my throat. Everything hurts. Robin has poisoned me with his filthy clams. I hope he is suffering this much.

I

I'm lying across the tumble drier to ease the stomach cramps. The vibration is quite soothing. My phone is in the kitchen, close enough to hear. Crawling to the kitchen table, the effort nearly kills me.

Melissa.

'Where were you last night?'

'I was here.'

'I called and called. You didn't answer. Have you got a cold?'

'I've been sick, hurt my throat.'

'*Sick?*

'Robin brought some shellfish round last night.'

'*You shouldn't eat that stuff if there isn't an 'R' in the month.*'

I don't want to think about it. 'I'm sorry I missed you.'

She's already gone.

♟

At least my sheets are clean now. And my bedside rug, and the paintwork, and the bathroom. Body-fluids neutralised by Dettol.

Boiled water, hot as I can manage, sipping it slowly in an effort to re-hydrate. My stomach's not ready for painkillers. The stiffness in my neck is so bad it feels like the dream was real. I need someone to look after me.

♟

The car park is full, it's busy today. It's going to be a good weekend for the Trust's funds. I walked here to clear my head, but the sun keeps lancing through the branches, making it worse. It's only a mile from home to the Castle, but even that has tired me.

The skip in front of the southern door is half full. No wonder I feel like this, I must have shifted three or four tons of debris yesterday. The light breeze raises miniature tornadoes of dust across the pile of rubble.

I walk around the west end of the Chapel, following the gravel path. It's cool enough in the shade to make me shiver. I'm still not well. The grass is an unnatural green, blazing in the glare of the sunlight. The lawn in front of the Castle is littered with tourists. Shrieking children hurt my head. Peter waves from the hut door. I wave back, and my shoulder twinges.

There is a new display board next to the information board. I can't read it without worsening the headache. I walk back to Peter. Wait until a small group of customers wanders off.

'What's that board all about?' I ask him.

'Ah. The fairies came in the middle of the night and erected that.'

'So I see.'

'The lineage of the rightful kings of England,' he says.

'Wow.'

'Oh yes.'

Peter has a degree in modern history. He has explained the Stuart claim to me at length many, many times. I didn't listen much more to him than I did to Dad, but I have a notion that there is some merit in it.

'Never really matters who's king; it's all the same to us peasants.'

'Are you alright?' he asks.

I'm going to be sick again. Or faint.

'Sit down.'

A fuss. Humiliating enough Peter seeing this, but now Juliet has arrived.

'It's that crypt. It's making him ill,' she says.

'It's not the crypt, it's the clams.' Just remembering them makes me throw up.

If one more person tells me when it's safe to eat shellfish, I shall be sick on their shoes instead.

Juliet drives me home. I let her tuck me up in a rug on the sofa. Even the smell of the wool makes my stomach turn. I push the fringed hem away from my mouth. Thank God I cleaned up this morning, I'm too knackered to do anything now. I want Melissa. Juliet looks embarrassed when I say it.

5. SUNDAY

Blackness again. Is this a dream? The feeling of unreality could just be light-headedness from yesterday. I can't even see the outline of the window, it's so dark. I'm too drowsy to worry. But the lights are there again, tiny pinpricks that aren't there when I close my eyes.

✗

'I just can't see why you want to go to a mass, that's all.'

I should eat some breakfast, toast or something, but Mel's phone call is standing between me and the breadbin.

'I don't know. To support Robin, I suppose.'

'Robin who's just poisoned you?'

'I want to go.'

'But you're an atheist.'

Am I? 'Plenty of atheists go to mass.' Look at Robin.

'Don't go.'

I know it's a matter of moments before she'll ring off, dashing to do whatever it is she does with those endless Sundays that she doesn't spend with me. I'm only going through the motions of the argument. Maybe I just don't care.

'I have to say goodbye now.'

I know.

✗

It's overcast and cold for May, so different from yesterday. Glad I put my coat on.

Robin's small, chilled flock are huddled round him outside the Chapel door. They can't get in. Only the elderly seem to feel the need to attend. Decrepit, lined faces almost translucent with the cold, so grey they seem to fade against the sodden stones. I must be the only one under seventy who comes here, besides Robin. Is it just a habit to them? Maybe faith grows with age, or fear. I suppose they're nearer needing the place for its final sacrament. Robin detaches himself and comes towards me.

'How are you?' he asks.

'Never eating anything that doesn't need lungs again.'

'Don't blame the food. I was fine. What do you think about this?' He waves his arm towards the Chapel.

'I did wonder how you'd manage with the trap-doors lifted up. I kept it as tidy as I could in there. Still, it would only take me a minute to lay the trapdoors again. I don't see why it should be a problem.'

'It's a private Chapel. I can't go in there without permission.'

'They won't let you go in?' I ask.

He shakes his head.

'You'd have thought the Jacobites would welcome a Catholic service in their Chapel.'

'I doubt it crossed their minds,' he says.

'Maybe it's just while the building work is going on?'

'Fool.'

What? What's that about? He's turned his back on me. The elderly communicants have already melted away. I would have to run to catch up with him as he strides back towards the car park.

I leave him to it.

✗

At least the Castle door hasn't been padlocked shut against the Trust. I could go up there and sulk in my tower. It's cold for loitering though. I might as well walk down to the bridge.

The path skirts the bank side beneath the Castle and is shady even when it's not misty like this. The moisture on the still air makes the loose chippings slippery and intensifies the smell of the Indian Balsam plants so that it seems to fill the wooded bank with a sickly miasma. The scent is strong enough now to make this unpleasant. The Trust hacks the balsam down every year before it flowers, but it's still spreading. I used to like popping the pods along the banks of the Ettrick when I was a kid.

> *Cam ye o'er frae France?*
> *Cam ye doon by Lunnon?*
> *Saw ye Geordie Whelps*
> *and his bonnie woman?*

I'm singing out loud. But why not? There's no-one around.

No-one but the other person singing. I stop. It was a woman's voice, a girl's perhaps. There she is, the girl from the Hall, perched on the parapet. Shit, she's seen me. Will she recognise me from Friday? I keep on walking towards the bridge.

She slides her backside off the stonework and comes to meet me. 'Do you like that song?'

'Not much.' I keep walking.

> *'Oh, weren't ye at the place*
> *called the Kittle Housie?*
> *Saw ye Geordie's grace*
> *a-ridin' on a goosie?*

Do you know what that means?'

Yes, I do, but I'm hardly going to talk to her about it.

'Is it silly?' she asks.

'Probably. Does anyone know you're here?' There are no

boarders at the Hall anymore, it's run as a day school now. She must live locally. She stops in front of me.

'I am allowed out by myself. I'm seventeen. Would you like to hear the rest?'

She talks so awkwardly, but she sings prettily. I suppose it's mimicry. I'd happily throttle whoever taught it to her.

'No, you're alright. Thank you.'

> *'I'll sell my rock, I'll sell my reel,*
> *My rippling-kame and spinning wheel,*
> *To buy my lad a tartan plaid,*
> *A braid sword, dirk, and white cockade.'*

'That's a new one on me.' I hope no-one else comes along. She's singing full throttle into my face. The bridge is narrow, enough room to walk on past, but not without side-stepping her first.

> *'Of all the money e'er I had,*
> *I spent it in good company.*
> *And all the harm I've ever done,*
> *Alas! it was to none but me.'*

'You've a good memory. I've got to go now.'

'All the songs. I know all the songs,' she says.

'That's good. I'd better get on.'

'I'll come and sing to you in your grave.'

'That's enough, now,' I raise my voice, 'let me past.'

'Fat lot of use songs are, bonny lad.'

Just keep walking. She has serious problems. Special Educational Needs aside, she's a bloody head-case. What the hell are they doing letting her out by herself? Whoever 'they' are. I don't much care. Jesus, what's wrong with people today? Cross or mad. Or both.

I

I have walked much further than I intended, following paths I didn't know were there. Not thinking much, just tramping along, the last few days playing through my mind like an overused tape, fading to nothing in places, distorted and loud in others. I want to pour my thoughts out of my head, flush them away so I can just *be*. When I try to stop thinking, though, my mind goes back to worse things. Maybe I'm better concentrating on the present problems, leave the past alone. Get some company. I'll go to the pub tonight. Walk into the village and make a night of it.

♟

I've ended up in the Black Bull, driven here by the live music elsewhere. I'm not in the mood.

I've got enough inside me to not want to stop, despite being sick all yesterday, but it's Monday tomorrow so I know I'll have to go easy. I never used to drink like this.

'Sorry.'

'Steady, there.'

I feel like I'm in a bubble, incapable of communication and surrounded by a pool of inaccessible noise. I don't know anyone in here anymore. The dark and warmth make me itch. Time to go home. Phone's ringing. Maybe this time I'll not answer it.

The guy I just bumped into is staring at me as I take the phone out of my pocket and turn it to mute. I don't switch it off.

The barman doesn't look up when I bid him goodnight. Glad to get rid of me without a fuss, I guess.

♟

The mist is rising on the Tyne behind me. Car headlights shine through the vapour like searchlights raking the skies for aircraft. My feet are soaking from stepping out of the way into ditches. I am a mile past the last pavement.

The lights are on in my cottage. Even through the beer, I'm surprised that this does not surprise me, I am almost expecting it.

Robin doesn't turn round when I walk in. He's concentrating on looking up a name in my book. My address book.

He pissed me off this morning. 'Can I help?'

He turns, flushing at my tone.

Have I overdone it? He looks fierce, makes me nervous for a second.

Then we both remember that he is standing in my sitting room without invitation.

'D'you happen to know Jason Holden's address?' he asks.

'Couldn't you have phoned to ask me that?'

'I was passing.'

Robin lives five miles from here. I can't think of anywhere he couldn't get to faster from his home on another road.

'Is it about the Chapel? I'll be seeing him tomorrow, I can ask if you like,' I say.

'I think this needs to be done in person. Did you have a good walk?'

'Very pleasant.'

I don't know why I said that. He puts my book down. The words hang between us for a moment, so obviously untruthful that it is rude. 'How did you know I went for a walk?'

'You always do when you don't want to face things.'

'It's a bit late for the analysis, Robin.'

'I brought some milk, if you're offering me coffee. You look like you could do with one.'

I'm tired. I would prefer that he just went. I can hear him lighting the fire while the kettle boils. It is freezing in here, but it's also nearly midnight.

I pass him the mug.

'Tell me about the crypt,' he says.

There's very little to tell. I thought we'd been through it all on Friday, though I was a little the worse for wear then, too. He listens intently. He must be really annoyed about Mass this morning, his eyes are black and his face is grim. Not that he ever looks particularly jolly, not with that aristocratic honk. How old is he? He always seems so vigorous, and his hair is thick and dark, though I suspect now that he dyes it. He speaks likes he thinks he's my contemporary, but he seems old tonight. I have lost the thread of the conversation. He stirs the fire. The coal bucket is empty. I won't offer to go outside and refill it.

'I'll let you get up to your bed, Mack.'

I'd better get up and see him out before he thinks of something else to talk about.

It's only after he's gone I find that he's swiped my address book. Jason will not be best pleased when Robin turns up. There is a strange pride in knowing Robin is the better man and I am on the winning team.

♟

This is ridiculous. I'm tired. I've had lots of exercise today and plenty to drink. Why can't I sleep?

The cottage is so small, but every corner seems strange tonight. I've spent five minutes now watching something move over there under the eaves. I stopped the mice getting in last winter. It's too big for a spider, and I can't be bothered to get out of bed to find out what it is for all the reasons that I should be asleep right now.

The movement is distinctive, a series of jerks that are gradually subsiding. Has it stopped? No, they've begun again, flapping dark against dark by the skirting. The drowsiness is stealing over me, finally, just when I'd rather have the energy to get out of bed and see what that is.

A light flashes across the room as I close my eyes and I'm too far gone to look.

6. MONDAY

Poor creature. A bit-bat, Dad used to call them. Why on Earth did it come into my room? Its body is tiny, folded up in its wings. I can hardly feel its weight as I carry it round to the compost heap.

The neighbours' ginger cat, a monstrous furry beast the size of a small cougar, crouches on the lawn. It is watching me with interest. I don't want the bloody animal to get a taste for bats – better bring the morsel back inside.

It's putting me off my breakfast. I suppose I could remove it from the table. I'm not hungry, anyway, this is just to stave off any hang-over from the beer.

I'm going through the motions of eating, really, waiting for Melissa's call.

This will be her now.

No, it's Clara, champing at the bit.

She wants a progress report. Everyone wants to know what's going on in the crypt. I don't imagine Jason will be too pleased with all this curiosity. Then again, I don't imagine Lord Muck and his sister are too pleased with Jason, now they know he's working for the opposition. Clara's barking mad today and it is a mistake to try to placate her, so I don't bother. She would see it as weakness.

'I don't know how I can help. I either do the job or walk away from it.'

'Well –'

Ah, so she expects me to resign. I try reason. 'The Jacobite Society would get another stonemason easily enough. Have you tried another angle?'

'I've spoken to English Heritage, of course, but they have caved in and agreed to the whole thing. It's insane. We own the Chapel.'

'I don't understand how they can do anything, then.'

'They're looking for something to prove otherwise, apparently. They're doing this through the courts.'

So Jason has sent me to look for hidden treasure after all. I am burning to know why the Jacobites think there is some evidence to support their claim beyond the wall, but I don't want to give Clara the satisfaction of appearing to be interested. I find I'm fiddling with the dead bat. Concentrate.

I have let a silence develop, which she has interpreted.

'Well, I can see you're showing your true colours, now, Mack.'

'I am not prepared to lose my job over this.' I nearly apologised there.

Clara saves me from finding a way to end the conversation by ringing off in a bluster.

I am being observed. I swing round to the window. The ginger cat is on the sill, glaring at me. Bloody thing must have an amazing sense of smell if it can detect the bat from out there.

'Shoo!'

Still it glares balefully in at me, doesn't even move when I flap the tea towel at the window.

I lean across the sink. 'Scat!'

It rises up to its full height, arching its back and spits at me. I open the window forcefully, knocking it off the sill. There's nothing at hand to throw at it. It's too fast anyway, diving under the laurel bush.

I drain the milk out of my bowl into the sink and scrape the soggy remains of the cereal into the bin, leaving the bin lid open so that I can dispose of the bat.

It's gone. It must have been playing dead all along. It hasn't crawled in amongst the clutter. I check the floor and behind the furniture, but it's disappeared. Who'd have thought it? So lifeless and cold, just waiting for me to turn my back.

I hope it doesn't find its way into my bedroom again.

♜

The padlock is off so I know Jason is already in the Chapel. He is waiting for me just inside the door. We barely acknowledge each other. His fringe is not slicked into careful alignment this morning so his receding hairline is exposed. His jacket is crumpled and his shoes are scuffed too, not his usual Monday morning appearance at all. Standards are falling. Maybe Lord Muck has given him a piece of his mind, or Robin may have caught up with him. It can't have been Clara; he's far too composed to have been savaged by her this morning. He follows me down into the crypt without a word. Our footsteps ring out on the stone steps. There is damp on the air in here this morning. The crypt seems dim, almost as if a fog is forming. Condensation perhaps? Surely it should be drying out down here, now the trapdoors have been lifted, not getting damper.

He is inspecting the ragged wall, crunching through rubble. He steps up onto my low platform, the plank across two breeze blocks, and teeters for a moment as though he were walking along a rope. He steadies himself against the wall and bobs up on the balls of his feet, vainly trying to see over into the dark void beyond.

'When will it be down?' he asks.

'Wednesday, maybe.' I am half a head taller than him, I shall see in before he does.

'Why aren't you using stone cutters?'

'The Stihl saw would make too much dust. Anyway, this way if the roof starts to come down, I have time to get some props in.'

'The roof won't come down. That isn't why the wall was put up.'

'You don't know that for certain.'

'Actually I do. We have the bill from the mason who put this wall up in 1732. It's in the archives in London.'

I want to see that bill, to connect with the mason who last worked this stone. Jason is off again, prowling, fretting about the time the job is taking. He should try doing some work, then he would understand, not need to keep asking these stupid questions.

'But you could speed the job up by using a stone-saw. If you had equipment to extract the dust.'

'Not really. See how thick the wall is?'

'But it has to be quicker than doing it by hand.'

'Are you telling me I don't know my job?'

'I-I-it's, no, you…' He has his back to the wall. His face is red, his eyes fixed on my stone-hammer. I am looming over him, hefting my hammer with a threat I didn't intend. I didn't mean to make a stand like this; my heart's jumping. So is the tick in his cheek.

'Here.' I pass him the hammer and broad, blunt chisel, 'See how much dust you raise just taking one stone out. Try this one.'

He takes the tools and turns to gaze unhappily at the wall. I point out the stone again. He tentatively pokes the chisel blade into the mortar and taps the pommel with the hammer.

I take the tools from him, 'Like this.' Metal rings against metal and a cloud of dust rises, leaving a useful cut under the stone.

I put the hammer back into his right hand. He hates this. He takes the chisel and nuzzles it into the soft mortar again.

The tendons pull taught and strain under the smooth skin on the back of his hand as he raises the heavy hammer. Despite my demonstration he's using his wrist all wrong, as though he's bowling a cricket ball instead of taking the strength from his upper arm. The blow lands with a dull *thwuck* on his knuckles.

The dust problem becomes more evident as he dances round choking in the powdery cloud, mouthing swear words, tears in his eyes. He staggers away from me, trying to regain command of himself.

'Let me look at your fingers.'

'Get away from me!' He scrambles backwards, his injured hand clutched to his chest, holding his right hand out to ward me off. He climbs up the steps still half-turned towards me as though he's being pursued.

The Chapel door slams above me. The dust settles. What was I supposed to do? The man is an idiot. And he was telling me my job, no matter what he thinks.

I pick up the hammer and scuff around in the grit to find my chisel. I resent his weakness, he makes me bully him, makes me complicit in his ineptitude. He turns me into something I am not.

I

This wall was put up too fast. The mason has pushed splinters from the stones he shaped between the rows of blocks so that their weight did not push the mortar out from the grikes before it had set. This wall would have been too weak to have ever borne the weight of the Chapel above it. It looks the part, but I know now what the mason must have known then. He was building too fast for the materials he was using. This wall couldn't stop a building from collapsing, but it's plenty to stop access to the back of the crypt. Or egress from the space behind. Is that what's behind this wall, a Georgian oubliette? That would boost the visitor revenue. I shut away the pictures of despair and thirst, the bleeding fingers and torn nails. I need to get out more.

I can get my pick in behind some of the larger splinters and prise them out of the matrix so that the surrounding mortar comes away in large powdery clusters. Mostly it's still hacking away at the firm surface of packed lime, raising a hazy landscape of cloudy dust-hills around me in the still air while I pound each stone block free enough of the mortar bed to be levered off and laid to rest in the dust.

The work induces a sort of dizzy euphoria, but after two hours of pulverising lime and stone, I have to stop.

Now I'm standing still my whole body throbs from head to foot. Gradually the hammer-rhythm subsides. Something has changed. There: a faint draught, very slight. I only feel it because my shirt is soaked and sticking to me. A waft of air, no more than a breath, from beyond the wall.

♟

The sun has come out. It's much warmer than yesterday. Peter is puffing towards the hut as I rub an alcohol hand-cleaner wipe from the first aid kit over my hands to cover the crypt-smell.

'You haven't seen her?' he asks.

'Seen who?'

'The girl. Melissa.'

Melissa? My Melissa lost again.

'Mack? Did Juliet not come and ask you? There's a kid gone missing from the Hall. She was dropped off at the usual time this morning and hasn't been seen since.'

It's happened before. The kids are teenagers, after all, as prone to bunk off as any ordinary child.

'Well, she's not been in the crypt, but that's as much as I can help you with. I haven't seen Juliet all morning. Is the geyser on?'

I sit on the hut steps in the sunshine while Peter makes my coffee. I pass him a coin. The coffee was free last week, but that was before I knew who I was working for. Peter accepts the money without the need of an explanation. Like Juliet, this place is his life too. I appreciate that he is bearing his anxiety with such composure.

'The girl is called Melissa?'

'Yes. Melissa Fawdington. Do you know which one she is?' he asks.

'No, I know a Melissa, that's all. Nothing to do with the Hall.'

'I don't know why the parents don't take them into the school. It's the third time this year,' he says.

'Giving them some independence, as normal a life as possible?'

He shakes his head. 'Anyway... she'll come back in time for lunch, she's a proper little porker, always hanging round the hut trying to nick sweets.' He models the bulky shape of the girl in the air with his hands.

'Ah, that one. Yes, I have seen her. Cheeky.'

'That's her. Yes, come to think of it, I saw you talking to her last Friday,' he says.

'She was hanging round here at the weekend too, down by the bridge.'

'Probably found herself a boyfriend. You know what girls are like at that age.'

There is an amicable lull in the conversation. I finish my coffee.

I have to admit I'm quite pleased the wretched child has gone missing. It means she won't be hanging around here. Something about her bothers me. I like her even less now I know her name.

♟

I have hit a hard patch of masonry. The wall is much better built lower down though I'm still working above my height. The original mason probably had some little job's-worth like Jason sitting over him, too, making him build more sloppily towards the top, to finish the job in a hurry. It's a pity he wasn't so lax earlier on. I'm finding this hard, unmaking his wall. Lugging out the rubble out seems like welcome relief. I wipe the grime off my watch at increasingly frequent intervals, looking forward to my lunch break. At least there's less dust now I'm going more slowly.

♟

Finally I emerge into the sunshine. It feels like breaking through the surface of a pond. Deep lungfuls of sweet air and the smell of bruised grass. Everyone is standing in a big group on the lawn in front of the Castle.

Another meeting about the Jacobites? Something's wrong. A police car is parked on the grass behind them. I walk across and stand beside Peter.

'What's happening?' I ask.

'They're organising search parties.'

'For the girl? Bit soon isn't it?'

'Some of the other kids said she's been upset recently. Talking about a man threatening her,' he says.

'Oh dear.' Hard enough to sort fact from fiction in what teenagers usually tell their friends, doubly so with children who have such a confused understanding of the world.

I would rather help with the search than keep on burrowing under the Chapel. I volunteer on the spot. It will annoy Jason and he will not want to lose face by showing it. I have no fear for this Melissa, she seems stroppy enough to look after herself, and it's only been half a day. But I suppose I am biased. To her parents, she is still a vulnerable little girl.

My Melissa wasn't a child, she was twenty-one. It was a lousy party, her twenty-first, relatives awkward with her friends.

I wasn't allowed in her bedroom. Her mother was a cow. I know Melissa was her little girl.

I join Peter's team. We stand waiting in the sunshine for our instructions while Juliet talks to one of the police officers. He beckons me over. Why is Juliet looking at me like that?

'Malcolm Macready?'

'Yes.' I can hear the caution in my own voice.

Juliet is blushing so furiously I can feel the heat.

'You know Melissa Fawdington?' he asks.

'The missing girl? I've spoken to her a couple of times. I didn't know her name until this morning, when our custodian told me she was missing.' I find myself reddening as if I've done something wrong.

'You didn't know her name?' He looks at Juliet significantly.

'My girlfriend's called Melissa.' I have nothing to hide.

'Melissa Stokes?'

I nod. Bloody Juliet has told him about Melissa. I needed a CRB check to work here because of the proximity to the Hall. I told her why there was a query. A formality. Ten years ago.

She was all tea and sympathy. I feel betrayed.

'Would you prefer to talk in private?'

'This is fine. Do I need my solicitor?'

'You're not under arrest. We're confirming everyone's whereabouts.' Is he smiling? Condescending little prick. 'Can you tell me where you've been since eight o' clock this morning?'

'I left home about quarter past eight, got here at five to. I met Jason Holden, and we discussed the work under the Chapel. I worked, had a coffee with Peter at half ten and went back down until lunchtime.'

'Before you left home?'

'I was getting ready for work. I live alone.'

I am glad that I cannot confirm where I was. It makes his job less easy. Juliet is quivery with treacherous excitement. I turn my back on them when he has finished and walk back to the Chapel. I don't think they will want me in their search party after all.

'Mack?' Peter calls after me. What's the point? I slam the door behind me.

♟

There is a kafuffle outside, but I don't care. Let them get on with it.

It's getting louder, shouting, and barking too. They must be right outside. Thumps and slams and a sudden draught. Both doors bang open at once, sucking the wind from north to south, stirring up the air down here in the crypt as it does so. Dust swirls up and envelops me. I'm blind, with only the manic yelling and baying above. Christ, they're going to set the dogs on me. Is it better to wait down here or go up there? The dust eddies round me as I climb up the stairs, wiping grit from the corners of my eyes.

The police dog-handlers are in silhouette, they become clearer every second as the heavy dust settles. Two of the dogs are making a hell of a racket at the Family door. I leave them to it. There are three more handlers at the South door, swearing and shouting, trying to control their bloody wolf pack. The dogs sound hysterical, terrified. They are trying to pull away from the Chapel, straining back on their haunches. The handlers are hauling on their leashes, leaning towards the doorway, men and dogs in furious equilibrium. One of them shouts at me in the same tone he uses on his dog.

'You, out here, now.'

I shield my eyes from the sun as I cross the grass, waiting while he drags his dog over to another handler.

'What's got into the dogs?' I ask.

The baying has subsided to an urgent whining now they have moved back from the door. Even so, I almost have to shout to make myself heard.

'Put that down, sir.'

I've carried my hammer up here. 'You can't bring the dogs into the Chapel.'

'Put the hammer down, sir.'

I don't want to. I might forget where I've put it. 'What's the matter with them?'

'They've followed something here. This is the last time I'll ask you. Put it down.' He pulls his truncheon out of his belt. As if.

I look him in the eye. 'I'm using it. I was using it when you arrived.'

One of the dogs is yelping repeatedly now, like someone's beating it. The noise goes right through my head.

'Shut that bloody animal up!' he shouts over his shoulder. He turns back and squares up to me.

Bugger this. 'Come in if you're going to, but you're not bringing the dogs in.' I turn my back on him, my hammer still in my hand.

He follows, has no choice. The petty victory steadies the sick feeling in my stomach until the nearest dog catches my eye. Its growl rumbles like a rock fall, still going as I pass into the cool sanctuary of the Chapel.

The handler hesitates behind me and I pause so he can give his eyes time to adjust to the comparative gloom. I cross the flags and shut the Family door; the draught subsides, but the air is cold. We are at the foot of the stairs to the gallery.

He looks around, 'What's upstairs?'

It's a real effort to keep my peace as we climb up the uneven whitewashed stairway. Is it universal, this need to make inane chatter with police officers under any circumstances?

There's someone sitting on the bench by the rail. It's not who we're looking for. Nowhere up here for a plump teenager to hide. Nevertheless, he strides around the small space as if he could make her bounce out of the floorboards. The exhibits in the cabinets tinkle on their glass shelves in time to his footfall.

The elderly visitor is ignoring the disturbance. She shouldn't be in here.

'Excuse me, the Chapel is closed,' I tell her.

No response.

I step in front of her. She stares at me blankly. I recognise her, one of Robin's regulars.

P.C. Plod is breathing heavily behind me. 'This some sort of museum?' Amazing level of contempt he gets into his voice, despising the whole concept of antiquity in a breath.

I give up on the old dear and turn back to the police officer. 'It's what the archaeologists have found over the years in the Castle grounds.'

'Valuable?'

Not in the way he's thinking. I shake my head. All I can taste is dust.

He sets off down the stairs. He actually looks under the pews, pushed up against the wall. Has he not read the description of her?

'Is that camera turned on?'

'Yes.'

It's trained on the only things of any monetary value in the place, a battered chair and the Jacobean cradle, black oak, carved with creatures to scar the infant mind.

'I'll need to see the recordings since midnight,' he says.

'Ask the custodian, Peter White.'

He grunts and peers into the choir stalls. He sets the fragile cradle rocking as he pushes past.

'Where else?'

I try to say, but I choke on spittle, the words lost as I cough. Grit gets into my eyes when I rub them. He waits then follows me down into the crypt in silence. His feet sound dull and flat behind me.

I make a point of laying down my hammer next to my chisel.

'What's behind this wall?' he asks.

'I don't know. She couldn't get through there.'

He is straining to look in, standing tiptoe on the plank.

'I need a ladder.'

'I don't have one.' I do. I was using it last week. Someone must have borrowed it. Jason had the key.

'And you've been down here all the time the Chapel was unlocked?'

'Yes, apart from my breaks.'

He builds a little step out of my breezeblocks so that his chin is level with the top stones. The wall is too thick for him to see anything but straight ahead. He shines his torch in. I can see the roof of the hidden section from where I stand. I'm no wiser, it looks just like the roof on this side, nicely finished stone blocks arching across the span of the room beyond.

'She couldn't get through there,' he concludes as he slithers gingerly down from his makeshift steps.

He rubs his hands, 'Bloody freezing in here.'

That's as close as he'll come to acknowledging my cooperation.

I walk behind him up the stairs, trying to seem calm, indifferent. The dogs growl as soon as I put my foot on the threshold. It can't be me that's setting them off like this. I stand in the doorway and watch the policeman leave. He's still in the shadow from the Chapel, but I know it's warmer than inside, he seems to grow as he walks away. A sudden through-draught slams the door. He'll think it was me.

Upstairs, the old woman has left; the gallery is empty.

♜

It's like an igloo down here. I'm shivering, and my breath's coming in clouds. My hands are frozen, the cold of the metal hammer shaft makes my fingers ache. It's like working outside in February, not inside in May.

The dogs were taken away over an hour ago, there's no sound from outside. Every time I stop hammering to listen it's quiet. Are they still searching? Have they found her? I will feel terrible if she really has been hurt. Stolen, raped, strangled. Jesus. The only thing worse than being down here would be to go up there and find out. There is no-one up there I want to talk to. I'm trapped, stuck in this freezing cellar until they all go home. Will this be interpreted as guilt, skulking down here?

I've removed six stones since the dogs. One every ten minutes. I estimate at this rate it will take me forty-two working days to take down the facing stones, the same for the inner wall. I should be done by the end of September, not allowing for the infill and rubble removal.

I'd get on faster if I stopped playing games. It's years since I did this, maths over reality, simple problems, a man digging a hole. Logic. No bloody logic about those dogs. They were scared.

There is a draught now. I thought I had imagined it earlier, but it's definitely there. Not constant, almost like the building's breathing. Is there a shaft beyond this wall? Bit daft having a priest hole under the Chapel. The archaeologists excavated the drains last year, five foot high and paved, opening into little subterranean rooms. The network stretched way beyond the Castle demesne. They reckon some might be Roman. Maybe this Chapel joins up with the drains.

It's getting too cold to work down here.

I've put down my tools and I'm hugging my hands under my armpits. It hurts as the feeling comes back. Someone's coming. Not police, the footfall's too hesitant. Too heavy for Juliet.

'Malcolm?'

'Down here, Jason.'

Better look busy. Christ, the hammer is so cold it stings my fingers. It clatters when I drop it.

Jason stands half way down the steps. 'Everything alright?'

I leave the hammer on the ground and look at him. Jason is looking right back at me. Someone steps on my grave. Strange, this is commiseration I'm feeling. There is an unspoken sharing of our woes. He is aware of it, too, I swear it.

Jason clears his throat. 'I'm sorry I wasn't here earlier to deal with the police when they searched the Chapel.'

What use would he have been? I'm so hunched up with the cold my shrug doesn't look as offensive as it could have.

He hasn't finished. 'And about before, I apologise for earlier, too, Malcolm. I was out of order. You know your job.'

'How's your hand?'

He is wearing a bandage, he raises it a little. 'Index finger broken. My fault.'

There's nothing to say.

He comes down to my level and stands next to me. We contemplate my lack of progress for a moment.

'It's quarter to four. You may as well finish in the crypt today. It's too cold to work down here.'

'Thank you.' I could go for a walk, try to enjoy the sunshine.

'You can fill your time in working on the tower.'

It's somehow reassuring when he's so consistent.

'Why are you smiling? Is there a problem?'

'No, Jason.'

He puts his uninjured hand up to his temples, probing with the tips of his long, delicate fingers for the epicentre of some pain. I hesitate to see if he has anything else to say, but he waves me away.

♟

The walls are as warm as flesh. It's good to be up here, above the trees. I swing myself up to the top of the scaffolding and begin to hack the old mortar out. There isn't really time to do much. I am starting a new section. The stones seem quite sound here, the south face, away from the prevailing weather. No complaints, the sun is shining, I can smell the big sycamore tree on the breeze and the balsam from the path below. Above the rumble of traffic noise, across the river, the bells of St. Andrew's in Corbridge chime four.

And then I hear her singing that bloody song.

♟

This is ridiculous. Sound carries up to the tower, further than you'd expect, but even so, she still has to be somewhere around the Castle. I thought I saw her a minute ago by the window upstairs, but it must have been shadows. Everyone has left. The search has moved on, and it's not time for David to start on his rounds yet. The car park is empty. I've looked everywhere.

'Melissa.' Can't sound too anxious, might frighten her.

This is hopeless. Maybe if I go back up, right up to the pepper-pot tower, I could get an overview.

These stairs are going to kill me. Sweat is pouring off me. Where can she have gone? Little cow has probably spent the day watching everyone going frantic looking for her. I check each level as I go, but she could slip back down past me, get down the steps each time I leave the stairwell. I can't hear anything when I stop, just the blood in my ears, but she knows this place probably as well as I do. Hide and seek, but I'm not playing.

'Melissa, come on.'

No reason to think she's in the Castle now, just I keep seeing things in the corner of my eye. She must be enjoying this. Blast her. She'll feel differently when she's all alone in the dark. Nearly there. I pause to catch my breath as I unlock the padlock to the top tower. A fragment of song? No, just birds.

It's cold in the little spiral stairway, and I almost lose my footing in the gloom. Steady. The day has lost its warmth. I turn around in the miniature turret, survey the tree tops, thick new leaves in the way of whatever it was I hoped to see.

I put my hands up to my mouth. 'Melissa. Come out wherever you are.'

There, on the platform below me, something pale shifts and slips. I can't quite see. I'll have to lean over. Damn, the stone crumbles as I try to get a better look. No good, it won't take my weight. There's a little sound. A sob or a laugh. I can't see anyone. I call her name again as I scramble back down the uneven blocks to the lower level. No-one's here, just an empty rectangular-decked platform with four broken walls, a small mediaeval fireplace in the only wall that is still full-height. She wouldn't fit in that. It's too cold to stay up here much longer. My shirt's soaked. The breeze is picking up and the sun has gone behind the clouds.

She's gone. I can feel it. Bloody stupid, I don't know that, I'm not psychic. She could still be here. I'm just tired with the search. I call out for her on each landing as I go down and wait in vain for a reply.

It's not my responsibility. They ought to have looked more thoroughly this afternoon. Should I ring the police? I should, but I won't. I must promise myself this.

There is nothing when I listen at the timber of the Castle door. If she is here, if she has chosen to stay here, then the walls will keep her safe tonight.

'This is your last chance, Melissa. I've locked the door. Can you hear me? You'll have to wait here all night now.'

Nothing.

The jackdaws in the sycamore mutter as I walk away on the gravel path. I turn by the corner of the Chapel. Yes, I expected that, a movement behind the big window in the Great Hall. It's my imagination, it must be.

'Goodbye, Melissa.'

Ⅰ

God, what time is it? No lights this time, no flapping injured bats. The room's dark and quiet. The joints click in my back as I stretch. Where's my watch? Blast, it's fallen onto the floor. Where's it gone? Fingertip search, one-handed round the legs of the bedside table.

My hand. Someone's got hold of my wrist. Jesus Christ! There's someone under my bed. 'Help. *Get off. Get off.*' The sheets won't let go. I twist over and flip right off the bed onto my back, wrapped up in bedclothes. I'm being pulled under. 'Help!' The stuff from my bedside table falls on my head, the water splashes into my eyes. I cut my free hand finding the lamp. I smash it down onto the fist that grips mine. Oh thank God. My hand's released.

Back on my feet, scrabbling for the door.

I can't find the light switch. There it is, slippery with my blood.

Safety in light. The room looks like a tornado just passed through it.

'*Get out!*'

I've no weapon, nothing to back up the shaky fury in my voice. I'm bleeding from both hands, but if I move from the door they might escape and I'm not going to let them get away with this.

'Get out of there.' I sound calmer. I can reach the chair with my foot and pull it towards me. I don't take my eyes of the bed while I put my jeans on. I must look ridiculous holding the chair like a lion tamer, but I'm not taking any chances. I stay between the bed and door and tug the bedclothes towards me. I crouch down, but I can't see. My lamp's broken, I can't get a light down here.

'Melissa?' horrible thought that she was in here while I was asleep. I try to remember the grip dragging me down. Could a girl have done that? I have four red marks across my wrist. The blood trickles down to my elbow as I inspect the damage from the glass. Stings a bit.

In the end, I'm on all fours peering into the empty darkness under the bed.

No-one could get past me.

But there's no-one here either.

7. TUESDAY

Robin doesn't sound like I've woken him.

'*I'll come over for you.*'

I am almost undone by his kindness. I can't find the words to express how thankful I am. He has already rung off. I didn't know who else to call. I couldn't ask Juliet to come out at this hour and Peter wouldn't get of his bed in the middle of the night even if it was on fire. Anyway it's not such an imposition, Robin is a night-owl, or rather a nightingale, the robin that sings in the dark so that no-one sees it has lost its red breast.

I'm not sure if I need stitches. The bleeding seems to have stopped, but it was so difficult wrapping both hands that I'm reluctant to unwrap them again to check. I haven't been upstairs since it happened. I can't even read while I wait for him, can't hold a book, can't take my mind off it. It was hard enough to get my trainers on.

Robin's here already.

'Thank you for coming.' I proffer my injuries, bloody tea towels bound round both fists.

'No, no. Keep them wrapped. I've brought nothing to deal with cuts. We'll get you back to my place.'

'I thought it might be best to go to A and E.'

'You think I can't deal with this?'

The sharpness in his voice makes my heart sink. 'I might need stitches.'

'Why did you call me if you didn't think I could help?'

My gratitude is dimming already. I am uncertain of the price of the favour I'm asking. 'I don't have any way of getting –'

'Ah, so I'm a cheap taxi service.'

'Robin –'

He's smiling to soften the chastisement. 'I'm sure it won't be bad enough for stitches.' He thinks I'm making a fuss.

'Yes, you're probably right. It's just both hands… you know.'

'Difficult.'

'Anyway, thanks for coming.'

He doesn't say I'm welcome, or reassure me that it's nothing. He ushers me out of the house, into the dewy darkness and locks my door behind us. It's awkward opening the car door, and I think my right hand is bleeding again. Inside his car smells of petrol fumes. It's almost new, a black showy Lotus, but it smells like an old banger. My feet settle in the compost of rubbish in the passenger footwell. For such a foodie, he has a remarkable number of fast-food cartons in here. He reaches across me to fasten the seatbelt. It is an uncomfortable moment, he is too close and his breath is foul, but then he's come out in the middle of the night to help me. I am an ungracious sod. I don't like being beholden to anyone. Still, better to be indebted to Robin than suffer Juliet's cloying interference.

Robin over-revs the engine when he starts. He always does this. The neighbours have mentioned it a couple of times when our Friday night chess games have stretched into the small hours.

'Ready?'

I mutter gratefulness once again as he pulls away from my gate. Christ, he drives fast.

'Anything wrong? Besides your hands.'

'No. Fine, thank you.' I want to cling to seat belt strap as he cuts every corner. Hedges fly towards us in the headlights. He's doing eighty, barely slows at the junctions. Thank God it's only five miles. Thank God we don't meet any other traffic. The last sixty yards up an untarmacked drive leave me shaken. He stops so abruptly it's all I can do to stay put.

He lives in an ordinary farmhouse, not a manse or whatever the Papist equivalent is. The windows were dark as we approached, but the lights turn on as soon as we cross the threshold. He must have some sort of gizmo. I've never noticed this before and it unsettles me. His house feels suddenly less predictable, less familiar, not that he brings me here very often.

The first time I visited it was like I conjured the whole thing. It was just the way I'd imagined his home would be. Not the outside, that's a plain farmhouse with an overgrown garden. But inside the hallway is far too grand for a country home, black and white marble and a sweeping staircase with a galleried landing above. There are only three windows upstairs, so it doesn't seem feasible that there is room for bedrooms as well as all this stately grandeur. His sitting room is walled in with heavy bookcases. Low piles of extra books that have no shelves spread like stromatolites across the dusty wooden floor. There are only two chairs, ancient and saggy. Little clouds of dust puff up when you sit down too fast, and they squeak and wheeze when you clamber out of them. I have a twinge of envy every time I come into this room. I don't think he reads as much as he makes out: the same books lie bookmarked next to the chairs, the dust thicker each time I visit.

I wish I could get the living room fire in my cottage to stay in like this. He pokes it briefly and sparks fly up from the blaze.

'Let's take a look at you, then.'

He stands next to me under the central ceiling light. The discomfort of proximity makes me fumble to unwrap the towels myself. He doesn't seem very impressed. The cut on my right hand looks nasty. A slice right across the palm cuts my life line at the heel of my hand and splits the skin between my thumb and forefinger, the slight webbing that shows my Viking heritage.

'I have something to fix that.'

Ointment? It's beyond a smear of Germolene. I wish he'd taken me to casualty.

'What's the matter, Mack?'

'Sure it doesn't need stitches?'

'It's nothing. What is worrying you? I do have medical training.'

'I didn't know.'

He smiles, modestly lowering those white eyelashes. 'In a previous life.'

All the same. 'This one looks like it might heal better with a stitch or two.'

He laughs at me. 'Don't be such a girl.'

'It's deep.'

'It's a scratch. Trust me. Back in a tick.'

Trust? But I can hardly ask for a second opinion when I've called him for help.

✗

'Mack. I thought I would let you doze, but maybe we'd better see to your hands.'

I have cricked my neck with starting up in the sagging chair. The fire roars, making me sweat. He is holding a tray of pots and bowls, more like he's going to prepare food rather than tend to damaged skin. I try to move some periodicals off the table by his chair so that he can set the tray down. I have to swipe them sideways in the end. My fingers are very stiff.

He's perched on the edge of the other chair, dabbing a white napkin into some sort of black goo that smells like seaweed. I really don't want this.

'Hang on –'

He takes hold of my right hand. Holds hard onto it. This is the second time I've been caught tonight. I thrash in the chair, squirming even before he wipes the cloth into the cut.

'Jesus Christ!' It stings like hell, hurts far more than the initial cut.

Robin throws my hand back at me.

'Don't use that name *here*.'

Bloody hell, I thought he didn't believe –

He's trembling. The fire blazes up, making shadows that distort his mouth into a snarl, his eyes just pinpricks of black in the ruddy flesh. For a moment I see something else, not my friend at all.

It's only the flickering light, tired eyes and firelight.

'I –' My pulse is throbbing so hard in my throat that it strangles my words.

'Give me your hand.' He is making an effort to calm down. Even for the sake of friendship I can't let him…

He's grabbed my hand so tight I can't turn it. The ointment burns the split skin.

'Please –'

'Nearly done. Brilliant stuff this. I would have used comfrey, but it's too early in the season.'

It's unbearable, beyond words. Maybe it will suddenly work, have an anaesthetic effect. Wish it would hurry up. No, not my other hand. I'm trying so hard not to wail out loud that I have no energy spare to protest as he does the same to my left hand. *Jesus Christ,* I repeat in my head. He shows me what he has done. The cuts have opened up like gaping mouths, and the surrounding skin is angry under the slime.

'Pennyroyal.' The bastard is studiously ignoring my distress. 'Bound to hurt, first part of the healing process.'

Maybe if I wash it off now…

'Sit down. I'll bandage your hands; we don't want them getting infected.'

He has two rolls of grubby crepe bandages. They look like they've been stored in a dusty cupboard for a long time. He's gentle enough now. I don't have a choice. He works in silence. I try to count the books along the shelf next to me to take my mind off the pain. Finally he's finished with me.

'Thank you.' The dressings look ludicrous. He's used a full roll on each hand so they are like big white galls at the end of my arms, with only my finger tips protruding. I can barely waggle my fingers. I'm getting used to the pain, but it's not getting any better. 'Should it hurt this much?'

'Don't be such a baby, Mack.'

I'll get Juliet or Peter to take me to casualty tomorrow. I hope it won't be too late to stitch them. I use the bandaging on the back of my left hand to wipe the sweat off my face while I hunt for a preamble to asking what else was in the muck he's rubbed into my cuts.

'I didn't think you went in for all this qua – traditional medicine.'

'I find it's very effective.'

I've hurt his feelings. He packs up the jars with quiet dignity and carries the tray back out. He did come and pick me up in the middle of the night. *Sweet Jesus*, it hurts. I imagine the skin pulling further apart, the sinews and flesh underneath tearing away from my bones. What keeps your hands together if the skin comes off?

He's back again. 'You'd better take some painkillers if you can't cope with the discomfort.' He waves the box of co-codamol in front of me and releases the tablets, placing them by a glass of water.

No more quackery. I get the point.

I can't touch my thumb and fingertips together, he has robbed me of my fine motor skills. He swoops on the pills impatiently and holds them in front of my face as I sit and he stands. He is looking down on me, celebrant to penitent. I open my mouth and he places the pill on my tongue, a Host I believe in, the grace of codeine. I swallow it alright, but he's passing me the next one already. I can't manage to swallow two without water. He passes me the glass, holds it to my lips, tips it too far, so that I choke and splutter. I wipe my mouth on the bandages. The smell of the muck he used makes me gag. I look up at him to avoid staring eye-level at his crotch. He scowls down on me, then turns and withdraws without a word, closing the door quietly behind him.

I must have really offended him. Can I ask him to drive me home? Should I get a taxi? I'm not sure I can even use a phone with these wretched bandages.

♟

Footsteps wake me. They hesitate at the sitting room door, then leave, softly.

I try to settle down again, but sleep won't come. No wonder, I can see daylight under the curtains. It's time to get up. My hands are throbbing sinfully. From the kitchen I can hear the chink of china. I settle back in the chair and pretend to be asleep when he comes in.

'How are your hands this morning?'

I mumble something, feigning disturbed slumber. I will not commit to the lie that my hands are better after his ministrations. I can barely believe that I have to be this disingenuous with Robin. He's forgotten we're friends, forgotten how pleased he was that he had someone to talk to on his own level. I want him to remember but I don't understand how it came to this pass, so I'm at a loss to make amends. I feel so helpless. His huffiness bothers me almost as much as my hands.

'I'll help you with breakfast, then I'll run you home. I have things to do today.'

'Of course you have, you've done more than enough already. Sorry I kept you up last night.'

He's looking at me across the toast and coffee. Grovelling won't help me.

'Actually, Robin, I do think I should get my hands seen to at the hospital, they are –'

'I haven't time to take you to casualty this morning. Do you think if I drive you home, you could get another of your friends from your extensive social network to run you down to the General?'

Shit. What can I say to that?

We ignore the breakfast tray by silent accord and he ushers me out of the room.

He never asked how I cut my hands. I hope he doesn't think it was on purpose. Not that it matters what he thinks of me. Not now. He hurt my hands when I needed help, and yet he's the one sulking.

I don't even attempt to fasten my seat belt, and if he notices he doesn't say anything. I close my eyes. If we crash I'd rather not have the anticipation.

The roads aren't as quiet this time of day. I imagine the angry mothers in their 4x4s squealing to a halt as he cuts corners and jumps junctions. I'm sweating by the time he pulls up at home.

'Thank you.'

'Get out.'

It takes a while. He does not assist. I bend down to talk through the closed window. 'Robin, look –'

He's off. Loose chippings scatter behind him.

The ginger cat is sitting on the opposite verge eight feet away, watching him go. I catch its eye. It hisses at me.

'Not you as well.'

Keys. Hell and damnation. He's got my keys. He locked the door last night. I can see my phone on the kitchen table. It's ringing. Probably Mel.

What now? Cap in hand to the bloody landlord. Actually, Clara has a set of keys. She's much closer, and human. A bad-tempered, selfish snob, but human all the same. I can't recommend her brother nearly so highly. She might even give me a lift to get my hands seen to.

The cuts have oozed a yellow liquid through the crepe.

♟

It's only a mile, but I haven't a coat, and although it's not raining, the air is damp and the breeze is strong. It's nine, now. I step into her driveway just as she returns from taking her offspring to the expensive private day-school that will hopefully compensate for their inherent stupidity. She hasn't done her face yet. Without lipstick she looks disconcertingly like her brother.

'Mack! Oh good, you've come to fix the water-table?'

I hold up my hands.

'Good God, what have you been doing?'

'I cut my hands last night and Robin bandaged them, but he's put some stuff on... I'm in a bad way, Clara, and he has my door keys.'

She wrinkles her nose. It's in the balance; she wants to distance herself.

'Well, if you could just give me your spare keys for the cottage.' I avoid her eyes, watch a blackbird on the lawn, half turn to go. Can I be any more pathetic?

It works.

'Oh, come in, then. See what we can do.'

I follow her to kitchen door at the side of the house. The kitchen is as messy as usual. God knows how she manages to pass hygiene control for the tea-rooms and her bed and breakfast business. Two obese Basset hounds shift and grumble as I step over them next to the Aga. Clara leads me through the back hallway to the old scullery. It's an interesting room, hardly touched by the twentieth century, let alone the twenty-first. It must be fourteen feet to the ceiling. There's a huge, crazed Belfast sink under the window, big enough to bathe in. The ceiling is hung with obsolescent metal work and tackle, all festooned with fat, fluffy cobwebs. The window is only cleaned to a comfortable height, curtained with dirt and webs above. Clara keeps her looseboxes in better order. A tabby cat, hiding among the jars of matted paintbrushes and tins of hoof-oil, jumps out and bolts for the door.

'Wait here.'

She isn't long. She's carrying the first aid kit she uses for the horses. I want proper medical care, not another –

Ah, Clara with a pair of sharp scissors is enough to scare anyone. I stand absolutely still while she cuts the bandages off my hands.

'Now then, my bonny lad...' I've heard her talk like this before, but only to her horses. The words don't matter, her tone is eloquent, '...there we go. Hold still. Steady does it. Gently. Gently.'

Ugh, what a mess. The skin is white and wrinkled, what I can see of it. The muck Robin applied is still slimed over the worst bits, the raw edges of the cuts. The flesh looks angry underneath. It smells bad. Gangrene? So soon? If anything, it hurts even more with the fresh air.

'Oooh what have we here, then laddo?' She's talking to herself, watching my hands as if they might go off somewhere on their own. She gropes behind her and brings out a nail brush. This is not good.

'Clara, I think-'

She rushes me. No nonsense, a pre-emptive strike. She thrusts my hands under the cold tap in her strong grip. All the while she is scrubbing she is chatting in her equine-vernacular, causing me so much pain I can't help but howl.

It's over. She was quick. My hands are bleeding and smarting, but the awful burning pain is gone now they're clean again. I lean against the sink while I get my breath back.

'Right, you need stitches in that one.'

It looks better than it did.

She passes me a towel that smells of her Bassets. 'What the hell did she put on your hands?'

'Robin?'

'Whoever. You said someone did this to you.'

'I don't know. He mentioned pennyroyal.'

She snorts unpleasantly. 'Cobblers. No use whatsoever. Use that for causing miscarriages.'

I don't even want to know how she knows that.

'Come on, then. I'll take you down to the General. I need to get some tea-bags anyway.'

She's plainly not interested in my gratitude. I manage a smile.

'That's better.'

She hasn't even mentioned the Castle. Shit, I might even have to revisit my prejudices on this one.

♟

Ten to three. Five hours to get six stitches. Juliet's late, pulling up at the kerb in her little yellow Fiat. I wonder if anyone has bothered to tell Jason. This is going to slow me down.

She opens the door for me and holds it while I climb in. My fingers are so clumsy from the local anaesthetic that I can't fasten my seat belt. I have to wait for her to sit down.

'We've been so worried about you. Here, let me get that.' She smells of soap and shampoo, old but clean. She leans across me and belts me in. 'What with one thing and another.'

She does a sixteen point safety check before we set off, even though she is mid-journey, adjusting her mirrors, fidgeting herself comfortable on her backrest.

'Peter and I think you need a good old-fashioned holiday. I don't know how you keep going on doing all that hard work. You're a bright boy, Mack; you shouldn't be doing manual labour like this.'

So she and Peter think I'm depressed. 'It's no shame to work with your hands.'

'No, no, I didn't mean that.' She stares earnestly ahead of us, doing twenty five on a straight road. Still, better than Robin.

'Things can get on top of you, especially when you're on your own.' She slows still further to glance at me. 'Sometimes we all need a little help.'

Worse than depressed, suicidal, even. Cowardice and incompetence making me flunk an attempt to slit my wrists.

I clear my throat. 'My hands were an accident.'

'Of course they were. I don't think you said how it happened?'

'I broke a glass in the dark and knocked my light off the table, then cut myself trying to turn it on.' Close enough.

'And you waited until Clara found you in the morning? How on earth did you get locked out?'

'Father Greene. I called Father Greene last night –'

'You called a priest instead of a doctor?'

'He's a friend.'

'Oh. Oh, I see. Well, that's good. I'm glad you're making friends here. Local, is he?'

'He lives past Whitley Chapel. I thought you knew him.'

'No, dear. I don't have a lot to do with That Side.'

Robin knows Juliet. I suppose he's around the Castle so much that they must have met. I should have guessed that she was staunch Anglican, all priests must look the same to her.

'I'm not a Catholic either. He's not my priest or confessor or whatever. Just a friend, like I said. We play chess.'

'I did wonder, you don't seem the type. Here we are.'

She has driven me home.

'I ought to get to work.'

'It's the middle of the afternoon. Jason hasn't been there today, anyway. And the police are all over the place. They still haven't found that poor little girl. Besides, you can't do anything with bandaged hands.'

Somehow she already has the spare keys. I follow her in. The cottage is always cold when the wind is up like this.

Juliet fusses and flaps. Puts the kettle on, lights the fire, finds a roll of freezer bags for me to put over my hands to keep my bandages clean. I haven't eaten. She makes me sardines on toast. Stays to wash up. Talking, all the time talking. I am so tired.

✚

When I wake up I can hear her above me. This is too much. I jog up the narrow stairs and catch her red-handed with a bundle of my sheets in her arms.

'You can't sleep in these.' She's blushing, but defiant.

I can see over her shoulder that she's tidied my room.

'Juliet, really –'

'You need help. Professional help.'

If the landing weren't so small and she wasn't so slight I might have missed her brushing past me. For Juliet that is extreme aggression. Or maybe fear –

On the wall behind the bed I have drawn a gaping mouth in my own blood.

✚

I am alone. I could call out after her receding footsteps, but she is lost to me. I am something else to her now, something sick, contaminated.

She slams the garden gate. Oh, Juliet, come back. No-one ever needed you as badly as I do now.

Right now it's too easy to remember last night. Is this what it feels like, madness? Insanity? But something real happened.

I have marks on my wrist still, turning to bruises already, stale blood lying under the surface of my skin. I can't remember what took place afterwards though, can't follow my steps downstairs before I rang Robin. Am I having blackouts? I don't remember drawing anything on the wall. Why did I do that?

One thing for her to tell me that I need help, another to actually stay here and help me get it. Out there she's finally finished getting herself ready to drive off. I can hear her tentative little motor pull away from my gate.

On further reflection, I don't think I want to stay in this house tonight.

♟

I have moved the bed away from the wall. Something has scrooged around under there. The carpet nap is ridged and ruffled, and my good shoes have been kicked out of the way.

Does this count as evidence?

I guess it depends on whom I'm trying to convince.

The blood didn't come off very well. I couldn't completely obliterate the mouth. I'll let it dry, then paint over it. I think I've some of that colour out in the wood shed. Plummet, it's called. A stormy grey to match the clouds the first day I moved into the cottage. Dark enough to cover these rusty stains, anyway.

Is that someone at the door? I wait for a second rap, walk to the window, stand to one side and move the curtains a little. A uniformed police officer is standing in the middle of the lawn, staring up at the windows. I withdraw my hand quickly. Another rap. There must be two of them. No car. Have they walked over from the Castle?

'Coming.' I jog down the stairs loudly to explain my shortness of breath.

They are standing side by side when I open the door.

I am too glazed with panic to listen for their names or check their ID. The shorter one, the one who was looking up at my windows, seems to be the senior of the two.

'Ah. We thought you'd be at work today. We looked for you.'

'An accident. I had an accident.'

'Nasty. Both hands.'

'I've been at the hospital, I needed stitches and I'm right-handed.' I'm talking too much. I sound like an idiot, blurting out details they don't need. I shut my mouth, but the silence is worse.

'This is just routine, sir. May we come in?'

I know I look guilty. 'Yes, fine.' I force myself to hold the door open.

The sitting room feels very crowded with them standing around. They don't sit when I invite them to. I follow their gaze, the dust, the cold grate where Juliet's mean little fire has gone out, the mess from my sardines on toast, crumbs across the rug. The room is cold and smells of fish.

'You live alone?'

I nod.

'Mind if we have a look around?'

Yes. 'There's nothing to see.'

'Just to check, to eliminate –'

'You'd need a warrant, then, and reasonable grounds.'

'A missing girl is reasonable grounds, wouldn't you say?'

'It's a small cottage; I would have noticed her.'

He jerks his head up. I have made a mistake.

'Do you hear something, Neil?'

'Upstairs?'

They barge past me. I don't know if they are allowed to do this. I have been set up. Is it better to follow? They go into my bedroom first. The taller one bars my way, stretching his arm across my door like a kid in a playground stopping me getting to the swings.

'Wait downstairs, sir.'

This is my house. I sit on the top stair. They walk past within touching distance as they search the spare room and the bathroom. It doesn't take long.

'Is this yours, sir?' My neck twinges when I twist round to look at what he is holding. It is Melissa's watch. I bought it for her twenty-first. It shows the phases of the moon. The strap is barely worn. You can't tell which hole she wore it on.

I shake my head. Let him work for his pay.

'Do you have a girlfriend?'

'No.'

'What is it doing here, then?'

'It belonged to a friend.'

'So why do you have it?'

'It doesn't belong to the girl you're looking for.'

He puts it into a plastic bag. 'We'll give you a receipt for this.'

The other one is standing behind him. I shift my position to ease my neck.

'Where are the sheets from your bed?'

'In the washing machine.'

'Having a bit of a spring clean?'

'I told you, I had an accident. They had blood on them.'

'Is the washing machine on?'

I don't know. I listen to try to hear it whirring. 'I can't remember.'

'Go and check, please, Neil.' He turns back to me. 'Mind telling me what was going on in here last night?' He indicates my bedroom door.

'I broke a glass in the dark and broke my lamp trying to turn it on and cut both my hands. It was an accident.'

'So what are the marks on your wall? They're still wet.'

'I must have smeared blood on the wall. In the dark. Before I found the light switch. I was cleaning it up when you came.'

'With bandaged hands?'

'I put bags over the bandages.'

He sucks his teeth, staring over my head as if the answer he is looking for is written on the sloping ceiling. 'You see, we were a bit concerned about you're attitude yesterday, sir.'

I stand up. I'm as tall as he is, even though I'm standing on the step below the landing.

Neil interrupts us from the foot of the stairs. He has an armful of my washing. It's still dry. Juliet could have put the bloody washing machine on for me.

♜

They've taken my sheets, too, as well as the watch. And photographs of the wet arcs on the stained wall.

They are rootling around in the outbuildings now. Maybe I should have asked them to look for the grey paint while they were out there.

The bathroom has been rifled through. They know what brand of shampoo I use and that I have electric toothbrush. More to the point, they also know I keep Melissa's cuttings in a shoebox under the spare bed, along with the birthday card she sent me and the ring she made for me the day we went for a drive up past Stanhope. She wound a single rush stem round my finger. I plaited a bracelet for her. The midges ate us alive as we rolled in the rushes.

They found her watch in my sock drawer.

I can hear them talking outside. They are asking my next-door neighbour questions. She's home from work, it's nearly six. What is she telling them about me? What does she know? We barely say hello if we see each other. I don't have any incriminating habits.

Their goodbyes are civil. The garden gate slams.

They must have gone by now.

My phone needs charging, but I don't want to hang round here that long. Sleeping bag? Spare bedroom, last time I saw it.

They have even unmade the bed. Did they think I'd ironed the girl flat and lain her between the sheets?

Maybe I won't take the sleeping bag. Better not look like I'm doing a bunk, just take the bare minimum for tonight. I'd go to a pub or a bed and breakfast, but I don't want this to look official. It's warm enough tonight, if I get out of the wind. Pity the Chapel's locked. No, the state I'm in, that's probably for the best. I shall go to Peter's hut, at least it's somewhere to go, better than sleeping under a hedge. Dear God, am I going to become a tramp because of a nightmare?

As I sit down on the bed, the shoebox with Melissa's clipping spills over next to my leg on the crumpled duvet. The ring she made has unravelled, lying amongst the leaves of paper like a shrivelled umbilical cord. A thin twine that holds me back, anchors me down so that my mouth is barely above the tide. Jesus, get a grip.

I fold the withered rush stem into my wallet, stuff clean underwear and a tee shirt into my rucksack, and put on a pullover. Better take my coat too. I pick up my phone, even though it only has one bar of charge left. I don't look back, and I don't lock the door. I'm not afraid of anything that a lock could keep out.

❧

It's cold. Not so cold I turn around. The wind is dropping, and there is some cloud coverage, so it shouldn't get too bad tonight. The rucksack's not too heavy, either. I'll walk over to the Travellers Rest for a meal. This won't be too bad. Might as well enjoy it. The stitches pull a bit. I should have phoned Jason. If he was that bothered about today he'd have rung me, anyway. I dial, but his number's unavailable. Just as well, I'd hate to use the last of the juice in the battery listening to him.

❧

The car park is full. It's always busy on Wednesdays, I should have thought of that.

The menu hasn't changed since last time. I'll have the venison casserole. Hope it's not road-kill; the chef always looks a little shady. I had rabbit here once with a lead pellet garnish.

'What can I get you to drink with that?' The lad stands behind the bar as if he'd studied it at college.

'Pint of Guinness, please.' We have to speak quite loudly because the bar is crowded and noisy.

'The draft's off. The guest ale is local.'

'Any stout?'

'Not on draft. I can highly recommend the guest ale.'

He doesn't look old enough to drink. Plump farming stock, with a round, juvenile face, all chirpy smiles and no brains. Pleasant enough, but I want something dark and bitter. Looking along the bar, I don't fancy anything they have on draft. Silly names, too sweet and too expensive.

'OK. A pint.'

He pours a glass of gassy orange liquid with foam that disperses instantly.

I take a sip before paying. It's disgusting. The lad turns red as he looks at me.

'Four pounds fifty.'

'Good God.'

'It's from our Artisan Beer range.'

'No kidding.' Shit, the owner's coming over. The thin, mean one, not the little friendly effeminate one that likes to chat about local history.

'Problems, Andy?'

'No, Mr. Archer.'

The owner shouldn't be in charge of a public house, not when he doesn't like having people on his territory.

'Everything alright with your pint, sir?'

He catches my eye. I don't have to reply. It's like I'm transparent today.

He tilts his head as though he's answering me. 'Lucozade.'

Did he really say – 'I missed that…?'

'Four pounds fifty.'

'Right.' I pass him a twenty. I'll have to get some money out of the bank tomorrow.

'I'll bring your meal over to you. Have you got a table?'

I shake my head. When I came in there were a few small tables free by the door, so I hadn't bothered to nab one. Now they have all been taken. He looks annoyed. He gazes towards an elderly couple sitting by the window that overlooks the car park. The old man is getting to his feet.

'You can sit over there.'

I have had to prop up the bar for fifteen minutes while both of them visit the lavatory and laboriously pay, forget their coats, chat to a neighbour, and generally take up space. The proprietor seems as impatient as I am to have me seated. The crowd is getting louder. I really can't drink this muck. I have to almost shout above the baying diners all around. The young barman is busy with other customers so the owner is serving me.

'Can I have a large whisky and a jug of water, please?'

'You should stay away from spirits tonight, sir.'

'Excuse me?'

He raises his eyebrows. I don't want to have an argument. I wait while he goes to the optics. We perform the transaction in silence. The general noise level rises to the point I feel like it's physically buffeting me as I weave the way to my table.

'Mack!'

Oh no, Clara. Clara and a husband so meek he has no name.

'How are your hands?' This is across three tables at ninety decibels. Several heads turn in polite enquiry.

'Six stitches. They'll be fine. Thank you for your help this morning.'

Nods of sympathy from strangers.

'I heard the police came around this afternoon.'

Even more interest from the intermediate eaters this time. I nod and sit down. She can't expect me to shout the details to her. People are staring. If they knew why the police were around, I'd be lynched.

I have barely picked up my glass and she's here, plonking herself down on a spare stool without waiting for me to invite her. 'Sorry, stupid thing to blurt out. Still, we're all friends here.'

They might be her friends. I just wanted a quiet meal.

'The police searched the cottage. They were looking for the missing girl. They didn't find her.'

'Of course not. She's still missing, then? Her poor mother, but then…it's difficult. Are you in trouble?' She manages to lower her voice without it being any less audible to the foursome at the next table. She smells of cologne and gin and an underlying whiff of Basset.

'I don't know, Clara. I haven't done anything, but that's not always a guarantee.'

She glances down at my rucksack. 'Well, anything we can do.'

The food arrives, saving me from making a reply. She stands up, getting in the way. The owner twists around her like a dancer and puts my meal down in front of me.

'Oh,' says Clara.

It's not what I ordered. It's some sort of vegetable broth, served in a wooden bowl, with a wooden spoon. I look up, but he's gone. I shrug just as my phone rings.

'I'd complain.'

'I'm sure you would, Clara. Frankly I just want to get out of here.' I pull my phone out of my pocket. 'I need to get this.'

She nods. Almost smiles, backing away, somehow missing the tables in reverse gear. 'Let me know if you need anything.'

I delete Mel's text and turn the phone off again, not that it makes any difference, just saves the battery so that I can use it too.

This soup is good. Tastes of herbs and garlic. The bread's not bad either. Possibly better than road-kill stew anyway. Could do with a proper spoon. Has no-one ever seen a man eat soup before? It's like feeding time at the zoo and I don't like being on this side of the bars.

♖

The wind has picked up, whipping the clouds into smoky tatters across the last light in the sky. The moon hasn't risen yet. It's a dark walk back to the Castle.

The roadside is soggy and there is a ditch on this side. Wish I'd thought to bring a torch. Cars don't pass me very often, but when they do I can't find a place to step off the tarmac until the headlights light up the verge. There's another motor up ahead. I must be as far as the bends already, the car's close, but I can't see the lights. Surely I should be able to see his lights by now. Shit, he hasn't got his lights on. There's no verge here, just an overgrown bank with a wall at the top. I scramble out of the path of the vehicle, nearly on top of me now, grabbing onto vegetation to pull myself clear of the road. Right at the last second his lights blaze into my face. Green discs swim before my eyes. He couldn't have done it on purpose, couldn't have known I was going to be here. Bloody fool driving around with no lights.

I can hear the car pulling up as I slither down into the road, still dazzled, dropping handfuls of crushed raspberry leaves and meadowsweet, the smell so strong it holds me up. Christ, he's turning round. Is he coming back for me? My fingers and toes remember the holds in the undergrowth. He cuts it fine, the slipstream tugs at my trousers, I'm only a couple of feet above the road. My palms are stinging with having to grip the stems, I let go as soon as I can and jump back down into the road.

'Idiot. Wanker.'

He slams the brakes on. He couldn't have heard.

Reversing light.

Adrenaline pushes me back up the bank and over the wall at the top. The long spring grass smothers me where I fall in the cool and dark. My rucksack twists into my shoulder. He brakes a few yards beyond down below on the road. The engine dies. Is he going to follow me on foot? What's he waiting for? I count my heartbeats, listening for the sound of a car door above the roar and hiss of my own breath. I get to fourteen before the engine starts again. An arc of light sweeps the branches above me as he drives away. I'm saying 'he' – could have been anyone. It wasn't Clara's Chelsea tractor, though, something low-slung and powerful.

I could just spend the night here, wrapped in the dark. The grass is not thick enough to cushion the lumps and bumps, though, and it is wet at the roots. This jacket's supposed to be waterproof, but the dampness is seeping through. Maybe it's just sweat cooling. Better start moving before I get chilled. My hands are tingling, but I can't feel blood, perhaps the stitches have held.

How the hell do I get back down? Is it wise to walk along the road? It was probably bored kids. Not personal, it couldn't be. Unless Clara has raised a lynch mob or yapped enough for someone to make the connection. Hardly anyone even knew the girl before she went missing. The car came from the wrong direction; if they'd left the pub, they'd have to drive all the way round to pass me. Sneaky. But then, they may have been driving round looking for me and struck lucky on the way back. Better stick to the fields for as long as I can.

𝕀

It's dark enough to have to keep the wall within arm's reach, brushing my fingertips against it every few steps for reassurance. Wish I knew how far along I've come. There's not enough light to get my bearings. Not sure I could climb back over this wall anyway, not without bringing it down into the road with me. The copingstones aren't packed tightly enough to do their job; they grind against each other when I lean on them. It's not properly bedded into the ground either, I can feel the loose footings through the toes of my trainers. I'd have worn my work boots if I'd known I was going to have to scale stonework. I started on dry stone walls. Uncle Jimmy would never have let me leave a job like this.

I wish I hadn't thought of him. I need to concentrate on getting to the Castle without breaking my ankles. From what I can tell, the boundary's bending round to the left, which would mean I am level with the sawmill. Could it have been Robin?

I smell the cattle before I come upon them. A sudden noise, a sharp breath only a yard away. A snort so close I can feel droplets of snot on the back of my hand. A sudden ruckus, I press back against the wall to avoid being trampled. They probably can't see any better than me, and they wouldn't care anyway.

'Oi.' They swerve away and stampede off, snorting and bucking, stopping a few yards away, waiting for more fun. I can't remember which field I last saw cattle in. I don't seem to be so far above the road. There is a faint glimmer, the moon is rising and the clouds are lifting. I have come further than I thought. I need to cross the road shortly to take the turning for the Castle.

The moon clears the trees, gibbous, fat and misshapen. The long shadows it casts lie in front of me, and its light bleaches the grass. I can see the silhouette of a gateway onto a farm track at the bottom of the field. It's a lot easier walking out across the turf than hugging the wall. I hadn't realised how tense I've been. My shoulders unknot, and I head for the gate.

The cattle circle for a while until they get bored and amble off, spattering shit as they go. They are fifty yards behind me by the time I reach the gate.

The moon is bright enough to see that there isn't a proper latch. My sore hands are too clumsy to undo the bailer twine. The bars creak under my weight as I climb over.

A motor starts behind me on the farm track. Not again. I am dazzled with brilliant light. I shield my eyes and press my back against the gate. The car rolls slowly towards me, the beam of light rocking with the uneven track. My heart is pounding in my chest, but I need it to, need to know that it can pump blood hard enough to save me. The car's not going fast enough to do me damage. I can get up on the gate if needs be. It pulls up next to me. Am I about to be ticked off for trespass?

'Mack?' The cattle thunder off behind me, back up the field.

I bend down to the window. The dashboard display illuminates his white eyelashes.

I have to make a conscious effort to unclench my teeth before I can speak. 'What are you doing here, Robin?'

'I could well ask the same of you. How are your hands?'

I pull them in against my chest in an involuntary gesture that tells him all he needs to know.

'Can I give you a lift?'

'I'm not going home.'

'Neither am I. Come on, get in, and we can talk as we drive.'

'Where have you been?'

'I'm up a dead-end lane, Mack, I'd have thought that is obvious. I was visiting. Come on, I've forgiven you for this morning.'

'Gee, thanks,' but I say this too quietly for him to hear as I cross in front of his lights to get to the passenger door.

'Put your bag in the back. Can you manage the seatbelt?'

'I'm fine. How long have you been here tonight?'

'Are you alright, Mack? What's with all the questioning?'

'Some prat tried to run me over on the way back from the pub.'

'And you thought it might have been me?'

'I really don't know, Robin. You were pretty hacked off with me this morning.'

'Trust me, if I had wanted to run you down tonight, I would have succeeded.'

Trust again. I have put such trust in Robin over the past two years that he could wreck my life more thoroughly by talking than by running me down with his car. And yet – he has forgiven me. Surprising anything can still matter to me.

I close my eyes.

♜

I wake as the car slews violently to a halt. Robin driving with his usual care and attention. He's parked at an angle on top of a thick tree root. We are in the Castle car park, amongst the stately sequoia trees planted by the people who built the Hall a century after the castle was abandoned. Their roots play havoc with the driveway and parking area.

'We're here.'

'Why?' I ask.

The drive can't have taken more than five minutes, but it feels like I've slept for hours; my neck is cricked, but the dog-tired muzziness has gone. I'm really thirsty.

'I thought this is where you were heading.'

'Why would you think that?'

'Because everyone goes somewhere they feel safe in times of trouble. And you are in trouble, aren't you, Mack?'

'I don't want to talk about it.'

'Yes you do. I'm here whenever you're ready.'

He turns off the lights. Outside, the moonlight falls in pools between the tree trunks, but it's dark here in his car, with only a small flashing red light on the dash. Robin's face is in shadows.

It takes effort not to do what he expects. Rubbish rustles when I shift my feet. 'Can you pass my rucksack?'

He struggles, pulling it awkwardly through the seats. It thuds down between us.

'Not running away are you?'

'Just wanted some fresh air.' I can feel his eyes on me. It's freezing, the temperature must have plummeted outside.

'It must have really frightened you.'

'How much did I tell you about last night?'

'Enough.'

'I can't remember.'

'Don't worry. It goes no further. I am as silent as the grave.'

I don't think I told him anything. I didn't mean to, but it's all a bit vague. I know his chess manoeuvres, and this feels like he's flushing me out, dangling hope in front of me so that I blunder on wholesale. I am rubbing the bruises on my wrist, drawing attention to them. I can feel him looking at me in the dark.

'Sorry, got to go.' I open the door and climb out, scattering several coffee cartons out with me. 'Thanks for the lift.'

'Another time.'

The door slams harder than I intended. The wind has dropped, and the clang echoes round the trees. A dog barks up at the Hall.

It's not quick, crossing the root-mesh in the patches of light. I am reluctant to walk across the middle of the car park, just in case. I can't go round the Chapel, he'll guess where I'm going. If I cross over to the stile, he'll think I'm going down the footpath to the river. Another eccentric moonlight wander. He knows about those, too.

Finally he starts the car and rolls past. He waves as he draws level with me beside the stile. I climb over in case he looks back. His taillights disappear beyond the main gates, and he floors the accelerator. A couple of days ago I would have smiled, now this irritates me.

It's safe to go back round to the path past the Chapel.

Someone's whistling. I forgot about David. Some night watchman. He didn't bother to investigate Robin's car very quickly. Still, I don't suppose I would either, not on his wages. I think he's by the Family door of the Chapel. Yes, I can hear his boots on the gravel. I wait in the shadow of an ancient lime tree. I recognise its scent in the dark.

David stops before he comes out into the open. The beam of his torch sweeps across the bumpy parking area. No-one there for him to worry about now. He'll go round the Hall next, checking the windows and doors, then he'll make himself a hot drink in his little cabin behind the Hall, then he'll start all over again. Maybe he whistles so that people get out of his way. See no evil. There, footsteps on concrete, receding into the quiet night.

I slip out of the shadows and stay on the grass next to the gravel path, making as little noise as possible. The walls of the Chapel are dazzling in the moonlight. I walk round to the dark side. I know my way so well I could do it blindfold. Peter leaves the keys to the shed under a bucket next to the fence. It's random enough, I suppose, to be some form of protection. They jangle as I lift them. I clamp my hand around them and straighten up, listening for David. A door closes at some distance, the metal door of David's Portakabin. Can't hear anything. I'm not doing anything wrong anyway. Just strange. Odd. Suspicious, even. I let myself in.

♜

It's very dark. The only window looks onto the deep shadow of the Chapel. This chair's not designed to sleep in; nevertheless,

I have slept, and something has woken me. A song, a fragment of that song. I'm not sure if it came from a bad dream or if it's outside my head.

> '...*Jocky's gone to France,*
> *and Montgomery's lady*
> *there will learn to dance;*
> *madam, are ye ready?'*

The voice is breathless, but it's holding the tune. Someone is singing as they walk along. Melissa.

I tear the door open. 'Hey, Melissa!', then remember she's a child as the footsteps turn to running, slithering over the cobbles towards the Castle. I pelt after her. The gate is shut. My arm crumples as I try to vault it, forgetting my injured palms. I roll on the cobbles and stagger to my feet.

'*Ah*. Wait. Melissa! It's OK, you aren't in trouble.' I know this will not convince her, coming from a grown man chasing her. What else can I do? This will look so bad if David finds me here.

No sound. She has stopped. I was only down for a split second, I would have seen her crossing the bars of moonlight if she'd gone past the front of the Castle. I won't sound so fierce when I've caught my breath. Can she see me? The shadow from the sycamore is deep, and I'm next to the fence to confuse my silhouette.

'Melissa? Come on, you know me. I wouldn't hurt you. I just want to get you back to your mum.' Is this the right tactic? 'Or anyone else you'd rather go back to. No-one's cross with you.'

The leaves are stirred by a slight breeze above. Is there something else? In the blackness beyond a door creaks. The Castle door. It isn't locked! Does no-one care but me? Walk, don't run. This is a rescue, not a pursuit. The door's too heavy for the wind to blow it. She must have pushed it. She must be in there. The cobbles are slippery and uneven. In the dark I miss the doorway, grope in the blackness, feel the rough edge of the coarse sandstone, follow the weathered folds back towards the huge door with my fingertips. The door is barely ajar. I have to push it further to let myself in. I meant to oil the hinges this week. The motion sensors haven't turned on the lights down here, so she must have gone upstairs. The barrel vault is the only place with electricity. I listen. She could be anywhere.

There, footsteps. Not on the stairs, on the flagged floor above.

The stairs go up in a series of short flights and quarter landings. I stop at each turn and strain to hear. I step into the huge dim hall above the barrel vault. I'm not out of breath, but my heart is thumping. I'm sure I would hear her go past me back down the steps.

'Melissa. Come on. It's me, Mack.'

I must have been wrong, the footsteps are still overhead. Now I can tell she's on the wooden decking, not flagstones.

It's lighter on the stairway further up.

Is it better to creep up to the top of the stairs or to sound confident? Which will cause least alarm? I can't help but tiptoe now, I'm so desperate to catch her.

The moonlight floods the roofless floor, shining on an empty space.

'Hello? Melissa?'

Damnation. I know she can't have gone past me. She's not in the fireplace, it's too small. Unless it isn't her.

'Hello? Anyone?'

She must be on the top level up by the door to the pepperpot tower. My feet clatter on the new wooden steps.

The platform's empty. I lean over the railings. Where is she? Hell's Teeth, she steps out from behind me, bold as brass.

'Christ! Melissa.'

The moonlight makes her skin look blue. She walks about four metres past me and turns to face me. Her tee-shirt is filthy and stained, and it clings to her lumpy adolescent bulk. She stinks. Even from this distance it turns my stomach. She smells of the river. Not the little stream under the Lord's bridge, but the Tyne itself. Her hair lies in bedraggled rat tails down her shoulders. She's dripping water onto the decking. A dark pool forms where she stands staring back at me. Her feet are bare. Neat, delicate feet, the only vulnerable thing about her. I drag my eyes back to her face.

'Have you been in the river?' I know my voice wobbles, but she's scaring me.

She opens her mouth and dark water dribbles down her chin. Christ. There is a familiar smell now, too, the underlying stench of death. Where has she been to get in this state? Has she been holed up in the crypt after all? Maybe she tried to wash herself in the river afterwards and fell in.

'It's going to be OK, Melissa.'

She shakes her head, slowly, like she's in a daydream. She takes a deep breath then tilts her head up to the moon and begins to scream. I can't shut it out even with my hands clamped over my ears. What happened to her?

'It's alright, it's alright. You're safe now.' I shout to make myself heard. Where the hell is David? I can't do this on my own. I can't bring myself to touch her, daren't anyway, how would it look? We're locked apart by revulsion and fear, and I know I should do something.

The scream falters, dwindles to a rasp and she lets her head fall forward onto her chest, her chin lost in marbled folds of fat. The light is fading. Thin, fast moving clouds filter the moon as it sinks westward. If anything this is even more unnerving, I can't distinguish her face in the gloom, just her solid outline.

'Please don't scream. I'm not coming any closer. I'm not going to hurt you. You need to come downstairs with me. You'll be safe and everyone will look after you.'

She raises her head, listening.

'Everyone will be so pleased you're alright.'

She chokes, splutters. She just stands there, aborted coughs wracking her body. My feet have taken root. Suddenly she spits out more black water. Disgusting, putrid phlegm, stinking of river silt. Jesus, she's trying to laugh.

'Stop it! Stop it, Melissa.'

Where's she going?

'No, come down from there.'

Too late, I run to save her. She moves with the lugubrious pace of a sleepwalker, yet she's at the wall before I can catch her. So fat and unfit, yet she's hoisted herself up the broken stones before I can grab her. She doesn't even look at me as she jumps. It's me screaming, not her.

A thud on the grass below. I am already at the stairs.

I trip three steps down, bang and bump. There's no moon now, but the faintest glimmer of dawn so I can see greyscale outlines as I career on. Still I tumble and scrabble headlong down the uneven endless flights, hard elbows of stone meeting me when my feet miss the edges. Bruised and battered I hurtle down to her, tearing the door open. Where's David? I can't go round the broken north end of the Castle without more daylight, I have to go the long way round, back through the gate and round to the west side. The wall she fell down.

♦

The encroaching dawn leaves her in shadow and the odd, flat light makes it difficult to judge depth and distance. She lies like a beached whale. Unkind. Poor child, revulsion clouds my thoughts even as I creep up to her.

She's dead; I know that, standing over her body. I am deeply unwilling to touch her. This nausea is from the smell, not queasiness at her death. She is so dead I can't quite believe I was talking to her only a few minutes ago. Did I do something wrong? What are you meant to say? I tried my best. I did.

Must check, confirm she's beyond help, then ring someone. Who, though? Police? Ambulance? Her doctor? Oh God. Why is this happening to me?

I'm gagging even before I touch her neck. She's icy cold. I have to poke my fingers into the creases of skin to find her pulse point. My stomach heaves. I crawl away from her to vomit herbs and water.

I don't know how long I've been here on my hands and knees when I notice a pair of muddy leather shoes just beyond my nose.

'I didn't push her.' Why did I say that?

I stagger to my feet. The man stares past me like I'm not here. Like he's numb.

I rub the bleariness out of my eyes. It's not much lighter, but vastly different. The flat pale dawn is held around us by the rising river mist.

There is a silent ring of people around her body. Some of these people are from the Chapel, Robin's regulars. What the Hell are they doing here? At this hour? Why didn't David call someone useful? I want the police here, don't care what trouble I'm in – I can't bear this any longer. I follow the man's eyes as I turn on my phone. He's watching the Chapel, but I can't see anything. Shit, the battery's flat. Shaking it won't help.

'Hey, has anyone called the police yet? Oi, I'm talking to you.'

They're walking away. For God's sake, there's a dead girl lying here.

'Hey!' I jog along beside them for a few strides, but it's no good, they just keep on walking.

I stop, reluctant to leave her alone. 'David! Where the bloody hell are you?'

He must have heard me. Surely help is on its way. Should have got here by now, though. Maybe he's been asleep, missed it all, dozing in his chair.

The dew is settling in large droplets on her waxy skin.

I have to get help.

My feet crunch on the path. The mist holds the sound close. David might not be in his cabin, maybe he sneaks home in the early hours. The vapour is thinner towards the back of the Hall. I expected to catch Robin's flock up by now. I think they must be local. They all walk to Mass on Sundays, they never seem to bring cars.

There's a light in the cabin.

Yes, David's in there. I can see his boots propped up on the coffee table.

I shout his name as I hammer on the door.

He looks like shit, oily strands of hair plastered across his forehead, his face flushed and greasy. There's an empty bottle of Bells next to his comfy armchair. Glad to know he takes security here so seriously.

'Fucksake, Mack. What time's it?'

'Getting on for five. My phone's dead. I need to use yours.'

'Why?'

'Just give me the bloody thing, can't you!'

'All right, all right.'

I snatch it from his fingers.

'What's happened? More vandalism? I didn't hear anything.'

'No, you wouldn't have. Hello, police. Does it matter? Just get someone over here.'

Why do they need so much information? I don't know the bloody postcode. I know I'm gabbling, but why do they have a total imbecile on the switchboard? He isn't making any effort to understand what I'm trying to explain. Halfway through, David cottons on and dashes out.

By the time I've finished he's come back leaning there in the doorway of his foetid hidey-hole, looking even worse than before.

'Mack, where did you say the girl fell?'

8. WEDNESDAY

'Mack! Hey, Mack.'

Peter.

Peter and a policeman. Several policemen. There is no degree of human misery that cannot be made worse by the presence of a policeman. I paraphrase.

'What was that?' Peter is crouching in front of me. He takes my hands away from my face.

It's wet, a depressing mizzle, not even proper rain.

'Mack, David said you saw Melissa jump off the top of the Castle. You told the police –'

No. I can't think about that right now.

'Sir?' I don't look up, but Peter has moved. Shiny black shoes in front of me. Reminds me of –

'Now then, Malcolm. Up you get.'

I can't stand. Peter is here again, propping me up between himself and the sandstone. I can feel the particles of quartz through my shirt. Where's my jacket? Oh yes, I left it in the hut.

'He needs a doctor.'

'We'll get him a doctor.'

'WHERE IS SHE?' God, what's happened to my voice?

'Mack…' Peter's speaks softly, in a tone which warns me not to say anything more.

I couldn't if I wanted to.

I let them take my arms. Peter stands back. I don't look at him.

'He needs help, can't you see that?' Peter calls after us.

I have my eyes closed most of the way. They guide me, but they don't need to. I know the path. They have parked on the grass by the South Door to the Chapel next to the skip. They will leave tyre marks in the soft wet turf.

I can't hold on to the journey, we're at the police station before we ought to be. I could walk unaided now, but they're on either side of me again.

This room is cramped, horrible. It smells of sick buildings, carpet and chemicals. My head is aching already.

'Do you want to see a doctor?'

I don't.

♟

Could be hours later. Maybe, maybe not.

'Malcolm?'

He's too young to be a doctor, too scrubbed and well-spoken to be police, though. How could I sleep in this chair? I would have been better off curling up on the floor. I can't remember the last time I slept properly. It is too easy to blame the pain in my back on the man who has woken me. His ID tag swings across my line of vision. He's nervous. Maybe I'm his first murder suspect. I could snarl, scare him some more for being so transparent. Better not.

'Malcolm?'

'It's Mack.'

'Mack. Good. I've been asked to take a look at you. We'll start with a few questions.'

Yes, I have quite a lot of those. 'Am I going mad?'

He whinnies with nerves. I wasn't being funny.

'I think I've been having hallucinations.' I wish my voice was steadier.

'Ah. Any head injuries recently?'

'It seemed so —'

'Head injuries.' He's shining his torch in my eyes, shrinking from the necessary proximity.

'No.'

'Stress?'

Just repeated questioning from the police about a missing girl, the one I saw kill herself, the one who wasn't there when I went back. 'Nothing out of the ordinary.'

'Have you had episodes like this in the past?'

How would I know if I think they're real? He's stuck a wooden spatula in my mouth before I can articulate this. It scratches the back of my tongue. He withdraws it.

'History of mental illness?'

For a moment I don't realise he means my personal history. He thinks if he uses as few words as possible he'll get out of here faster.

I shake my head.

'You saw things that couldn't have happened?'

'It could have happened. I'm not sure now, though. It felt real at the time.'

'Right. Roll up your sleeve. Drugs?'

Might help. That's not what he means. I cooperate. At least he's not treating me like I'm a cretin. Yet.

'No. Not prescription, not illegal. Don't even drink that much.' I've drunk quite a bit recently.

He doesn't ask permission before he draws blood. Fills four phials.

'What are you testing for?'

'General tests, check you out.'

'This isn't a mineral deficiency.'

'Go on then, what do you think it is?'

We look at each other properly for the first time. He isn't nervous anymore. It is I who am scared now. This is really happening. This man could have me sectioned.

'I think I saw a girl throw herself off the top of the Castle. But then she wasn't there.'

'How real was it?'

'I touched her. After she fell.' My mouth is parched. I drain the tepid water from the disposable cup.

'Where did you touch her?'

Jesus, where does he think? I bring two fingers up and place them over the point where my blood is pounding along my jugular just above my collar bone. 'Here.'

'And what did it feel like, when you touched her?' He perches on the corner of the table, hands resting on one thigh. He's interested now, enthusiastic, even.

'I haven't washed my hands.' I know I can't explain the state she was in, not calmly enough. I shouldn't have said that, about washing my hands. His face has gone tense again.

'I don't wash my hands. Not like that. It's not compulsive.'

His mouth twists. 'So why did you say it?'

'I touched her, she was dead.' There's no basin in here. I need to wipe my hands on something. The effort not to wring my hands like Lady Macbeth means I have no attention with which to elaborate. He doesn't wait for long.

'Anything else? Did she speak to you before she jumped?'

'She was trying to communicate.'

'In words?'

I don't think so – I can't remember, did she speak? He gives me very little time to think.

'Do you hear people talking to you? People who aren't really there?'

'Voices in my head, you mean?'

He twists his mouth again. 'Yes, voices in your head.'

'I'm hallucinating, not schizophrenic.'

'Is that a diagnosis?'

'Isn't that what you're here for?'

'No, not really. You're fit for questioning as far as I can see.'

I crush the paper cup in my hand. The noise as it collapses surprises both of us.

'Malcolm? Mack?'

He waits until I look at him. He does not know whether I am a killer or not, yet there is enough sympathy here to make my eyes sting.

'A young girl has gone missing. The police have searched your workplace and your home; you're anxious that you're a suspect. You panicked and had a fairly severe hallucinatory episode. I'm just the doctor on call, not a psychologist, but it doesn't seem an entirely unreasonable response to me. You need to speak to your G.P. when you get out of here.'

I remember to breathe, letting the air in my lungs go with a ragged exhalation, too loud to pretend it's normal.

'I can give you sleeping pills, or antidepressants, but they won't do you much good.' He bins the used equipment with his back to me. 'Good luck.'

I wish he had more presence, more kudos, something to hold on to that makes his opinion of my sanity more trustworthy, more likely. I want a second opinion.

✗

I can hear him in the corridor. He talks down to the police, squashing them so they have to listen. He's young, but he'll make a fuss if they don't accept what he's saying.

Back in the interview room they pass me a sheet. It's a statement I haven't made. I didn't imagine *this*: someone with the mental age of eight has written down approximately what they think I meant. Do I want to put my name to a piece of prose this bad?

At least the facts are roughly right. When I returned to the place where she had fallen she wasn't there. There were witnesses, of course. Why haven't I mentioned them? Robin's grim little flock. If something as solid as that girl was just my imagination –

Fool! Of course it didn't happen. She was cold from days rotting in the river. She was long dead when I got to her.

'Malcolm?'

'Yes. I need to wash my hands first. Please.'

✶

And now I'm back here. The rain is running down the back of my neck. Proper rain now. Peter is talking at me, but I can't be bothered to listen. Jason isn't here. The Chapel is locked, and I'm so dog-tired there's little I could do down in the crypt anyway.

'I'm sorry, Mack.' Peter is looking aggrieved. 'The keys.'

I wipe the rain out of my eyes. 'What about the keys?'

'*The* keys. For the Castle. Have you not been listening to me?'

A rhetorical question.

'You left the Castle unlocked. The Committee has suggested that David should look after the keys. It makes more sense now you're busy with the crypt, anyway. You don't need the keys at the moment.'

My torn hand hurts from clenching around the rusty key. This is the key that has been stretching my trousers out of shape for the past two years. I know its contours so well I could pick it out blindfold from a pile of ironmongery. It's the only original key for the Castle door, the Committee's keys are copies.

'David was drunk last night. I found him curled up with a bottle of whisky. He wouldn't have known what was going on at all –'

'I know. He smelt like a distillery. And he drove home.'

'And you think he's going to look after things better than me?' The awful vagueness that has tangled round my brain for the past two days finally dissipates with the urgency of retaining the key. 'The whole point is that the Castle was unlocked when I got there.'

'I locked it!'

'I've never known you not to, Peter. I'm just saying, it wasn't locked by the time I...' Bloody rain, I swipe my fringe back.

'Exactly. You can hardly claim to have been a reliable witness last night. Sorry, but...'

I hang my head, ignoring the cold rivulet of water which runs down between my shoulder blades.

Peter is as drenched as I am. Has he been standing out here because of me? I start to walk, heading for the heater in his hut. 'Have there been any visitors today?'

'In weather like this? Just as well, anyway. The police had another search, called it off five minutes before you got back.'

'Can I have a coffee?'

'Don't be daft. You can even have a biscuit.'

I let him go in first. My jacket is where I left it, on the back of one of the chairs. At least I have something dry to put on.

I don't pay for the coffee this time. Right now it feels like it did before everything changed, we are outside time, beyond strife, sheltering in Peter's little wooden hut. The window mists up. We steam by the small heater waiting for the coffee to cool, listening to the rain bouncing on the roof.

I still have my key.

I

At midday, I ring Jason and leave a message. No point hanging around – Peter closes up at half two. The grass squelches as we cut across the lawn to his car. He gives me a lift home, but I don't ask him in.

I

The door swings open at the lightest touch. Rain has blown in and pooled on the quarry tiles. It is cold, and I can feel the damp on the still air. It smells damp, too, and there's a more subtle odour of age and disuse.

There is a sharp sour smell as soon as I open the fridge.

The milk has curdled. The fridge seems to be working alright. Has there been a power cut? The loaf I was eating two days ago is covered in velvety turquoise mould. I fetch a bin-bag while the kettle boils and slide all the food I have into it, all spoiled, all rotten. My hands stink like blue cheese. There is no hot water. I have to use the first kettleful for washing my hands.

It doesn't take that long, really, to scrub out the kitchen. No-one else is going to do it.

I'm exhausted, but even the sofa looks comfortless in the gloomy chill of the sitting room. The fire is sulky with the cold chimney, and coal-smoke billows out into the room as it finally catches, the tiny tongues of flame producing little heat, but lots of thick yellow fumes.

♜

There's still a lingering smell of neglect in the sitting room, even now I've tidied up a bit. I'd rather sleep downstairs tonight. Don't want to think about what's happened, not yet. I'll leave the room to warm up while I sort out my bed. I need to fetch the bedclothes from the spare room, the police have the sheets from my bed.

God, what's that smell? Is it dry rot? How the hell? My bedroom door is open and the pungent smog of fungus is so strong I can taste it on the back of my tongue. Jesus, what a mess. Thick black mould has grown where I swabbed down the wall. The cottage has no central heating, I'm used to the odd patch of mould round the windows, but this is some giant mutant cousin of mildew, multiplying in folds of sooty excrescence that ripple down the wall. In several places powdery lumps have fallen to the carpet, exploding into miniature black sunrays. It's probably bad for me standing here, breathing in the spores.

There's some mould-killer in the bathroom.

Aim and squirt. It's too late to bother to try to protect the carpet. The smell gets worse, the bleach doesn't seem to be working.

My phone. I thought she had forgotten me.

It's not Mel. I thought the batteries were dead. But I used it at the Castle today to ring Jason… it just wouldn't work when I really needed it last night.

'Hello?'

'*Thank God –*'

'Jason?'

My phone gives a pathetic beep and dies. Again. Maybe there's something wrong with it? I don't look after it very well.

I give the wall another blast of bleach. The sodden black mass seems to be slumping, but it's hard to tell. I'd better charge this while I remember. The smell seems to come back down the stairs with me.

Stupid, but I feel uneasy with my back to the door as I rummage for the charger in the kitchen drawer. I feel the draught before I realise the front door is open.

'Are you going to hit me with that thing?'

'Jesus, Robin. Can't you knock?'

He flushes. I remember his prohibition on blasphemy.

'I did knock.'

No he didn't.

'I heard about your adventures.'

'From whom?'

He visibly jolts at this; I don't often challenge him.

'Actually, Mack, I'd rather not say. Your performance caused quite a stir. I came over to find out if you were intending an encore.'

My hands are shaking. It makes it difficult to slot the male and female parts together. He's watching me. That's it. I click on the switch, and my phone lights up.

'Would you like a cup of coffee?'

'There's a terrible smell of bleach in here. You haven't been trying to do something foolish, have you?'

'Like what? Housework? The place is damp, the roof must be leaking. I was trying to get rid of some mould, that's all.'

'You should complain to the landlord.'

I hold up the jar of coffee. He nods. Coffee is about all I have in. No milk. No sugar, even – it was so damp I chucked that too.

'Do you need to go shopping?'

'They'll be closed by the time I get there.' That's the drawback of having only a village within walking distance.

'I'll run you down to town; the supermarket's always open.'

Should I? Oh, this is stupid, we've been through a rough patch, but he's still Robin.

'Thank you. That would really help.'

I pretend to need to go to the bathroom so that I can go upstairs and check on the mould. It looks like a heavy black velvet curtain now, slithering downward from gravity or the inadequate action of the bleach. There's enough to need a shovel and bucket if the spray doesn't work. The wall is filthy where it has slid away.

I only lock the door because Robin is watching. Must I vet every action to make sure my behaviour goes unremarked?

♟

Robin insisted on buying the wine. It doesn't go with sausages and bacon. I can't drink much tonight, I have the bedroom to sort out before I can go to bed. I didn't really want him to stay, but I can't ask him to go when he's been so kind. Despite this solicitude I feel wary, though, on tenterhooks. He's leading up to something. A lecture I don't want to hear.

I'm so hungry I'm eating bread and butter while I fry the sausages. He starts while I am at a disadvantage, my mouth full of crust.

'So what really happened last night?'

I wave the tongs indicating that I can't answer.

'I was wondering…'

The bacon spits loudly as I add it to the pan.

'This is nothing to do with the missing girl, is it?'

The strips of meat contort with the heat. I pin them down with the tongs and continue to chew.

'That's what the police don't understand: that the stress you're under comes from what Jason has asked you to do. From being asked to find what has been walled up.'

Suddenly I have no saliva with which to lubricate the bread.

Robin laughs. 'Have you have bitten off more than you can chew there, Mack?'

I pass him the tongs and unbolt the back door. I spit the bread out into the bushes. When I come back in, Robin is slicing up the rest of the loaf.

'Shall we eat in the kitchen or the sitting room?' he asks without looking up.

'In here.' I fetch the bottle of Worcester sauce from the pantry.

'Eggs?'

'Forgot.'

'Oh well. There's plenty here.'

I make the tea while he serves up. Sulky domesticity confused with companionship. I wonder if he has ever lived with anyone, but then I haven't either, if you don't count student lodgings.

His choice of subject matter has taken the edge off my appetite. I swallow the first glass of wine in one long swig. He's watching me and shrugs slightly as I put my glass down.

I

Here he is, an hour later, back to the subject like a dog to a bone, sitting in his usual armchair.

'It doesn't take a degree in psychology to understand why your work must disturb you so badly.'

'Would you like a whisky?' I bloody need one if he's going to go on like this.

'The water of life,' he says.

I pour the Scotch. Robin's examining his drink when I return from the kitchen with a jug of water.

'Anything wrong?'

'Look at this glass, Mack. Can you see the tiny flaw?' He holds it up to the lamp for me.

'I can't see anything.'

'Look closer. It's like a tiny face, staring out.'

I still can't see anything, but I follow the movement of amber liquid as he swirls it around.

'You'll spill that if you're not careful.'

'There's your mother talking.'

'You never met my mother.'

> *'Cam ye o'er frae France?*
> *Cam ye doon by Lunnon?*
> *Saw ye Geordie Whelps*
> *and his bonnie woman?'*

His voice is soft and he sings in falsetto, mimicking a woman's tone.

He looks at me. What can I say? If I ask him not to sing it, he will know too much about last night, more than I am willing to discuss. He has seen enough, anyway.

I rub my eyes. 'Look, Robin, it's been a hell of a couple of days. I think I'd better just go to bed.'

'How can you sleep with this festering? Talk to me, Mack. I'll listen – I always have done.'

I spill the water as I try to dilute my whisky. He takes the jug and pours it for me.

'Is that enough?'

'Thank you. I'm not being rude, Robin. I do appreciate it, but I can't see how picking at old scabs will help. I have enough worries in the present, without going over past problems.'

My phone rings in the kitchen. I'm glad of the excuse. He seems to think that he owns me because I have burdened him with my past. I should find a polite way to put this to him. I pull the charger out and pick up my phone.

'Hello?'

Deep silence, the sound sucked out, rather than absent.

'Hello, Mel?'

She isn't going to speak to me tonight. I put away the plates we washed earlier; it delays going back to him. He's lying back with his eyes closed when I return.

'Anything important?' He opens one eye.

'No.'

He laughs, a low rumble like an asthmatic cough. He can't know about Mel's calls. Surely I haven't told him about them? I flop into the other chair and pick up my glass.

Robin sits up. 'So, Mack, what do you reckon is behind that wall? Some long-dead uncle?'

The whisky burns the insides of my cheeks. I swallow but don't speak. There is nothing to say.

'Lost your voice? Or are you going to throw me out?'

Could I physically throw him out if he won't leave? I bet he's stronger than he looks. That temper, too, and the aggression of a short man.

'You have to come to terms with what you've done in the past.'

'Or I could just quit this job and move on.'

He shifts in his seat, taking his time. 'The past will always catch up with you, no matter where you run to. You have to face it some time.'

'Like you say, you haven't a degree in psychology.'

'Like I say, it doesn't take one to see what this is doing to you. Come with me to the Chapel now. We'll go down there, and you can confront what you are really scared of.'

'Don't be stupid, it's after eleven. The Chapel's padlocked

and Jason has the key. I'm perfectly fine about it. In fact, I'm looking forward to finding out what's behind the wall.'

My hand twinges with a fresh pain. The glass slips from my fingers before I can adjust my hold on it.

'Look, you've cut yourself.'

I haven't: the stitches have opened up, blood is seeping through the dressing. He takes my hand before I can get away and pulls a shard of glass out of my finger. The pain stops as abruptly as it started. I jerk my hand away from him. I was mistaken, I panicked, the blood is just from the new cut. I put my finger in my mouth, suck at the taste of iron.

He fusses round at my feet, picking up the rest of the glass.

'Leave it. Leave it, Robin. I'll do it in the morning. I want to go to bed now.'

'Are you going to work tomorrow?'

'Of course.'

'Are you expecting Jason to be there?'

'No idea. I'll get on outside if he's not.'

'If it stops raining.'

'Yes.'

'Go to bed, then.' He gets up from the floor.

He is stiff as he walks, seems bent over, more tired than I've known him. Maybe I should have been cooperative, he was only trying to help.

'Robin –'

What's happened to his eyes? They are so bloodshot no white shows. 'Are you OK?'

He turns back to the door, talking over his shoulder, 'My health is the least of your concerns.'

Is he ill? We hardly ever talk about him. I should ask. He's gone.

𝕀

My knees are shaking with tiredness, so I lean against the door jamb, surveying the mess in my bedroom. The reek of bleach is too strong for me to sleep in here even if it had worked. Fresh mould is blossoming on the arcs of smeared blood. The filth that has fallen away from the wall is piled in thick black pleats against the skirting. I'll deal with it in the morning. Better phone Lord Muck in the morning, too, tell him that there is a problem with his property. I close the door to shut in the smell.

I cram all Mel's stuff back into the shoebox and push the box back under the guest room bed. How long is it since I last aired this room? The duvet feels cold with the damp. I can't sleep in here. Not upstairs. It feels like a long time till morning. A lot of dark to get through.

The stairs are narrow. I don't think to roll the duvet up first, so it fights me all the way down. My phone's ringing, but I can't get to it before I've tugged the bedding into the sitting room.

'Hello.'

Bloody hell, she's got nothing better to do tonight. Christ it's cold in here. I wrap the quilt round me before I slide down onto the sofa. So cold, yet I'm drifting off to sleep. She's still there. I can hear her breathing when I press the phone to my ear.

9. THURSDAY

The thing is, when I got there he was still talking to me, even though he was plainly dead. I didn't hear what he said, m'lud, his fingers were crammed in his mouth. He'd been sucking the blood from his fingertips where he'd torn them prying out a stone.

I can't answer your questions while I'm stuffed in a box.

'Ahhh!' I crick my neck with a sickening wrench. I must have had myself jammed deep into the sofa. It's dawn, my sitting room, not a court with a coffin for a witness box. The annoying ringing is my phone, not bells to call the jury. I've lost it somewhere in the duvet. My neck twinges again as I stand up and shake my bedding out. The phone falls, landing with a thud on the rug. My neck twinges more with stooping to pick it up.

'Hello?'

'Mack? Mack, it's me. Don't hang up. Can you get to the Chapel for eight?'

'Jason? Sorry I missed your –'

He's rung off. No explanation, probably thinks he doesn't owe me one. Probably thinks it's me who has explaining to do. Probably right. Bloody little man. Still, work will do me good.

It's only quarter past six. Is it worth trying to go back to sleep? Now the relief of waking up in the light has worn off, I'm feeling so tired still I might sleep through the alarm. Can't keep Jason waiting…

Lights, better than the last dream. Little lights, faint dots twirling round and round and… I've been here before –

Jesus!

Someone's at the door.

'Alright, alright, I'm coming. Don't break the bloody door down.'

Groggy dash, no time to bother to pull on my jeans. It'll only be Robin.

It's Clara, not Robin. Wakes me up like a bucket of cold water.

'Well hello, Mack.'

'Sorry, thought it was –'

'Obviously.' God, she's like her brother, same voice, same build. Better legs.

'I'll just –'

'No need. I just popped round to see if you were alright. That ghastly Holden person is in a flap down at the Chapel. Says he has to see you. He's been very rude to Peter. And Juliet. I've had to smooth a lot of ruffled feathers on your account.'

'I slept through the alarm. Is he still there?'

'He was when I left.'

'I need to…'

'I'll tell him you shan't be long if I see him.'

She appraises me long enough to embarrass us both. Again I feel transparent. It amused me last summer when she lingered near as I worked shirtless. Now it feels worse, but at the same time it's vaguely reassuring.

She pulls a face. Can't tell if it's meant to be a shrug or a flirtatious smirk, not when she looks so like her brother.

'Thanks.'

'My pleasure.'

I should feel more sullied than I do. A happier me, deep inside, untroubled by the past, smirks back at her before I can stop it.

✠

The memory makes me shudder as I shower.

It's ten already. I should have asked Clara to help me with this dressing. There's too much tape on, it's going to make my hand stiff. The cuts have closed up, but they look angry, and the whole of my right hand feels hot. I'll have to hack out with my left hand. Anything to get back to work. That's all I am now, a mason. My job defines me, there is nothing else.

Mel rings, but I don't answer. This time I lock my door as I leave.

✠

It's cold today. The sun is out, but it is filtered through high clouds, and the wind cuts through my shirt. The morning feels washed clean by yesterday's downpour. The sky glints back from water at the far corner of the field. It takes a lot of rain for water to lie on this field. I should have brought my jacket.

Jason's Land Rover is still in the car park. It's alone, no visitors, no little yellow Fiat, and no sign of Peter's car either. The archaeologists aren't here today. It was too wet yesterday. Maybe the police sent them home, anyway. Jason's Land Rover is muddy, looks like he's actually been off-roading.

I walk around to the Family door. It's not shut properly. I can hear Jason talking to someone in the Chapel. Sounds like they're having a row. Should I get my tools out of the lock-up first, or tell him I'm here? Curiosity killed the cat.

I knock, but they don't lower their voices. Carefully I pull the door closed, then make a lot of noise opening it. Their conversation breaks off immediately.

The two men are standing by the communion rail. Jason is facing me. His cheeks are flushed, but the colour drains when

111

he sees me. I don't know who he's talking to, whoever it is has clearly upset him.

'Hello, Mack.' Robin turns around. That explains it: Robin's enough to upset anyone.

'You –' Jason stands there like one o' clock half struck, as Mum would say. He mustn't want me to see them together. Colluding with the enemy, perhaps?

'If I'm interrupting?' I walk forward, stand next to Robin, facing Jason.

'No, we're just catching up,' Robin says.

He seems different this morning. I can't put my finger on it. Jason interests me more, though. He is pressing himself back against the rail, holding on to it and staring at me like he's seeing a ghost.

'You know Christopher?' his voice is so high it almost makes me laugh.

'Christopher?' Ah, Christopher Robin. 'Really?' I turn to Robin, he bows his head. I see his teeth glint, but he hides his smile from Jason.

Jason is smiling at me like rigor mortis has overcome him. 'Christopher was my brother,' he says through clenched teeth.

'Oh. I didn't know.' Interesting use of tense. No brotherly love lost there, then.

It's Robin's hair; it's almost ginger in this light. I wonder how I missed the familial resemblance before. That patrician nose. Why didn't he tell me? All this time he's talked with me about Jason like he didn't know him. He needed to look up his address –

'So, you've met him before?' Jason is breathing heavily, squeezing his words out.

'Well, yes. Are you alright, Jason?'

'How long have you known?'

I look at Robin. He looks back, amused. He's enjoying this. I almost feel sorry for Jason.

'How long have you known about me and him?' Jason grinds the question out again, fixedly looking at me, not Robin.

'I didn't know he was your brother, I told you. We met when I started work here two years ago. Did you not know he was here?'

'Why would I?' He's almost in tears now. 'Why would he be here?'

This is awkward. Time to bring the conversation around. 'You said you needed to see me? I'm sorry I'm so late.'

'Yes, yes, of course.' Jason stays where he is.

'About getting back to work on the crypt?'

He licks his thin lips and glances at Robin. Christopher Robin. '*Not while he's here.*'

Good grief.

'Robin, you seem to be upsetting your brother. Can you come back when we've sorted out my work?' I must ask him about his name some time. He teases me enough.

'Of course. Let's not be strangers, eh, Jake, now I know where to find you.'

Jason makes a sort of whimpering sound. It sends ice up my spine. His eyes are fixed on my face, as though he's refusing to watch his brother's departure. The effort is making him sweat.

'Bye, Robin.' I call over my shoulder. I can't tear my eyes away from Jason; he's shaking from head to foot. I've never seen a man so close to crumpling like a paper bag.

'What's the matter? D'you owe him money or something?'

The door slams behind me. The whole building seems to tremble.

'Has he gone?'

I look around. 'Yes.'

'*How do you know my brother?*' At least his colour is coming back.

'I didn't *know* he was your brother. Look he's my friend, but I understand –'

'You understand?' Jason pushes himself upright from the communion rail. Actually, they don't look that much alike. 'Is that why you were late?'

'No. I slept in. I haven't had a lot of sleep recently.'

'You should –' He runs his hands over his face, takes a moment, 'It doesn't matter. You're here now.'

'OK. What do you want me to do today?' My neck muscles ache at the prospect of work.

'How are your hands?'

'Fair enough. How's your finger?'

'What happened? I heard about…'

He trails off as I straighten up, look down on him.

'There was an accident. I cut my hands.'

'I mean the police.'

'I know what you mean, Jason.'

'It affects the job…I need to know…'

'I've got some history, a bit of a past, that's all. My girlfriend disappeared ten years ago. Obviously I was questioned, as I was close to her. No doubt you've asked Juliet about this. I spend a lot of time here; you can't help meeting the kids. I knew the missing girl.'

'Knew?'

It takes a second to understand him. Oh. 'Yes. *Knew.* Nobody really thinks she's still alive?'

'Peter said you thought you'd seen her.'

'I was mistaken.'

'So what are the police doing with you?'

It's a fair question. I've given a statement. They haven't asked me to stay here or report back to the station. They are waiting to see what I do next. I could just tell him this, but I won't. 'I think I'm still their only suspect.'

'Unless she's found alive and well.'

'Unless she's still alive, yes.'

'Poor child.'

'I didn't like her.'

He starts to laugh, a horrible nervous giggle, sees my face and thinks better of it, clearing his throat instead and fumbles for a handkerchief.

I can't watch this feeble attempt to pull himself together. I turn away. I have a strong urge to walk out, but there's my job, responsibilities. I head down to the crypt. His footsteps follow me.

It's warmer down here than in the Chapel. Muggy, or at least it will be once I've worked up a sweat.

'Do you want me to start from where I left off on Monday?'

'Can you finish it today?'

'No. Obviously I can't, Jason; there's twenty tons of masonry here.'

'How much longer? We've lost a lot of time.'

'It takes as long as it takes.'

Somewhere beyond the wall, a shower of stone dust patters down. Jason flinches.

'It's OK, it'll just be a mouse.'

'A mouse!' He can't be scared of mice. 'A mouse, eating –'

'There's nothing for it to eat. It'll just be exploring.'

'We need this finished. *Vermin.*'

'We must have frightened them.'

The scrabbling is getting louder. Jason follows it with his eyes. Something small and light scampers across the width of the wall on the other side of the masonry. Its friend follows it. Jason shrinks back from the sound. Immediately there are more of them, more and more, it's like the rustling of dry autumn leaves now with little avalanches of dust sporadically scattering down. They must be taking out the mortar on the other side faster than I could.

God, for a moment I thought it was the mice laughing. Jason covers his mouth to smother the sound. He is as white as a sheet, gulping for air, panicking. 'What are they *eating*?'

I knew the crypt scared him. 'What are you worried they're eating?'

I can't make out the reply, but it clearly distresses him.

'One thing about mice, Jason, if you've got mice you know you don't have rats.'

'*Why*?' I can barely hear him, he mouths the word.

'Because the first thing rats eat is the mice.'

'Oh, God.'

The tide of vermin slows to a trickle. We both follow the sound of the last straggler scuttling after its brethren. It's quiet now, so quiet I can hear his breathing ease, even the little creak as his shoulders slump.

'What's behind the wall, Jason?'

He straightens up, the skin drawing tight across the bridge of his nose. 'Just do your job.'

'Fine. We'll need another skip by tomorrow morning, then. I'll be a bit slower hacking out with my hands like this, but I can shovel fast enough.'

I'll find out what's back there soon enough, anyway.

'I'll order another skip. I'll be back shortly after lunch,' he says.

His footsteps ring out on the stone stair. It sounds different. Hollow. Has there been some sort of collapse on the other side of the wall?

I hate working in gloves, but there's no way to avoid it. The first job will be to carry out some of this dust. I forgot to fetch my tools.

♟

I thought I'd left them in the lock-up. They aren't here. Surely I can't have left them in the Castle? The last job I did was up on the Tower.

116

That was Monday.

Has it only been three days? Heavy droplets splash from the sycamore as I pass under it. The last few days creep up around me, incoherent and jumbled. I stop by the Castle door and try to remember.

I heard her. That's right, I heard singing and left what I was doing.

Surely I didn't just leave my tools up there? Good job I still have my key, because Peter's left the door locked. I hope my things are OK. There has been so much rain. It won't have done either the blades or the handles much good. I don't think anyone would take them but you never know these days. I shouldn't have been so casual with my livelihood.

♟

The rain has dribbled down the walls and soaked the stairwell, leaving little puddles in places where the steps are worn. There's the occasional drip still. I've never seen the Castle look more dreary. My footsteps clang as though on metal, a dull repetition that jars up my spine.

I haven't left anything up here on the scaffolding. It's a relief that I wasn't so careless even when there were other things going on. I wish I could remember what I did do with my tools, though. Did I really hear her singing? Wasn't that just my imagination too? It doesn't matter. It happened, or didn't. Was she still alive when I heard her on Monday, though? It's immaterial if she's dead already. I don't know she isn't alive now – why am I so sure? It seemed so real.

The grooved boards are full of rainwater. The wood's more slippery than the stone flags underneath, now they're slimed with dirt.

God, her face. The image won't go away. I don't know why I came all the way up here. I never brought my tools up here. The lichen's scuffed where she went over the wall.

It had to be my imagination.

An hallucination. The doctor said so.

The wind is cool. I breathe. I'll wait until I can hear the birds above my own blood thundering in my ears.

The lichen is definitely scuffed. Arcs from the soles of someone's shoes as they hoisted themselves up. Up and over.

It could have been anyone, posing for a photo, maybe, in the rain, with the police.

♜

A car slows down over by the main gate. I watch through the branches of the sycamore as it pulls into the drive. A cavalcade follows, fifteen cars. Even from up here, I can see they're posh saloons, dark blue, silver mink, graphite, tasteful, heavy on the gas. Nursed into spaces between the tree roots in the car park.

Peter's not back. I'd better go down.

♜

The key to the shed is still under the bucket. I have time to get behind the counter before the first of them arrives.

It's the Jacobites. We're being invaded! Suits and overcoats and gleaming city shoes. There isn't room for them all in the hut, only seven or eight have crowded in. They don't recognise me – why would they?

The leader stands in front of me, begins before I can say anything.

'This is a courtesy.'

Should I tug my forelock?

'We represent the Jacobite Society of Scotland and England. Can I have your name?'

'Mack Macready.'

'Right, Macready, we expect the entire site to be made available to us. I would appreciate your keys as well.' He has that lowland Edinburgh accent that is almost English, a soft burr that sounds insincere and so easily turns into a whine.

'I don't have any keys. The curator's not here. I'm just the stone mason.' Did I leave the Castle unlocked when I came back down?

'This is very inconvenient. We need to take an inventory.'

'Do you have an appointment?'

He makes a sort of scoffing noise, like a camel about to spit, and turns to an older man behind him. He's murmuring, but the shed is so small I'm close enough to hear across the counter. 'I thought you said Holden had sorted this out. I don't want to waste the afternoon talking to the bloody yokels.'

He glances at me. This is my best vacant peasant expression.

Distrust flickers across his face. 'Have they done this on purpose?'

'Who?'

'Have your –' he points to my chest so I'm sure he means me, '– superiors left you here –' a little hand-mime to demonstrate the cabin surrounding us, '– on purpose?'

It never occurred to me before that I had superiors on this Earth. That's my upbringing, though; we are all equal in the eyes of the Lord. I will think of the perfect reply to him in the shower tonight; it's always the way.

'You have missed Jason by about an hour. I'll try to contact a member of the Trust Committee for you. Meanwhile, you can either wait here or buy an entrance ticket and enjoy the Castle. It's three-fifty for adults, two pounds for concessions.' Peter would be proud of me.

'Don't be so bloody silly.' He can barely get the words out he's so cross.

When I straighten up I am as tall as him. He must be about fifty, hard as iron, but I'm younger and have only just realised how much better I would feel after a fight: 'Well, if that's your attitude, you can wait here until Jason comes back. We don't have to take abuse from members of the public.'

'Do you know who I am?'

'Obviously whoever you are, you're not as important as you think if you have to tell me.'

He snatches at my shirt across the narrow countertop. I chop down on his wrist without thinking. The side of my hand smarts and the healing cut twinges. Shit. Suddenly my appetite for scrapping has diminished.

He rubs his wrist, glaring at me. 'Macready.'

'That's right.'

'You're fired.'

I hope I don't show any reaction. I'm going to have to breathe soon.

One of the suits behind taps him on the shoulder and murmurs something in his ear. I breathe out as unobtrusively as possible.

He shifts a little and fixes me with a glare. 'You will be fired if you continue to obstruct us.' Now this is where us peasants just can't compete for bald-headed hypocrisy. He doesn't turn a hair, simply changes his imperative. 'Consider this a verbal warning.'

'I'll telephone Jason, shall I?'

'If you would.' He is actually snarling now.

I use the land-line. My hand shakes a little, but he doesn't notice. The others are shifting uncomfortably. Two of them shuffle outside to pass the proceedings on to their comrades.

There is some satisfaction from making Jason squeal with the information. He assumed that Peter would come back to comply with instructions. Peter isn't paid by the Jacobites though. His absence is a tactical manoeuvre. No curator, no keys. No keys, no occupation, not legally, anyway.

I turn back to the bastard who's just tried to fire me.

'Jason says he will be here in about half an hour. I'm sure he can deal with your enquiries more satisfactorily than I can.'

He makes the scoffing noise again. The little cabin has steamed up. I want to get out, it's making me feel claustrophobic. Is he going to just stand there until Jason gets here?

Someone is trotting towards us along the gravel path.

'Hugh,' the newcomer calls past the throng, 'the Chapel's open.'

They had keys to the Chapel already; it's no victory, but there's still a sinking feeling.

'Good. Macready, you can show us the progress down there.'

The walk from the shed is uncomfortable. The path is narrow and the grass is wet. I can't avoid the appearance of being marched to the Chapel by this tosser.

It's really cold in here. There will be condensation in the cases upstairs if they don't turn the heating up. I suppose the exhibits may all belong to them now, no longer the Trust's concern.

'Show me.' He puts his hand on my arm lightly enough, but even that's too much.

'Take your hand off my arm.'

We glare. Upstairs, someone laughs very quietly.

He jerks his head to one of his party, and they hare off to the spiral stair. I can hear them clattering up to gallery. He drops his arm to his side.

'You first.' He makes an exaggerated gesture to usher me forwards so he can follow me down to the crypt.

The stone steps do sound different. There is a layer of dust floating about five feet from the floor. Someone has been down here very recently. We step down into the hazy air.

My tools! The small pick, the old brush I use for dry work, my masonry hammer and cold chisel. I know I didn't leave them here. I couldn't have missed them. Someone's brought them down here while I was looking for them in the Castle. What the hell's going on?

I need time to think about this, but they're crowding down here, the whole lot of them, like a troop of bloody kids on a school trip. My friend tramples the dust in front of my kit before I can even look for footprints. I bet he bullied the weedy boys, probably still does.

They take turns to try to look over the wall in a disordered scrum. They won't be able to see any more than I could.

I pick out the weakest looking one, early forties, short, earnest, can't even get a look-in at the wall, too hesitant. 'So what are you expecting to find behind this wall?' I practice an affably stupid expression until my cheeks ache.

'Well, as far as we know, this is the last resting place of the heart of James Radcliffe.' He's pleased to be asked, can't help but inform me. Some men are born to teach.

'So it's really just more of the crypt?'

'Oh no,' he pushes his glasses further up his nose, 'you see, his heart was terrifically symbolic. It was supposed to have miraculous healing properties. There was all sorts of folklore about it. So much, in fact, that the authorities became scared it would form a rallying point for the cause and came after it. It was officially lost, but our researchers think it was put in here with all the other documents.'

'Ah, the documents, what are they about, then?'

'It's –'

'It's confidential, Archie.'

I hope I don't blanch like Archie when that git comes up behind us. Archie looks at me properly. I like to think he sees me for what I am, not just a surface to bounce sound off.

The older man turns his attention to me. 'Why the interest, Macready?'

'Look around. You tell me.'

'This is of purely archaeological significance. There is no monetary value.'

'I won't steal your heart, don't worry. My interest is purely historical, too.'

'Your interest begins and ends with the removal of this wall.'

'You and your friends had better let me get on with it, then.'

'Hugh!' upper crust diction peals across the echoing chatter, 'Holden's here.'

He sort of snarls at me and shoves some of his friends until the ripple passes through them and they all get out of his way. The air is thick with stirred grit. Several of them are beginning to cough.

I try to loosen the tightness in my shoulders. The men begin to drift up the stairs. The place smells like a locker room in an expensive leisure centre, cologne and testosterone, and the underlying rank reek of suppressed perspiration. I preferred the smell of grave-liquor.

♜

No more mice. Still and quiet, peaceful again. The dust has settled. There's only the aroma of damp stone and old mortar now, and the smell all subterranean rooms have, the memory of wet earth and worms. I reassemble my breezeblock platform so that I am working at a comfortable height. Outside, well, the dispute is nothing to do with me. I have no say in anything, no part in these decisions. I ignore the occasional argumentative noises that drift down here. This is my job, my wall for that matter, when no-one else is around.

Maybe I should just make a hole big enough to squeeze through, rather than taking the whole wall down. Nobody's really interested in removing it, just getting behind it.

Ah, stupid, automatically used my right hand. That stings. There are my gloves, scuffed into the dirt by expensive leather soles. I slap them together, raising a cloud that nearly chokes me.

I can't work in these bloody gloves. How do they expect you to hold things properly?

Even with my left hand, I need to try to keep my shoulder as rigid as possible to reduce the impact on my wrist and elbow and the cuts on my hands. I swing my whole body to put some weight behind each blow. I shift the little pick from right to left and back again. I don't think I'm damaging the cuts too badly, but it hurts each time I hack at the mortar using my right hand.

It's taken fifteen minutes to get this one stone out. Stupid trying to time my progress; it takes as long as it takes. Patience. If I get these three blocks out and the ones on the other side, would there be room to crawl through?

Wonder what Radcliffe's heart would fetch on eBay.

Wonder how long I'd last if that lot found out I'd taken it.

The stones are barely even bedded in on the other side. This one's loose already. The mice couldn't have done that, surely? Can't get a grip with gloves, useless sodding things. That's better. Ow, banged knuckles. Daren't risk pushing the stones down on that side, something might get smashed, something good. This one next to it is loose too, waggles like a bad tooth. Just– there. Inching the stone towards me, my shoulders and elbows cramped and bent in the gap, standing on tiptoe, my cheek resting on the powdery stone surface, breathing in the smell of decaying mortar. Then the stone tilts towards me. I rock back on my heels and pull it out. There still isn't room to climb over. It's quarter past eleven. I'll give it till lunchtime.

Four more stones on the other side. I'm hurting my hands, but I am close now. I can reach the inner face more easily as I've come down a whole course on my side.

The stone on the far side teeters with very little pressure. I mustn't let it fall into the chamber. The stitches tug as I stretch my hand wide to span the top of it. The stone's so loose it comes away with less force than I am using. I lose my footing, scrabble and slip, twisting as I fall to go forwards as best I can rather than keeling over onto my back. I land hard on my right knee and the heel of my left hand. Chips of stone stab through my jeans and puncture my skin. It feels like they have embedded themselves into the bone of my kneecap, but I am familiar with this sort of injury. The pain will pass soon after the pressure is removed.

The stone came with me. I lay it down and sit in the thick dust to pick the little pieces out of my knee. The blood flows well enough to flush out any remaining dirt. These jeans are finished, though. They were already ripped from saving Jason last week. Uncle Jimmy always wore knee pads, but I never got on with them; I'd rather have the odd mishap and bloody knee than be permanently hampered as I work with straps round my legs.

Something about that stone caught my eye even as I was falling. I drag the newly retrieved block towards me. It's heavy and awkward. A rough cube, dark on top, but this is not the facing side. I turn it over – the next plane is dark also. Another turn, it lies with the surface that faced the chamber now uppermost. There's something... words – HELP ME – two words scratched on the stone. Someone was down here, trapped behind this wall. The stone is too heavy to hold in front of me for long. I put it down carefully and rest my forehead on my knees.

Hell's teeth.

I close my eyes and count to ten. When I open my eyes the words are almost there but so faint, so ephemeral, I can't be sure. Did someone die down here? Is he still here, behind the wall? What's left of him, that is. Dust and bone and despair.

The door bangs above me in the Chapel. Shit, someone's coming. Ow, my knee. I clamber over the pile of stones towards the stairs. I'm too stiff to get up quickly. I think it's as much from using the pick the wrong way as from the tumble.

'Mack?'

The relief, it's only Peter –

'Down here.' My voice is shaky.

He clumps down the steps and breaks through the dust clouds, peering at me. 'Bloody hell, have you had an accident?'

'Give me a hand.'

'OK.' He crunches past the stones I have brought down today and pulls me to my feet through the swirling dirt. 'No broken bones?'

I shake my head. 'Just a cut knee.'

'Come on. Get cleaned up and I'll tell you all about the Jacobites.'

'Have they gone?'

'Oh yes.'

He leads the way. Even his footsteps sound happy. My left side aches, less used to doing work. I knew it was a mistake to favour one side, but what choice did I have? They'll get another stonemason in if I can't do it.

There's no point swabbing down my knee, I'll only end up with soggy jeans. The basin in here is too small to be much use, in any case. The place is in a bit of a state. Peter hasn't cleaned the toilets again.

I'll have to get fresh bandages anyway, so I let the dressings on my hands get soaked while I dig out as much of the muck from my knuckles and under my fingernails as I can. There's always a full first aid kit under the counter in the hut.

Peter has my coffee ready. It's too cold to sit outside, so I pull up a chair next to the heater and lay my hands on the table, palm side up.

He fetches the green plastic box and sets it down on the table in a businesslike manner. He cuts the soiled dressings off with swift snips. The stitches have held, the cut on my right hand hasn't opened up, but the holes around the sutures are dark, almost black.

'They'll take longer to heal if you keep bashing them like this.'

'Can't be helped.'

'Well, at least the Jacobites won't be badgering you any more for a while anyway.'

'Tell me what happened.'

He cleans my palms with several sachets of disinfectant wipes. I try to concentrate on what he is saying.

'His Lordship came over to see what all the fuss was about a couple of hours ago while you were down in the crypt. I may have inadvertently mentioned to Clara that they turned up earlier this morning wanting the keys.'

'You knew about that?'

'Jason and I had a short discussion on the topic.'

'So you went to fetch the cavalry.'

'Just as well, really. Sorry, need to get this clean.'

'It's fine.' I flex the fingers on my right hand. The pain makes me stop experimenting. 'Go on.'

Peter picks up my hand like it doesn't belong to me and examines the stitches again. 'Apparently the Jacobites are not going to have it all their own way, after all. There's an injunction on the injunction now or something daft – anyway, our team still has the keys.'

'Did they go quietly?'

'You know, I think they might have if Jason hadn't been so loud. He set off old Billy. His Lordship has a short fuse, as you know.'

'*Jason* made a fuss?'

'Like his life depended on it. Hysterical. I think he embarrassed the Catholic gentlemen to the point they were prepared to retire from the field. Then all hell broke out, right there in the car park. He said something to his Lordship, I didn't quite catch it, something about the Radcliffes, but it sent our brave knight right up in the air. I thought he was going to hit Jason. The school's been reopened today, you know, so all the kids came out to watch. Very entertaining. When Hugh Latham and his crew scuttled off some of the kids cheered, bless them.'

'Where's Jason now?'

'Is that too tight? Jason? I'm not sure. Come to think of it, his Land Rover was still there, last time I looked.'

Gingerly, I straighten my fingers. It feels better with a firm pad of protective swaddling across the palm. 'That's great.'

'Let's see your other hand. You've opened up the cut, twit. They should have put a couple of stitches in this one as well.'

'It's fine.'

'Wear gloves – don't just rely on the dressings. You don't want to get the cuts infected.'

'I was wearing gloves. Initially. Was Clara there?'

'Boudicca? You don't think she would have missed that scrap do you? She left with her brother; you've missed her. Hold still, nearly done.'

He cradles my hand, gently wrapping the gauze round, passing the roll from hand to hand like a weaver's shuttle, finishing the bandage with a neat tuck and a small pin.

I can't work like this. My hands aren't ready.

Peter seems expectant. There is a pause. I turn my hands over.

'No need to thank me.'

'Oh. Yes, better than the professionals. A lot better than I managed this morning. I ought to get back.'

'Do you think that's sensible?'

'Not to take any more wall down. I've made a hole through. I'm going to have a look.'

'Bloody hell!' Peter starts to slam the stuff back in the first aid box. 'You go ahead. Get down there!'

'What –'

'Jason's still around. He'll be in there like a rat up a trouser leg, nicking anything that isn't nailed down. Go on, I'll be there in a tick.'

I

Peter doesn't know how timid Jason is. He's just standing there, staring at one of the stones. *That* stone? He has his briefcase in one hand, like he was on his way out when he noticed the hole in the wall. He's been still long enough for the debris to start settling. Like me, his hair is white with powdery dust, there is even a layer on the upper surface of his leather case.

I'm out of breath from rushing over here. I slow to a stop three steps from the bottom and clear my throat.

He looks at me. 'Did you do this?'

'I found it.'

He glares back down at the stone by his feet. 'Have you been through?'

'Not yet. I was going to climb over now.'

That look again, commiseration. I don't like it. I'm not on his side. We are on opposing teams, even if they pay my wages. That's why I don't talk about the stone or speculate about what we might find, or who.

He stands back to let me past. The crypt suddenly feels warm and clammy.

I take two steps forwards to the hole and stop.

My knees are shaking. I can't help it, and it's not for the poor bugger who asked for help, nor does the proximity to death bother me. I shake because I feel his horror. Empathy is a terrible thing, from blushing at another's transgressions in the classroom to imagining too well how it feels to die of thirst in the dark.

'Have you a torch?'

He clucks with irritation. I face the wall while he rummages in his briefcase. The tops of the lowest stones are level with my chin. My mouth is parched. Stale air wafts out of the chamber.

'Here.' He thumps the torch down hard onto my sore hand.

I take another two steps forward and stand with my chest pressed against the wall. I shine the beam across the ceiling to get my bearings, then methodically sweep the light from side to side, but there's nothing. The back wall can't be more than twenty feet away.

'Go slower. This is hopeless. Here, let me.' He snatches the torch and steps up onto a couple of breezeblocks.

He angles his elbow so that he is shining the light on the floor. I catch glimpses, disjointed images. There is a lot of debris, probably from the original builder. I know I should dread what we will find, but I suddenly experience the flutter that Howard Carter must have felt at the hole in Tut Ankh Amun's tomb. I almost expect Jason to tell me he can see wonderful things. I can't anticipate where he will shift the light next, so I have little time to decipher each pause into existence. It is frustrating and disorientating.

He drops back down to the floor beside me.

'Nothing.' He sounds bereft.

I take the torch again and try for myself. Nothing. Even three hundred years of dust could not hide a skeleton. I hoist myself up so that I am at waist height to the hole. I cannot get my knees up, there isn't sufficient headroom. I have to lean across the wall and hold the torch above my ear to see the area close to the foot of the wall. It would be easy to miss something. One of us will have to go over. The air tastes sour. Still no body, no skeleton, just... footprints.

'Jesus, Jason, someone's been in here already.'

'Obviously.'

'Eh?' I drop back down to the floor and tug my shirt back down.

'Someone got in there when the wall was higher and scratched that on the stones.'

No.

He watches me returning to the stone. My knees creak as I crouch down over the message. It's very faint, only the angles of the letters showing. I hesitate. He could be right. Looking at it now, the scratches might not be that old.

'What, did you think someone had been walled up and managed to find a tool to write this? In the dark?'

'Yes. That's exactly what I thought, Jason.'

'Then you're more stupid than you look.'

'Piss off.'

'Don't be such a brat, Malcolm. We have bigger problems than this.'

'We?'

The door bangs above us.

'Who's there?' Jason calls past my shoulder. He sounds all authoritative now he's managed to tick me off.

'Are you alright, Mack?' Peter calls down.

'Yes. Where were you?'

'Someone telephoned for you. I couldn't get him to shut up. Some priest guy.'

'Robin.'

Jason is staring at me. I ignore him.

'Yeah, something about a chess game tomorrow.' Peter's voice echoes, and his footsteps ring out as he descends. The acoustics have changed. We are spoiling the Chapel.

Peter glances round at the mess, then focuses on the hole. 'May I?'

He scrambles up and squeezes his whole body into the gap before we can stop him. He is not built for small spaces.

'Take your jacket off; you'll never fit.'

His reply is lost in his collar. He'll throttle himself. Loose mortar scatters everywhere. Finally he manages, wriggling

131

sideways then slithering down the other side in the dark. I'm surprised – I did not think of Peter as plucky. He swears on the way down. I hear his jacket scraping the walls as he descends and the slap of his feet in soft dust as he lands. I can only see the top of his head now.

'Pass us that torch.'

Jason scowls at me as I stretch forward to pass the torch over. He clearly blames me for Peter's pre-emptive search. The beam of light sweeps round the chamber for a few seconds.

Peter whistles through his teeth. 'What were you expecting to find, Jason?'

'Have you found something?' Jason's voice is tight with anticipation.

'Zip, just footprints. Not mine. Size eight or nine. Small feet. Like yours.'

Jason is dusty, but he's not scruffy enough to have climbed over. Anyway, he doesn't have the balls.

'It wasn't him, Peter.'

'The message was meant for one of us,' Jason says quietly.

'How do you know that?'

'What message?' Peter asks from behind the wall. There is something comical about only being able to see his hair as he shuffles around.

'Someone scratched 'help me' on the wall in there. It was on one of the stones I took out this morning.'

'Well, bugger me.'

'Somebody has been in there,' Jason musters indignation, 'the security is useless.'

'What for?' Peter asks.

His disembodied question hangs in the dusty air for a moment between Jason and me. What for? Was it meant to give me a fright? If it was, it worked.

'Mind you, it is quite funny.' Peter's hair disappears and his voice in muffled, just the faint squeak of the nylon jacket rubbing against itself, '— must have been expecting a body —'

I look at Jason. He's biting his lower lip.

'That sounds more likely, doesn't it? A joke?' I don't sound as casual as I should.

Jason shakes his head, uncertain, unconvinced.

'Oh dear,' Peter sounds mildly annoyed, like he's forgotten to put sugar in his tea, 'I can't get out.'

'Seriously?'

'Seriously, chaps. There aren't any footholds on this side, and the batteries are going in the torch.'

'I don't know where the ladder is – Jason?'

'How should I know?' He pulls a face and turns to look around as if we could have missed it in the crypt.

'Well someone's managed to get in and out recently —'

'Maybe you could find them, then, and ask them how they got out, or, here's an idea, Mack, just pass me something to bloody stand on.'

I've never heard Peter sound like this before.

'OK. Hang on.' I pick up the plank and manoeuvre it so it slides through the hole. Jason is more of a hindrance than a help, lifting it up too high so that it knocks the roof on the other side, jarring my hands. His face is wet with perspiration. I let him lift the breeze blocks up. He passes six of them over. I hear Peter efficiently assembling a platform on the other side. He grunts and his head and shoulders appear.

'I hated PE at school. Never took to rock climbing, either.'

I reach forward to help pull him up.

'No, it'll hurt your hands.'

'Just get on with it, man.'

He grabs hold of me and we heave and hoist and thrash around until he flops onto the top of the wall like a seal onto a rock at low tide. There is no room for him to swing his legs round, even if he was fit enough to do it. Jason recognises the problem and helps me to haul him into the room, a ludicrous birthing, Jason swearing now too.

We are all lathered and gasping, grime in every pore, hair plastered, nostrils stuffed, wheezing and gagging on the humid air.

Peter starts to laugh. His lungs are so clogged he nearly chokes. He staggers away from the hole and sinks down onto one of the coffin benches, lying flat out on his back, still giggling sporadically between coughs, too knackered to take his jacket off, even though he looks like he's cooking himself, boil in a bag.

Jason follows Peter as soon as he can straighten up. He sits down on the bench next to him, resting his elbows on his knees and holding his head. The sweat drips into the dust between his shoes.

I lean against the wall, watching.

'Nothing.' Jason doesn't even look up he's so dejected.

'That's right. There was nothing there after all. A lot of effort to go to all for nothing.' Peter's amusement grates.

'Could whoever left the footprints have taken anything?' Jason asks.

I wondered about that, too.

Peter rolls onto his side, propped on one elbow with his face inches from Jason's. 'There was nothing to suggest that, just a few prints by the wall, no scuffs or scrabbles.'

'Of course we can't check that since you went galumphing around like an elephant.'

'Hey, I went over to help.' Peter levers himself up into a sitting position, 'There were only a few footprints, that's all. No outlines of bejewelled caskets, or rolls of parchment.'

'Leave him alone, Peter.'

They both look up at me. I've had enough. It's my labour that took down the wall, and like he said, it was all for nothing.

Just some ill-informed whim on the part of some stupid quasi-political group stuck in a three hundred year old feud. We have spoiled the Chapel for this.

I feel bitterly disappointed. 'Oh, let's just go home. I presume we can use the Trust's keys to lock the Chapel now?'

Jason shrugs. He looks dreadful.

I crunch across to Peter and pull him onto his feet. His hands are slippery with sweat. He slaps me on the back. I herd them up the stairs, leaving my tools where they lie. In a lifetime of petty failures I have rarely felt so deflated.

The sky is grey, but the comparative brightness still makes me blink. Three old men are standing on the gravel at the corner of the Chapel. They are looking at us: our appearance must be bizarre, staggering out of the Chapel dishevelled and tired. Jason fusses over his clothes. Peter unhooks the Jacobites' padlock from the hasp and trots off to get the Chapel keys from the hut.

Jason stops slapping his suit and straightens up at the edge of my vision. I am trying to keep an eye on the men without staring at them. He clearly wants my attention. It is irritating.

'I don't know what to do,' he says as soon as I acknowledge him.

'You and me, both.'

'You know it was Christopher. He got in there first.'

'What, your brother? Why?'

'To leave us a message.'

I repeat, 'Why?' but I can make a good guess. It's what passes with Robin for humour. I'm getting tired of his jokes.

'If it was for me, then I have a fair idea,' Jason says. 'Do you know why he would leave a message like that for you?'

'Because he wanted my help, presumably.'

Jason walks right up to me, looks me in the eye, almost cricking his neck with the angle. 'You're lying, Malcolm.'

I lean back, look round, embarrassed. But the old men have gone, and Peter is too far away to have heard.

'Back off, OK.'

'If that's the way it is.' Jason lets me past.

'Everything all right?' Peter has tidied himself up somehow. He has taken his sweater off, but he's still wearing his fake Barbour jacket. I can smell it before he's even close. The jacket is foul with more than sweat, soaked with the atmosphere of the crypt.

Jason stalks off, barely acknowledging Peter's existence.

Peter waits until he is round the corner. Why is he holding his jumper like that? He reminds me of a silver service waiter with a napkin to catch the drips. He really smells.

'Come with me to lock the Castle.'

He makes a pantomime out of locking the Chapel door, how hard can it be? 'Has Jason gone yet?'

'Don't think so.' I haven't heard his car start.

Peter still doesn't look at me. The keys go in his pocket, not back in the shed. Something's up.

The breeze makes the top branches of the sycamore creak. Sycamores don't bend away from the prevailing wind as they grow, they weather it or fall. The Trust wants to cut this one down because it's too close to the Castle.

Peter is walking so fast I can barely keep up with him. We jog up the stairs. I'm used to it, but he is suffering by the time we get to the top. He's not really checking for stray visitors. I follow him onto the decking. It is already drying in the wind. I look away from the wall she climbed over.

The wall I thought she climbed over.

'Why did you bring me up here?'

He's confused, frowns, 'Just wanted somewhere private to talk.'

'Oh.' It's bloody cold. The wind is picking up.

'Look, Mack, I didn't find nothing.'

I'm lost in syntax.

'Down there, there was something in the crypt.' He pants for air between the words.

'You said—'

'I said to *Jason*.'

'What was it? What did you find?'

He takes a big gulp of air. 'There's a trapdoor.'

'Good God.'

'Yes, see why I didn't want to say anything in front of Jason?'

'You put on quite a performance.'

'Thank you. The effort nearly broke me.'

'Are you sure?'

'Bloody positive. A trapdoor under all that dust.'

My watch is so filthy I have to wipe it to read the numerals. 'It's not time to lock up yet. Shall we go and have a look?'

'I have stuff to do. I'm closing early today.'

'Oh.'

'It's not something I want to risk on my own. You shouldn't either, Mack.'

'No… not very safe.'

'Could you take down some more of the wall tomorrow? It would make it much easier.'

'But won't the archaeologists want to be in there? I've done enough damage.'

'Those prats?' Peter straightens up. He's flushed, maybe from the stairs, maybe from the excitement of the afternoon. 'Why would you want to go telling them?'

'Because the whole site is important?'

'But finding this is just good luck. Our good luck.'

'Luck?'

'I didn't have to tell you about it.' He kicks at the decking. 'Wish I hadn't now.'

'You won't manage on your own.' That's why he told me: he needs me. I refrain from saying it, but it's there all the same.

He gives me a sour look. I don't like this Peter.

'It's freezing. I haven't got my jacket.' I turn to go.

'Wait!' He's actually trying to block my way.

'Peter –'

'Promise.'

'Promise what? It's archaeology, not some treasure hunt.'

'It's my find.'

'It's the Trust's decision, surely. It's history, it doesn't belong –'

'Don't you dare spoil this for me.'

The wind thrashes through the new sycamore leaves. The whole wood is alive, all around us. You can almost hear the sap rising in these heart beats. I want to flatten him. Harmless, hapless little Peter.

Greedy little Peter, guzzling up history like he guzzles Mars Bars in the hut.

'Let me past, Peter. I don't want to fall out with you.'

'Promise.'

I shake my head and start walking. He stands back.

I am on the quarter landing when he calls after me. 'Help me, Mack.'

♜

What's got into him? I could lock him in the Castle overnight, let the ghosts talk some sense into him. The key is in my hand. I pat the timbers of the door. Not tonight.

Bloody hell, it's cold. I would feel better if the weather wasn't this bad. It's called a depression for a reason. It's like I'm on a path that's getting narrower. The Brig o' Dread. I don't even know if it's the panic that makes me feel this way, or if being like this makes me panic. This is a maelstrom about to suck me down into it.

It's not depression – I've got too many worries, too much to contain in one mind. One tired mind.

Come on, none of this will matter in five years. It's a job. I can get another one.

It's no good. It doesn't work, trying to pull myself together. It's only words. Sometimes the light at the end of the tunnel really is an oncoming train. We're spoiling something here, and change feels terrible because I have nothing else to hold on to. I slam the wooden gate beneath the sycamore so hard the heavy padlock swings and clunks against the timber.

At the corner of the Chapel I stop and reach out to touch its stone. Cold and dry. The surface catches the bandage as I spread my fingers. I let my fingertips rub into the gritty little pits pecked into the quoin stones four hundred years ago. There is no need to pretend the stone can understand. I feel enough resentment for both of us.

Hell, Peter can see me fondling the wall if he's still skulking about up there. I pull my hand away. I mustn't look back. I hurry round the Chapel to be out of sight. I would never have thought Peter was capable of being like this. I'm not going to help him tomorrow, that's all there is to it. I'll have to tell Jason.

'Tell Jason what?'

'Christ, Robin!' Just standing there by the South door, waiting to pounce. How long have I been talking out loud?

'Just Robin will do.'

'Or Christopher?'

'Or Christopher,' he agrees.

'You didn't tell me.'

He shrugs and draws his black jacket round himself. 'It's not like we tell each other everything.'

I set off towards the car park. He falls into step beside me.

Maybe I can explain why I feel he ought to have told me. 'After all I've said to you, all my grumbling about Jason - I wouldn't have gone about him so much if I'd known he's your brother. You should have said something.'

'Nothing much to say. You're right: Jason is feeble, he is a fool.'

I remember how Jason looked at me. 'Were you in the crypt today?'

'No. What made you think I was?'

'Or yesterday?'

'Why do you ask?'

Should I tell him? If he wrote the message on the stone, then he'll already know I suspect him. If he didn't... well I'd rather he didn't see how much it has upset me. Or Jason.

'Mack?'

'Sorry. Miles away. Where's your car?'

There are only two cars, parked side by side, Jason's and Peter's.

'I'm getting a lift with Jason.'

Lucky Jason. We walk over to the vehicles. The windows of Jason's Land Rover are fogged. He's been waiting all this while. I go round to the driver's side and knock on the glass.

'Everything OK?'

He can't open the window, the electrics aren't on.

'Jason, can I have a word?'

He's just staring back at me. I'll be damned if I'm going to bellow through the glass. I reach out to the door handle, he shifts, reaches for the ignition. The door's locked.

'Jason.'

I hear the gears engage and I let go of the handle as he skids away.

Robin gazes across the space where the Land Rover was. He's amused, not annoyed. It's a long walk back to his place on a day like this.

'Family. Almost more trouble than they're worth, eh, Mack?'

'Most families don't scare the shit out of each other.'

I didn't think. I'm left standing wide open to whatever he has to say.

'Death by misadventure, now how scary must that have been?'

'I'm not –' Not what? What is there to say? 'Don't start, Robin. Not today.'

'Steady there.'

I bang my arm against the passenger side door of Peter's car. I almost fall.

Robin lurches forwards. 'Are you alright?'

'Leave me alone.' I brush at my clothes, at the sudden feeling that I've walked through cobwebs. My scalp crawls, my whole skin is in revolt.

He takes a step back. 'Look at you. Let me get you home.'

'This has to end, Robin. I can't take anymore.'

'Do you need to sit down? I can fetch Peter.'

'No! No thanks. I'll be fine.' Anyone but Peter.

'Are you sure? Shall we get you home?'

'I need to get some money out.' It's true. I also need to be among people, normal people on a pavement in a busy place. I can't run my fingers through my hair – the bandages snag. The children are making a racket on the far side of the Hall. Adults shouting instructions over voices too loud to listen. Home time, half past three.

Robin is thinking. 'I'll walk you home, then drive you down to town.'

'Your car is at my house?'

'Seemed sensible. The car park was full with all those gentlemen and we aren't allowed to use the school's car park during term time. You don't mind, do you?'

He smiles, but he must see that I do mind. The car park wasn't full this morning, not when I first met him with Jason.

'What's the matter now?'

'Nothing.' I head up the drive. 'Do you still have my set of keys for the cottage?'

He slaps his pockets. 'No, they must be at home. Why? Have you lost the spare set?'

'They aren't spares. They belong to my landlord. Can you bring mine back?'

'I'll fetch them over tomorrow. Slow down a little, I'm an old man.'

I slacken my pace and try to watch him without being too obvious. Yes, he looks like an old man now.

'What's the age gap between you and Jason?'

He laughs, 'Jason is my older brother.'

It's not much of a joke. I wonder how old he really is. I could just ask, only I don't. It's too cold for May, and the wind is picking up, carrying the first smattering raindrops belonging to another cold front. A miserable day.

'Not far now,' he says like I'm a child. The cottage will be cold. I'd forgotten about the mildew – I ought to ring Lord Muck. I might have more luck with Clara.

✗

It must be ten minutes since we last spoke. I am trying to prioritise anxieties as we tramp along. The Chapel comes first, even though, for practical purposes, it should be the mould problem. I can do something about both of those. I will feel better once I start to sort them out. Maybe I should think about sorting everything out once and for all.

'Well, look at that.'

'What?' It's an empty lane with empty fields on either side.

Robin pounces into the verge and comes back holding a blackbird's egg, pale, pale blue and speckled with brown, like it's been dusted with cocoa powder.

I grunt acknowledgement.

He holds it up between thumb and forefinger. 'It's a blackbird's egg.'

'Yes, I know.' I'm too cold for a nature lesson.

He squeezes, the egg bursts, watery slime and dark blood slide down his fingers.

'What did you do that for?'

He takes out his handkerchief and wipes his fingers, glaring at me down his nose like I somehow did it to him.

I shake my head and walk on, hunching my shoulders. It begins to rain harder. I hope he found the egg in the grass, not in a nest. He's at my side already, whistling very quietly. I catch the tune. He's doing it on purpose. We are a good five-hundred yards from the cottages, and his car is indeed parked there. I clench my fists and speed up. He manages to whistle even though he's almost trotting to keep up with me now. I stamp my feet down on the tarmac in rhythm to the words that drum inside my head. It's a song to teach a man to hate.

♟

He's been in here. He's lying about the keys. The place has that special chill I have come to associate with Robin's presence.

'Do you need to change first?' he calls from the kitchen.

It must be obvious that I'm checking the house. I've been in every room. The mould has made a hell of a mess, and the smell is overwhelming. Most of the black mass has slid down the walls under its own weight. It must be a foot deep at the skirting. Since this morning it's sent out white fluffy tendrils, exploratory roots, pushing across the carpet. Can fungus feed on skin cells, like dust mites? Is it foraging? I hope I get a new carpet out of this.

'Are you ready?'

I need to do some washing. This is my last clean shirt. 'Hang on.'

♟

He's sniffing the milk. There must be something wrong with the fridge, I only bought fresh milk yesterday.

'Oh dear,' he says with an odd tone, like I've done something wrong.

The kitchen feels grimy. Despite the thorough cleaning yesterday there is a feeling of neglect about it, unhomely. The rain dashes down the pane, grey beyond and grim in here. Even my African violets have succumbed, shrivelled up in their pots on the window sill. The cold probably did for them because their compost is still moist.

I pat my jeans to check I transferred my wallet. I have lost weight enough to need a belt with these jeans. They are new— well, a few months old— but I tend to wear a couple of pairs out before I change them. The button is stiff. What the hell is he doing now?

'What are you looking for?'

He pulls his head out of pantry. 'You've mould starting to grow in here, too.'

'Oh shit. Can you hang on a minute? I need to ring Clara while I remember.'

'Well…'

'Fine. You go. I'll walk down to the village. It's not a problem.' I click on Clara's number.

'No, no. You sort out the mould, I'll wait.'

I wish he wouldn't stand so close. It's embarrassing having the house in this state, even if it's only rented. 'Hello, Clara?'

'*If it's about this morning –*'

'No, it's the cottage, there's a problem.'

'*Well I can't sort that out now. William is furious, Mack, absolutely furious. That jumped up little –*'

'Clara, I have mould growing down the walls; I can't use my bedroom.'

Robin is laughing. I angle my body so he can't hear her end of the conversation as well.

'*Mould? Why did you wait until now to ring?*'

'I've been... it's grown really quickly, I've never seen anything like it. It only started yesterday.'

'Well, surely it can't be that bad. Can't we talk about this tomorrow?'

She's rung off. It would be a different matter if my rent was late. I'm sick of the way they behave as though they were doing me a favour here rather than treating it as a commercial transaction. I step away from Robin.

'All done?' he asks.

'Yeah. For all the good it did me.'

'Another night on the sofa?'

'Looks that way.' That feeling again, as though I've pushed through cobwebs. 'Let's go.'

♜

Mel calls as I'm putting on my seat belt. It takes a second too long to turn off my phone.

'Who was that?'

'No-one, I'll take it later. We'll be there in five minutes.' Two, at the speed Robin drives.

'So how are things down in the crypt?' he asks, pulling out in front of a lorry at the lane end.

My door misses the front of the truck by inches, then we're whisked away, swerving down a left hand turn, going so hard we leave the road for a moment as we cross the little hump-backed bridge over the railway line. I hope to God he stops at the junction.

'It's going well, but I suppose it will all stop now the Jacobites have left.'

'Oh, once you start –' He swerves straight out onto the main road.

'Look out!'

The oncoming vehicle squeals to a stop, the horn blaring. I stamp my right foot down amongst the empty coffee cartons in the footwell. Robin accelerates, brushing the kerb with his nearside tyres. He overcorrects the steering. The car rocks like a small boat before it returns to our side of the road. The car we nearly T-boned is right behind with its lights on.

'What's the matter with you, Mack?'

'I just don't like being nearly killed, that's all.'

'Relax. You're heading for an early grave.'

We sweep past the large Victorian cemetery.

'So have you been over the wall yet?' he asks.

'What wall?'

The traffic lights are against us on the bridge over the Tyne. The other car is so close behind that the driver risks Robin bumping him if we roll back a fraction when the lights change.

'The wall in the crypt you've spent a week trying to take down. Are you all right?'

'Yes.' I sound sulky.

'So have you been over the wall?'

'No. Peter went over. There wasn't anything to see. Just some footprints. Small feet, like yours.'

'And Jason's.'

'But Jason didn't go over.'

'Sure about that?' He pulls away as the lights change. We cross the bridge, and he turns into a narrow street with wide pavements.

'Just drop me in the market place.'

'And you're sure Jason's not been over?'

'Positive. Here will do.'

Robin pulls up, not bothering that he's blocking the one-way system. The car we nearly crashed into is still behind us. I glance at the driver as I get out. It is a woman, seething at this further discourtesy.

I duck my head back into the car. 'Thanks for the lift.'

'I'll wait, give you a lift back.'

'No, I'm fine.'

'No, I'll wait.'

'You're holding up the traffic. I want to walk home.' How much more does he need?

'It's raining. Don't be stubborn –'

'Good bye, Robin.' I close the door.

He pulls away at a crawl. The driver behind passes me slowly. It's a woman with kids in the back. I need to cross the street and have to stand at the kerb while the children we so nearly killed stare out at me from the back seat as they glide past. I can hear the tone of the driver's voice from the pavement. The tone but not the words. I am sick of getting on the wrong side of people.

Better zip my jacket. It's not raining hard, not much more than drizzle. I'm cold, but the walk home will warm me up. I want meat for tea. A big steak bleeding on my plate.

There's a problem with the cash machine. It's not five yet. I can catch the bank if I hurry. I've time to spare, but I jog along the road to my bank anyway.

It's not very warm in here; the windows have steamed up. There's only ever one teller at the windows. There is one customer in front of me. She looks vaguely familiar. Oh shit, it's the driver. No, it can't be, unless she's ditched the children, or left them unaccompanied in the car. She glances round, aware of the attention. Yes, it's her. I know her from somewhere, somewhere else.

I smile. She frowns and turns back to discuss her direct debits. She sounds anxious, apologetic. I'm sorry about Robin risking her family's life. I want to tell her I wouldn't drive like that. But then I'm not allowed to drive at all now, so it's irrelevant.

I smile again when she turns around. She mumbles something, but I miss what she says. I step forward into the space she has left.

'Sorry to keep you, sir.' The lad at the window manages not to look at the clock. In another minute it will be his time, not the bank's.

'That's OK. The cash machine wouldn't accept my card. I'd like fifty pounds, please.'

He clatters the amount on his keyboard.

'Would you just like to put your card in the slot and tap in your PIN.'

There is a pause. I feel an unreasonable wave of panic.

'Can you put the card in again, please?'

'Is there a problem?'

'The machine can't read it. Are you sure this is one of our cards?'

'What?'

'Perhaps the chip's been damaged. How long have you held an account with us?' He's smiling but I saw the quick movement he made to press the button to summon assistance.

'But I only used it a few days ago. And last night at the supermarket.'

'Not that card, sir, it wouldn't work. How long –'

'For two years.'

I pass him the card. There's nothing wrong with it. He examines it. He taps in the number. His face clears a little. A middle aged woman in a hideous corporate blouse and skirt cautiously looks round a door behind him.

'It's alright, Flora, thought we had a fake card here. It's just not scanning.'

She smiles at me and retreats back through the door.

'If you just fill out a withdrawal slip. Are you aware you're near your overdraft limit?'

'I didn't realise I was overdrawn. I'll make sure I put my wages in tomorrow.'

He counts out five ten pound notes. How have I gone through so much money?

'Can you check any recent withdrawals, please?'

'Do you think there has been some unauthorised use?'

'Possibly.'

He angles the screen. I have taken out two hundred pounds every night for a week. Or rather someone has. He shares my alarm which is reassuring. We go through my usual banking pattern. There is no record of my paying for shopping last night. Surely I didn't let Robin pay for my groceries? I can't remember.

'Well, we can sort it from here,' he says. 'We'll need to call the police. We'll retain the card. It's not legal, and you can't use it anyway. The police will probably want to call you as well.'

It's after closing time now. I've made trouble for him. Made more trouble for me. The last thing I want is to be noticed by the police again.

He watches me as I leave.

Three morose children are standing on the pavement opposite. I recognise them.

'Are you waiting for your mother? She isn't in there, she left a few minutes ago.'

The oldest can't be more than seven or eight. They are all in school uniform. They look hungry and cold. The little boy has a nasty bruise across his brow.

'Maybe you should wait for your Mum where she parked the car?'

A pedestrian swerves past me, stepping off the pavement in order to avoid me. Once she's past she looks round and stares right into my eyes. Maybe it's not a good idea to be seen talking to children. Not with all this trouble with Melissa. When I turn back the children have gone anyway.

✶

The butcher's is closed.

There's only the Co-op open. I don't fancy their meat as I rifle through the freezer cabinet. The cold is making my hands ache. Frozen stuff will take too long, anyway. No point getting sausages if half the pack will go to waste. I'm sick of fry-ups. I might be better off with tins if the fridge is broken.

This is ridiculous. I've been in here for twenty minutes. I might as well wait for the pub to start serving evening meals. I get paid tomorrow and the bank will sort out whatever's happened with my card.

The girl behind the tills gives me a filthy look as I leave. I'd make an inept shoplifter taking this long over it.

What do you do for half an hour after the shops have shut in a village in the rain?

There are lights on in the library.

I try to look casual so that I'm not humiliated if it's closed. I peruse the notice board before honing in on their closing time: 7.00pm every weekday except Friday. Who'd have thought it?

It's warm. And noisy. Half a dozen small children are squabbling over picture books. A person who presumably passes for a responsible adult is leaning against a bookshelf nearby, deep in a novel. The librarian says hello. You get a better class of book-borrower in the village than in town. I can put up with the kids in exchange for the warmth.

'Natural history, please?'

'In that corner, past the infants' art display.' She points into the recesses of the long, low room.

'Thank you.'

Dad collected the New Naturalist series. I open one at random, *A Country Parish*. The same feeling again, my scalp crawls, so bad this time I have to resist the temptation to throw down the book and shake the dirt out of my hair. Steady. Put the book back carefully. Calmly comb my hair with my fingers. Try to look casual, not like I'm searching for lice.

One of the children stands by the librarian's counter, watching me. I pull a face. The child looks away. I move along to the local history section to put some distance between us.

The local history section is large, arranged by source rather than topic. Little plaques show which collections have been bequeathed to the library. There are three whole shelves dedicated to the Castle. Always go for the most dog-eared book. It's either so good it's always being borrowed or so old it may be interesting. This book is… 1807. Last borrowed 1973. That good.

I take off my jacket and sit down at the nearest table. This is all about the Radcliffes. Not the flamboyant history Peter has told me, but an account of their family after James Radcliffe, Earl of Derwentwater, was executed. Officially there was some suspicion that he cheated the axe and that his cousin took the blade. I knew that story, but here the villagers are adamant that he died and came back to haunt them. It seems to be a mixture of folklore, testimonials and a series of accounts told by old men who would barely have been born when the Fifteen Rebellion failed. Radcliffe's heart is mentioned several times. The local people stayed Catholic until 1738 and still used the Chapel even when band of brigands took over the Castle. Eventually the habitable end of the Castle was blown up to stop it being used by 'thieves and murderers, although there were nonesuch living there'. The pages are worn thin and soft. I don't want to tear them, so I can't flick through. Maybe I should start at the beginning.

♜

I walk home with wine, bread and cheese and the book, choosing cold food and the company of words over the proximity of strangers in a pub. The book fits nicely in my jacket pocket, wrapped in its protective, recycled plastic bag. The rain has eased, the cloud is high, but it's still cold and it seems closer to dusk than it really is. The lane looks fresh this evening. Hemlock and sweet cicely fill the ditches, the may blossom is just opening on the outer twigs of the hedge. The whole world is washed green and white, even in this overcast chill.

This timeless quality is illusionary, I know. It is a picture of early twentieth-century agriculture, and it all looked different before that, but it still twists me with longing for peace and permanency. The pain of it is piquant, this enjoyable nostalgia, and I am lost outside myself for a mile or so.

I

The wind has changed; the fireplace isn't smoking tonight. The bottle is warming on the hearth, ready for my next glass. I have my duvet ready, but it's warm enough for now, sitting in my tee shirt as I read. The washing machine is chugging away. There's no traffic. I can't even hear the neighbours as I read.

The Family at the Castle played with fire. They were enormously wealthy, owning vast tracts of Northumberland. This book makes out it was their devotion to the Catholic Church that caused them to help the Jacobites. I don't believe for a moment that they risked it all for religion. It's the power that goes along with the faith, that's what beguiled them. Less scripture, more king-making. Our Chapel was one of the last Catholic churches to be built after the Reformation. It was a statement of intent.

Some of this is heavy going. I'm feeling sleepy. Gases in the coal click as they expand and escape. A good blaze.

I know the myth behind the Grey Lady. Juliet told me on my first day at the Castle. Radcliffe was reluctant to go to the Jacobite cause and his wife reputedly challenged him, throwing down her fan and saying she would ride to support King James, and he should take up his fan with the women. When he was caught and later executed, remorse made her return to wander the grounds.

Here they have it differently. When the Earl was captured and sent to the Tower of London, his wife demanded that someone take her husband's place on the scaffold, challenging a series of impoverished relations with the promise of land and pensions for their wives and children. Not one member of the family would do it, so she put a curse on them, and the whole clan perished. They have James Radcliffe as a saint and his wife as a witch.

The woman I saw last week at the Castle door?

The hair rises on the back of my neck. My hand shakes a little as I pour another glass. This is more the woman I saw, malicious and potent and so bloody real, not some romantic, floaty vision of a Grey Lady.

The wine is the temperature of blood. I can hardly swallow it, my throat is so tight. It's just a story. A melodramatic story written for a different audience. I concentrate on the history while I finish the glass, waiting for the warmth to return before I pick up the book again. The night is black outside, but I won't close the curtains. I stay within the circle, the sofa and the fire and a pool of light from the standard lamp.

So, Radcliffe went to his death in 1716. His head was put on a spike to rot and they let his family bring his body home. The steward cut out his heart, and a joiner working on the site made a little box for it. The joiner's account is recorded.

> The coffer was of boisewood the grain so close it did not need to be sealed. I was given a brass hasp and bindings and the good Father took the key from the little lock to keep. When the new priest opened the coffer this day His heart was as fresh as it was when I put it in myself this sixteen year past.

Here are the accounts of the miracles. Three healings just from touching the heart, each accompanied by several testimonies. Now I don't know much about Papal malarkeys, but wouldn't they have rushed this to Rome to have the Earl beatified or something? No account of that. There's a line drawing of the box, complete with stylized heart, suggesting the picture was not drawn from life.

More testimonies. Should I stop reading now? Will I sleep? One more glass, maybe finish the bottle to be sure.

These next accounts aren't about miracles.

They cut off James Radcliffe's head, but he still came home.

At first, the retinue of servants still managing the Castle noticed a beggar man loitering in the grounds. If he was challenged, he gave strange answers and disappeared. Something bad invariably befell the questioner soon after. Superstition blossomed, a legend grew and the more faith they put in their Lord's heart, the more frequent the apparition became. The serving girls ran away; one was found strangled in the snow on the second winter. The saintly Earl cannot have been that good to his people, for it was the general molestation of young girls that led the remaining servants to decide that the revenant was their Lord Derwentwater returned. This continued for a few years. Law and order were breaking down in the area, with reports of troops of brigands camping at the vicinity. The annals of the people still trying to live in the Castle record troubles from an entirely less mundane source. The priest was unwilling to convene an exorcism because the Sheriff would not allow him to contact his bishop in Newcastle. The people begged, the attacks got worse, girls lost, babies smothered, dogs and cats slaughtered, neighbour set against neighbour. Finally in a cold, late spring, much like this one, the priest was forced to take action.

My Lord Bishop,
Please forgive me for what I am about to do but I have no other Christian recourse. My parishioners' faith in me is at a very low ebb, yet what I do is for their good, not to win back

their favour, but to save their souls. To save us all. I must rid this place of the demon that besets us and have but one recourse left.

I pray to Saint Jude that you will get this letter. The roads are bad this year and things more foul than the usual cutthroats are abroad. Pray for me, Monsignor, as I commend my soul to the Virgin and ask only for good judgement in my task. I do not ask permission, lest you refuse from not understanding the straits in which we find ourselves. How could any man, even with your wisdom, comprehend what we suffer? God knows I would have applied to you ten years ago, but have been refused permission to write hitherto, and now I fear it is too late. As I write I hear the bells for the service to lay to rest an infant found torn apart not twenty four hours since. It was not dogs, no animal will come near the place. Evil abides here.

I can scarce speak the services for the laughter which begins as soon as I kiss my Bible. It is not in my head, only the steward and his wife dare enter the Chapel now, but they hear it too. I have their testimony which I send in mitigation, along with several others.

There are few alive here, but since last Sunday the dead walk among us. The churchyard is emptied and we are visited by ghosts that seem so solid many have fled in terror, but worse was to see those who did not run. The poor mothers trying to catch hold of their lost sons and our gamekeeper who fell senseless in front of his dead wife all wasted and rotted from the grave.

May God have mercy upon us.

Please do not condemn me, but pray for me and if I fail I beg you will say Mass for my soul. I send this with the last groom. Please give him his keep until he can find employment. He is a good and honest lad and I would not wish him to spend another night in this place. I go now to bury the latest victim of this curse. Then with the help of the Virgin and all the saints I shall lay this spirit as our Holy Church has decreed, by bell, book and candle.

Forgive me, I go unshriven. There is none left to do it for me. I have no other help nor council but my own conscience. God grant me courage.

Yours in Christ,
Richard Radcliffe, priest of this parish.

The original letter and testimonies were stored in Newcastle Keep at the time my book was written, seventy years after the event. I wonder if they still exist?

The priest must have been a family member – otherwise his name is too big a coincidence. It says when he died but not how. The Bishop sent a new priest that summer. He took the Earl's heart, stabbed it with a knife and had it sealed under the Chapel. My book concludes that this ended the superstition once and for all. Parliament blew up the major portion of the Castle, leaving only the fifteenth century tower, and the grounds were given to the Greenwich Hospital. The book finishes by describing the Castle as the most picturesque ruin and recommends it as a pleasant place to picnic. A nicely reasoned laying of antique imaginings from before the Age of Reason. The End.

Not really. Look at the thriving ghost walks and the log book of supernatural occurrences. I far as I can see, the Grey Lady was never lain to rest; it was too good a story. She is a victim of her own success.

I wonder if the Jacobites have read this account of their hero and antecedent? They are hoping for some sort of rallying point, a relic. Not so good having some nasty shrivelled bit of meat with a knife sticking out of it and a whole load of peasant superstition attached.

I have let the fire go out. Never mind, I'm tried enough to sleep. The duvet's warm from where I have leant against it. It must be late. I left my watch upstairs in the bathroom. Where's my phone?

It rings the instant I think of it.

'Hello? Hello. Mel, is that you? Mel?'

Has she stopped talking to me? She used to let me see her. Losing her voice now… it's almost a relief.

I return the call, banging the numbers in. Even though the battery must have died ten years ago, it still rings for me. But she doesn't answer.

I hope she's somewhere safe. The images from the priest's letter clog my mind for a moment. I shouldn't have read the book. Very little was credible, there wasn't much to learn and it has made me maudlin. Pathetic.

The house is very quiet.

There's one more glass left. Will it help me sleep? Better turn the lamp off. I am reluctant to break this circle of light. How ridiculous, a grown man sleeping downstairs with the light on. I click the lamp off at the socket. Three steps back to the sofa, feeling my way with not even starlight from the window.

Is that smoke? No smell of burning, no glowing embers rekindling. The room is pitch black, too dark even to make out shapes. There by the fireplace, a pillar of smoke or faint lights. Maybe it's my eyes. Maybe she is here after all.

10. FRIDAY

She's here in my dreams. She has her head in my lap. I smooth strands of hair back from her cheek. She has been crying – or is it raining? We are so close I am nearly her, watching myself looking down. This is not a great love, we both know that, but it will be her only one, and I will have to live with it forever, so we make it bigger than it is. She begins to cry again. The rain washes us both. I look up at the sky and know it is Scotland. The rain splashes on my face. It pelts down, hurts my skin. She is so very cold. I stroke her hair again and some of it comes away in my hand. I close my eyes and hold my hand out so that the rain washes it clean. I won't look down. Not at what she is now.

Jesus, let me wake up.

I'm still trying to rid myself of the horror of the thing in my lap, even when I know it is only my duvet.

Oh God.

I swing my legs to floor and sit up. Deep breaths, deep breaths. I can't go on living with this. I need to get home. I need to speak to the Lothian and Borders police. If I talk to this lot here, they'll think I'm mad.

The truth of the dream slams home; this was never a great love. If Mel had not been lost it would have fizzled out long since. We would have gone on with our lives. This makes me shrink down and hide my face in my hands. I want to howl at my past. What the Hell did I think I was doing? That poor girl out there somewhere. Her parents. Christ, her mother as she spat in my face at the memorial service.

My phone rings.

'Mel?'

Is that anything? The faintest noise? Is she there?

I can't just sit here all day. Come on. Can I risk leaving my hands unbandaged? The dressings need replacing more from showering than from grime. Most of today will probably be spent in arguing with Peter. Can I ask him to bandage my hands again?

My watch is where I left it in the bathroom. It's nearly eight. The dressings will have to do. I clatter down the stairs, won't think about Peter, no time. Quick breakfast.

I open the fridge. Jesus. Eugh, the reek fills the whole kitchen. Why the hell didn't Robin chuck the bloody milk when he found it yesterday? What did he do with the lid? The milk is green. I hold my breath again while I unbolt the back door.

I can't make it; I have to exhale but try my best not to breathe in. The bolt is stiff. Ow! Buggeration. I caught my bloody thumb. The smell makes me gag as I finally wrench the door open.

Damn, what do I do with this? I can't pour this out near the house. Or the neighbours' house. Or my sheds. I'm left holding the carton at arm's length and turning round on the tiny lawn in the back garden, looking for the best place to pour it out. Probably in the ditch over the road. I carry it out in front of me as I walk around the side of the house. It's basically cheese now, but it smells worse than anything I can remember and I've been stuck in a crypt for the best part of the week. I pity the wildlife in the overgrown ditch.

I pour slowly. If I tip it out too fast, it will splash on me. The stench fills the whole lane. Nearly done. There's still a thick coating inside the plastic. I shake the last curds out as carefully as possible. Thick globules slide and dribble. I skip back to save my trainers.

Someone's behind me. I spin round, carton in hand. It's the woman from the bank. No, it must be my neighbour. I can't remember her name.

'Hi.'

She stares back at me, closes her lips and looks questioningly at the carton.

'My fridge has broken, the milk's gone bad.'

'Oh.' Her voice is low and anxious. Are they the same woman? Did we nearly crash into my neighbour yesterday?

'Well, I'm late for work, I'd better…' I feel my face muscles pulling into an unnatural smile.

'Mack –'

'I'm sorry, did we meet in the bank yesterday? I've had a lot on my mind recently.'

'I know we don't know each other very well, and this isn't the best time, with you being late –'

'It was you, wasn't it?'

'Yes, but it's just I only wanted to say I'm sorry. If I made things worse with the police on Tuesday. It's difficult to know what to say. I just tried to tell the truth.'

What did she say, exactly? She hardly knows me. I straighten up; she flinches. I wish I could remember her name. She seems utterly nondescript, small and skinny in jeans and a patterned smock. No wonder I didn't recognise her yesterday.

She's not finished. She's steeling herself up for a longer speech.

I haven't time for this.

'It will be alright. Like I say, I have to get to work.'

I start to walk back across the lane to my gate.

She trots along next to me, 'Wait, Mack. Please.'

'I'm late.' My hand is on the latch. She holds on to the top of the gate. All I have to do is push it open, she's not

161

strong enough to stop me. I can't do it though. This is my mother's indoctrination: manners maketh the man. I sigh and look down at her.

'You seem like such a nice man. I know we don't know each other very well.' She swallows hard. Does she always repeat herself so much? 'It's only, well, I don't know if you know much about that man who comes round, your friend?'

I almost deny having any friends, but I know who she means. I nod.

'Well, I know he's your friend, but *please – he drinks –* he's a drink-driver... he used to be – well, I know people can get better – reform – but he never showed any remorse, never ever, and we were told he'd hung himself in Durham prison three years ago, and now we see him all the time, and it's brought it all back, and *I can't bear it*.' She drags in a deep breath impeded because she is crying. Suck and spew.

Robin? 'Are you talking about the priest who comes round?'

She has her hands over her face. She's beyond talking to, hysterical, silent tears and mucus dripping through her fingers between hiccupping breaths. I put one hand on her shoulder and the other on her elbow and gently turn her round in a brief waltz so that she's facing her house. I propel her along to her own gate and up her short garden path. She moves like a sleepwalker. I hope her husband hasn't left for work yet. I think he's called Geoff. Should I open the door or knock?

For a brief moment she leans back against me as we stand in front of the white woodwork. Her flesh is warm through the printed cotton. She starts to drop. Shit, she's fainted. I grab at her clumsily, she's so much shorter than me. I shove my hands under her arms and she still slithers down my legs, so I'm left holding her wrists. The stitches tug in my right hand.

The front door slams open.

'Macready!' her husband tries to thunder, but he is too hollow.

Gravel pokes into my sore skin as I get down onto my knees beside his wife on the damp path.

'She's fainted.'

'I can see that. Go away!' He flaps at me like he scaring away a pigeon, 'I said go! Go away and take your bloody evil friend with you. Can't you see this is destroying my wife?'

I scramble backwards, push myself to my feet. What have I done? I don't understand what I've done wrong. He's not knelt down to her, he's too afraid of me, shaking like his wife was.

I can't leave her lying here. He can't carry her.

She's no weight when I lift her.

He backs up the steps into his own house. This cottage is a mirror image of my own. I nudge open the door into their sitting room with my shoulder and step back to let him through. He throws a couple of magazines and a remote control off the sofa and I lay her down with her head on a cushion. All this is done in silence. What can I say? He sinks down next to her head, stroking her fringe back from her wet face. Her colour is coming back. Seeing them now, like this, I realise they aren't as old as I thought they were. Not really much older than me, forty at the most, but her hair is mostly grey, and he is bald and hunched and his face is lined. His eyes, though, they are outside time and black with outrage.

He twists his lips thin and clamps his jaws so tight his teeth grind. 'What are you waiting for? *Thanks?* It's your fault she's like this.'

He's scared of me, but brave enough to fight. I am ashamed of bringing the man to this.

'I'm going. I didn't know.'

'Yes, go. Out. Now, before she sees you again.'

I almost tiptoe back out, closing their front door as softly as I can. I leave the milk carton lying by the doorstep, where I dropped it when she fainted.

They can't mean Robin.

Do they know about me? All I hurt was the car and my arm and the bus shelter I demolished. No-one could get upset about that. There was never any question of a custodial sentence. But Robin? His driving is bad enough when he's sober. I can't picture him in jail. God help the other inmates. It doesn't seem possible that he hasn't mentioned it, but then there's all this business with him being Christopher Robin and Jason being his brother. He never mentioned that, either. Is this mistaken identity? I need to speak to Jason about this before I accost Robin. It would explain why he hates his brother so much.

I'm stiff. I'll have to sit on the stairs to change into my boots. How well does anyone know anybody else? Married couples live for decades with lies between them. What do I know about Robin?

These bandages do need changing, but it's already ten to nine.

My phone rings. No, not Mel, not now. I will leave my phone at home today.

♟

It's not raining at present, but it's so cold that we are standing in Peter's hut to argue. Sam, the head of the archaeology team, is very angry. I have never seen anyone outside a cartoon go this colour before. Even Lord Muck can't get this angry. Sam's face is puce, his eyes screwed up with rage, his fists clenched by his side, waiting for Jason to make one more wrong move.

Juliet is quivering with indecision next to Jason: she hasn't picked sides yet. Peter is standing behind Sam with a couple of other members of Sam's team. I can't even close the door behind me the place is so cramped. Their outdoor gear stinks of sweat and Gore-Tex.

'We have to have access to the crypt, Jason.' Sam repeats for the tenth time.

'I can't authorise it.'

'He can't,' Juliet agrees.

I look across into Peter's eyes. This wasn't what he wanted at all. Still, it saves me having to refuse to help him. I shrug as sympathetically as I can, pressed up against the door like a sardine. He pulls a face back, friendly enough. I don't think it occurs to him that I wouldn't help him pillage the crypt.

'Your lot pushed for this,' Sam won't let go, 'and you went ahead without consulting us, without getting proper permission from English Heritage. You are in deep shit. You haven't heard the last of this from them, either, believe me. Mack's not qualified to remove something this important. We only have the original survey drawings of the wall. God knows how much damage he's done.'

'You weren't on site, so I couldn't discuss it with you. I was only doing my job,' I say.

Sam swivels round to me, 'Yes, and you have no phone? You couldn't have rung me at the office? At least Holden didn't know what damage he was doing.'

Whoa. 'Now wait a minute, Sam –'

'This is my responsibility, Sam, not Malcolm's,' Jason says. 'He put your case as clearly as you have.'

I don't look at Jason, but I can feel his eyes on me. He needs an ally.

'But if I'd known…' Sam's storming rage is blowing itself out, levelling off at his usual bluster. Even the timbers of the hut seem to creak slightly in relief.

'Can I make everyone a nice cup of tea?' Juliet asks. Surely she isn't that simple?

Sam looks pained. The rest of his team begin to shuffle out. The hut empties rapidly. I have to step outside to let them past. Jason follows Sam. Maybe Juliet does know what she is doing, after all.

Her invitation wasn't extended to me. She sets two mugs down next to the geyser, one for her and one for Peter.

I remember I need to speak to Jason, excusing myself before she has a chance to snub me.

He has a quite a head start. I have to run round the Chapel after him.

'Hey, Jason!'

He waits for me next to the big lime tree. It's still dripping from the last shower.

'Malcolm.'

'Hello. Thank you for that. In the hut.'

He looks down at his shoes. The rain begins again. He follows me into the pale green shelter of the lime's soft new leaves. The lowest branches are above my head. It was only a sapling when Radcliffe died. We breathe in the smell. He closes his eyes for a moment. He looks like he hasn't slept. His eyes are sunken and his skin is greasy.

I ask, 'What's happening with the Jacobite Society?'

He shifts this weight from one foot to another. 'At the moment they are not permitted to enter the premises. English Heritage has served papers on them to make good the damage in the crypt. I suppose we will need you for that.'

I would like to do it. I have more pressing matters though.

'So who pays my wages now?'

He raises his eyebrows. 'I have your pay for last week and this week lying-on.'

I get paid with a week's delay, paying off all they owe indicates that I am no longer employed.

'Oh.'

'I haven't deducted money for the times you couldn't work this week.'

'Right. Thank you…What about rebuilding the wall?' I clear my throat and pocket the brown envelope he passes me.

'I imagine we will contact you when we need you. If you are still available.'

It's really happened.

He glances up from his shoes. 'I'm sorry, Malcolm.'

'If you knew this was happening why did you let me go on taking down the wall yesterday afternoon?'

'Because your friend told me to.'

'Robin? Why?' I thought he disliked everything the Jacobites were doing.

'He hasn't discussed it with you?'

'There's a lot he doesn't tell me. Like going to prison for drink driving.'

'You've lost me.'

'I think he did something to my neighbours once, when he was drunk. He was sent to Durham prison for it. They told me this morning.'

'My brother? That's ridiculous. Why would my brother have known your neighbours? And he never went to jail. Who are these people?'

I hope it is as simple as mistaken identity. But they seemed so sincere, my neighbours, this morning. I take a deep breath. The heavy orange-blossom perfume from the tree is becoming sickly. The downpour can't percolate through the leaves, but the tree itself has immersed us within a verdant susurration that suddenly intensifies to the applause of a million leaves clapping at us.

I almost have to shout. 'My neighbours must have been mistaken.'

'Very likely.'

The noise is deafening. Outside, someone shrieks and splashes past towards the car park. I can see their feet beneath the lower boughs. The rain bounces back up from the ground as though the ground is boiling. A sudden mist rises all around the tree. The saturated air cannot hold any more moisture. It's like being inside a great green drum.

'Maybe we should move.' I almost have to shout.

'What?'

'I said, maybe we should get out of here.'

'I can't hear thunder.'

Neither can I, but I'd rather get wet than fried.

I start to speak and the rain stops as though a tap has been turned off. Heavy drips patter around the outside of the tree, but everything else is abruptly hushed.

'Look!' he says.

All around us, thousands of tiny leaf-coloured caterpillars are letting themselves down out of the branches on silk threads. They twist and flail with the grace of trapeze artists. When I put my hand out to the nearest one the flailing becomes more rapid and it swings out of my grasp.

For a moment we smile at each other. I think that's the first time.

'Peter found a trapdoor in the crypt,' I say without thinking.

'Did he? I think he also found Radcliffe's heart.'

Would Peter do that? Would he steal? I wonder.

'You think your friend's immune to greed?'

'Peter?'

'He had the opportunity.'

Maybe. The caterpillars continue to descend between us, swaying more now their strings are longer. Will they be safe when they reach the ground?

'The box wouldn't be very big. He was wearing his jacket.'

'I noticed that,' Jason says quietly.

'Shall we go before the next shower? I don't want to have to walk on a carpet of these little things.' I hold up the outer twigs for him.

The tree soaks us both as we duck under the leaves. The light out here seems blue and drear after the green light beneath the tree. There are puddles of standing water on the grass.

'Was that what you were so anxious about when Peter was over on the other side of the crypt, the heart?'

He doesn't answer. He's heading for his car, walking briskly. I have to splash after him to catch up.

'Jason? Yesterday. Was that what you were looking for too?'

'Do you know where my brother is when he's not with us?'

'I know where he lives.'

'Good. Let's start there, then.'

⧚

We are lost. I've only been here with Robin, and you don't exactly concentrate on mapping your journey when you're been driven at silly speeds round these lanes. I don't know the address, so we can't navigate by satellite.

We are deep in an area known as The Shire, the medieval hinterland that fed the Abbey's coffers when the monks still ruled these lands. It has steep little valleys and remote farmhouses with roads barely fit for motor vehicles linking them like a web across the fields and spinneys. Dandelions sprout through the tarmac and hedges scrape the car windows. Several times we cross swollen streams through fords which have risen over a foot up their red and white imperial measuring posts. I would have noticed a ford on the way to Robin's house.

Finally, there, that ash tree – I recognise it.

'You said it wasn't this way,' Jason protests, pulling over rather than committing his vehicle to the steep uphill track on my whim.

'It looks familiar.'

'I'm not surprised. We must have been passed this way at least twice this morning.'

He is curbing his irritability as best he can. I know I must be annoying him.

'These roads all run into each other. I should have fetched my map.'

'It won't be on the map,' he says vaguely, letting off the handbrake.

He's been saying stuff like this for the past half hour. I have stopped bothering to question him.

This is the way.

Ancient ash trees dominate the hedgerows, bare branches cross above us, naked except for fat knobbly clusters of brown flowers on their outermost twigs. The leaves are late this year because of the dry winter.

The Land Rover climbs steadily up the hill.

'I hope there's somewhere to turn round at the top if this is a dead end.'

'It is up here. Not far.'

We rise out of the valley. The hedges give way to dry stone walls. In the fields on either side soggy lambs shelter under wet, grey ewes. The tarmac ends between two stone gates posts. We are nearly out of The Shire. In front of us the moors begin at the boundary behind the farmstead. Straight over that hill, somewhere, is Blanchland, or Weardale, depending how far west we have come.

'Is this it?'

'Yes. Must be.' It looks different from up here in the Land Rover; I'm used to bouncing along in Robin's car, skimming over the potholes.

Jason hesitates. 'It's an awful track and this cattle-grid doesn't look terribly robust.'

'Your brother manages it in his car. At least it's on the level.'

Jason drives so slowly that we rock and creak across the hoggin. He flinches each time the tyres dislodge a stone and send it clunking against the underside of the car. Good job it's a diesel; he would have stalled a petrol car by now. The track is less than a hundred metres long. It would have been quicker on foot.

Oh for pity's sake! He fusses over turning round in the space where the track widens in front of the garden gate. I jump out and slam the door while he manoeuvres at the speed of colliding tectonic plates.

The rain has stopped for the moment. Behind me, Jason revs his engine, flooding the air with the smell of diesel. The wrought-iron gate screeches on its hinges as I push it open.

Robin has done something to the plants. The lank roses and cotoneasters which overhang the short path are all dead. He must have used weed-killer. Now there are only bare stems with curled brown leaves fluttering in the breeze. Even the daffodil leaves have shrivelled up. I've seen it less bleak even in the middle of winter. The house looks deserted.

Jason turns off the motor. There is only the wind blowing across the empty field and the bleat of lambs in the heather beyond and the melancholy bubbling cry of the plovers as they guard their chosen territory.

'Are you sure this is it?' he asks.

I doubt my own eyes. I am more sure that this is Robin's house, but it looks less like I remember it. 'It's different inside.'

'Let's see.'

'But Robin isn't here. His car's not here. Jason!'

Jason brushes past me, scattering drops of water from the blighted shrubbery.

'It is my *brother's* house.'

The front door is locked. The windows are blank, the rooms hidden in gloom behind them.

'We can't just –' Where's he going? 'Oi, Jason!'

The path round the side of the house is slimy with decaying vegetation. It's bordered with cracked salt-glazed, rope-topped edging. Someone once tried to make it pretty. Round the back the garden ends in a small stock yard. Beyond this, a few paces at most, there is a row of derelict farm buildings. Some of them are used as sheep pens still. A ramshackle fence with skew-whiff poles and two strands of sagging barbed wire separates the domestic from the agricultural function. There was a wall here. You can see the foundations, but the rest of the stone has been taken away. The yard is deep in stinking mud, the surface pocked by hundreds of ovine hoof prints. The overpowering reek of sheep carries on the wind. Why does Robin put up with it?

The back door has a plank nailed across it. I wonder how anyone thought that would keep anything out. Even Jason is making headway, prising it off with a piece of rusty angle-iron.

'You could help,' he says.

'Help you break into Robin's house?'

'You may learn something.'

'Here, give me that.'

In the name of education I lever off the plank. The iron bites into my hands. It leaves a stripe of rust across my tatty bandages. They smell unpleasant.

I turn the dented metal knob. It opens. Robin is not careless.

'Do you think he guessed we were coming?'

Jason grunts.

I give the door a gentle push; there's nothing else I can do now. It swings open slowly onto a dark passageway papered with a brown floral pattern that shows a greasy line where elbows have rubbed against it for decades.

'You first,' says Jason.

'You're family.'

That's a nasty look. He brushes past my chest. The cracked, cigar-coloured lino is tacky underfoot. It's hard to reconcile this with the scholarly sitting room at the front of the house that I'm familiar with. The kitchen is on our right.

'Jesus.'

'Quite.'

'But I was only here on Tuesday.' I've eaten food here. I wouldn't if I'd known it came from this. The room looks like no-one been in it for years. The red Formica worktops are filthy with mouse droppings and grey, crumbly detritus. The doors hang open on the empty wall cupboards. It serves me right for never offering to do the dishes.

But this is wrong.

There is a pile of yellow plastic eartags in thick dust on the table in the middle of the room. I know these can't be Robin's. There are drifts of dead leaves blown against the skirting board. It's not the mess, it's the undisturbed-ness of the mess which makes me doubt. I back out of the room as Jason opens the door at the end of the corridor.

I am reluctant to go any further inside. We are trespassing, what if someone comes?

'Jason, this must be the wrong house. I must have got it wrong.'

He steps through into the front of the house, the bit I know.

'Oh, this is where he comes from, alright,' Jason says quietly from beyond the door.

I follow. This is not the hallway I know: the tiles are not black and white, there is no sweeping staircase. It is easy to see how there could be only ordinary bedrooms above.

'This isn't his place.'

Jason opens the door into the room on the right that would be Robin's study. There is the big desk I have glimpsed once or twice. In my memory, it is burnished walnut, glowing in the light from the desk-lamp and standing on a red and blue rug. The walls behind should be deep red and there ought to be an ornate plaster fireplace.

This is a distortion, a burlesque parody of my familiarity. The walls are greenish grey, with the paper peeling back. The fireplace is boarded up and a cheap old-fashioned electric fire has been fitted. The desk is an art deco partner's desk, 1920's dark, split oak with missing drawers, so I can see through it like a broken skull. There is an angle-poise light on top with a smashed bulb, bent upwards. The jagged glass catches the little

173

light that filters in. The carpet is in holes and the floorboards have rotted through by the window. Thistles have pushed up under the decaying frame and died in here. The smell of rot is mixed with a tang of rats so strong I almost sneeze.

'How?' I ask.

'Do you really not know?'

'But I was here. It was nothing...' There's no point repeating myself. This is Robin's house, but it is not. Jason does not seem as shocked as me. But then he has not been here before. I am not well.

'I have stopped being surprised by Christopher. It's the only thing that upsets him.'

'I don't know what's going on, Jason.'

'It's alright. You're not going mad. I thought I was, but I'm not.'

'You don't understand. I've been here before. It was nothing like this. It can't be.' I cross to the baluster and take hold of it with both hands to shake it. It is frustratingly solid.

'It shows how much hold he has over you. You said you've known him for two years. I only met him a couple of days ago and he almost had me fooled.'

Something...

'You even play games with him. He's told me about the chess. You leave yourself right open.'

'How can you only have known your brother for a few days?'

Jason laughs. A horrible little titter, the sort Juliet would make if she was trying to be impressively polite in front of Lord Muck.

'My brother Christopher died fifteen years ago.'

Jason has gone mad. The front door is locked. The only way out is through the door behind him.

I'm bigger than he is. He can't stop me.

'You're talking rubbish.'

'Your friend Robin is my brother's ghost.'

'Don't be stupid.'

'You want to know how I know this is his place?'

I shake my head. I really don't.

'I can *feel* him here.'

I feel the cold, the bitter cold. But that's what you get in old empty buildings in a May that feels like February.

'Robin is no ghost.' I am speaking quietly now, calm with truth and reason.

'They're nothing like I thought they were, either. More demanding.' That bloody laugh again.

'Let's go.'

He ignores me. He's walking to the sitting room door. My exit is clear.

'I need to look round,' he says over his shoulder.

'Why? What can you possibly hope to find?'

'I want to know how to get rid of him.'

'OK. Well that's a job for a priest or a psychologist. I'm going now.'

Jason hesitates, his back towards me as he opens the door. 'Malcolm, you need to be rid of him too.'

I

My eyes sting with the acrid ash of the burnt paper in the grate as I stir through the fragments Robin left with the toe of my boot. The charred corner of my address book lies on the hearth. He had no right to burn my book. Was he expecting us, clearing up before we got here?

The sitting room is like Robin's study, only worse. The shock is greater because I knew this room better. There are no bookcases, no books, only a pile of filthy old ledgers by the hearth, their cloth-bound board covers curling with the damp. There are bales of straw where there should be armchairs on either side of the fireplace. One end of each bale is blackened from exposure to the elements before they were dragged in here…I slept here on Monday night with this rot, the smell of wet straw, uric acid, rats. No.

It can't be. Have I been hallucinating all this time? Is this real now? My stomach growls. I haven't eaten today.

'I saw it – differently – I can't have imagined it? This is another…' The idea's gone, evaporated before I can finish the sentence. I shake my head, but my vision doesn't correct itself, the desolate room remains in comfortless dereliction.

Jason's as close as my shadow; I almost knock into him when I turn.

'So where the hell does Robin live, Jason?'

'He doesn't live anywhere. He isn't alive.'

'Let go of my arm.'

He won't let go. 'You see him.'

I don't see things the same way other people do. I shake my arm free. Jason's fear is repulsive. His whole body is trembling.

'You have to understand. You have to listen to me. He looks like Christopher, but Christopher's dead.'

'If he's dead, why are you so bloody scared of him?'

'Of course I'm scared. Are you mad? My dead brother is walking around talking to me.'

The sitting room door slams shut. We both jump, turn to look, but there's no-one there, only the echoes reverberating round the house.

'It's just the wind.'

But Jason's off, loping across the floorboards. He rattles the handle. It still turns.

He sidles back to me, right up to me, trying to make eye contact. He's so close I can smell him, over-groomed and under-exercised. Unhealthy.

'He's not my brother. He's pretending,' he whispers urgently, spraying spittle in my ear, 'But he's not the one I'm really scared of.'

I step back and wipe my ear and cheek. His fear contaminates me. My heart is thumping, my vision blurry. If he's about to confess he's scared of me –

'There's something else at the Castle, something worse than Christopher. Evil, true evil. *He's* frightened of it. It came the day we began to take down the wall under the Chapel, last Friday. I've seen it.'

He's mad. I mustn't listen. My heart is in my throat, the whole room pounds to its beat. I haven't seen this thing, but I know it, now he speaks of it. The place reeks of it; you only notice when you get away.

I

I sit on a bale, wishing I wasn't. Moorland sounds drift in through the ill-fitting window, lonely wildfowl and lost lambs. I have no idea how long we have been here. I don't know what time we arrived. Long enough to get used to the smell. Jason's muttering frays my nerves. I'm afraid I won't hear Robin's car over the top of him. He has passed me a heap of ledgers to look through, but I can't find anything, just old farm accounts written in faded ink.

Now he's trying to prise open the cupboards next to the fireplace.

'Help me get these doors open, will you.'

'What with?'

'That iron thing you used for the back door?'

I drop the ledger back on top of the pile. I don't want to go outside by myself. How stupid. No, it's not stupid. I know what I'm scared of: Robin's anger scares me.

Robin is no ghost. I should know; I have enough of them in my life already. Perhaps he has hypnotised me, grown some sort of Svengali influence over me, and I do not know what for or why I let him do this.

The passageway is dark. The through-draught earlier must have slammed the backdoor closed at the same time it blew the sitting room door shut.

My boots clack on the lino. I stop. No noise, but there's this feeling. And that's called imagination. Straighten up. Best foot forward.

The door opens onto a cold breeze and the stench of the sheep pens. No outraged tenant, no vindictive priest or angry landlord. Only a sleek carrion crow, blue-black in the flat silvery light, perched on top of one of the teetering fence posts. It takes to the sky, steel feathers cracking the air. The length of angle-iron is where I left it. I feel better holding it as I walk back down the corridor.

The wood splits as I jemmy the cupboard door open. The cupboard is empty except for a roll of packing tape and a wad of crepe bandages.

'Too late to pretend we haven't been here.' I can hear the anxiety in my voice.

'You really think he wouldn't know anyway?'

I hadn't considered it before. Our footprints are everywhere, and Jason's moved stuff around.

I sit down on the bale again and pick up another ledger. This is a lunatic quest. We have no idea what we are looking for.

And then we do.

As I open the ledger several newspaper clippings and a few folded sheets of paper spill out, cascading to the floor. At the same instant by the window Jason scatters a handful of yellowed bits of paper from the ledger he is looking through.

The straw digs into the backs of my legs as I crunch down over my knees to pick up the pieces. Jason's brother is dead, that much at least is true. I'm holding his death certificate. His local school raised money to send him to America for a bone marrow transplant. In the faded photo he doesn't look much like Jason. He has a kind face, soft and smiling. You can follow his slow decline through the sad little reports in the local papers.

'Good God!' says Jason. I don't ask what he has found.

♟

He still won't drive fast. We are so lost that we can't even get back out of the Shire. All the roads are recognisable, all the unique features identically familiar, no help whatsoever to steer by.

'Would you let me drive?'

'Stop it, Malcolm. I'm doing my best.'

'I grew up driving on roads like these.'

'I'm not going to let a banned driver drive my car uninsured.'

'There's a sign ahead.'

'Whitley Chapel. Three quarters of a mile. That will do.' He indicates to the empty roads and swings down the left fork at the junction. This is the first time he's been in forth gear since we left the house.

'What shall we do with all that?' he asks.

My life in newspaper clippings slides out across the upholstery of the back seat. I don't know. I shake my head.

'Malcolm? Because we can't take it to your house. He'll know.'

'I'll burn it.'

Jason thinks about this. He slows down while he thinks, takes the turning for town rather than back to the Castle. I want to scream at him to hurry. He pulls over next to a farm gate.

'What's up now?'

'I don't want to take you back to my house, either. You can burn them at your cottage. If he isn't there already.'

He reverses into the muddy track and turns around. For a moment there I thought he was going to make me get out and walk.

♖

It feels safer now we know where we are. This isn't the route I would have taken – it's longer by two miles. It has stopped raining but the clouds are low and dark. The ditches are overflowing, splashing up the sides of the car doors. Jason sits bolt upright, gripping the steering wheel like a toddler grips a swimming float.

Is he mad? Have we both gone mad? I try to swallow down the panic, not wail out loud, why is this happening to me? All the time I am conscious of those cuttings, the past festering on the seat behind me.

I ask, 'Did you read much of it?'

'Would it matter to you if I had?'

'I saw Christopher's obituary.'

'It's unfortunate we came across each other's paperwork.'

'I'm sorry for your loss.'

'Yes, well.'

'It must be awful watching someone you're close to waste away like that. My aunt –'

'I didn't watch him die. I lived two hundred miles away.'

Oh.

The route he has chosen takes us past the Castle entrance. It is taped off, two police cars flanking the stone gateposts.

My stomach heaves. 'They must have found her.'

He turns to look at me.

'I had nothing to do with the missing girl.' I clear my throat.

He turns back to the road. We drive the last mile in silence.

There are no cars outside my cottage.

He picks up the sheath of ageing paper, his and mine, while I'm still digging in my pocket for my house keys. He rolls the collection up and carries it like a club.

Did I leave the place unlocked? The hinges squeal like an injured animal as I push the door open. I oiled them last month. The cold and damp hit us, even with us standing on the doorstep in a keen wind. The icy breath from inside my cottage is colder still. Cold and silent.

'You first,' he says.

This is my house. It's so small I don't have time to register the emotions separately, fear that it will all be different and relief that it is the same. In the kitchen at any rate. The sitting room looks alright too.

'He isn't here.' The aftermath of adrenaline makes my voice sound wrong.

'What's that?' Jason points at the corner of the sitting room next to the fireplace.

A thick fan of mycelia has eaten its way through from my bedroom above and crept a few inches across the wall bringing a filtered taint of the familiar mushroom smell.

'If you think that's bad, Jason, come and take a look at this.'

Are the stair treads more springy than usual? The paint on my bedroom door is peeling away in long vertical blisters like I've put stripper on it. The door frame is slimy. I pull my hand away sharply. The door handle shrieks as I turn it. I'll have to put my shoulder to door the get it to budge. Ah, it bursts open with less force that I anticipated. Surprisingly sharp flakes of paint shower both of us.

Jason chokes behind me.

The wall where my bedhead used to stand is black with mould again, but that's just the flowering bit, the plant itself has spread halfway up the other three walls and across the carpet and is beginning to probe the window frame with fine white filaments.

'What the hell is it?' His voice is muffled and he is holding his jacket collar across his mouth.

'You see it too?'

'It would be difficult to miss, Malcolm. How can you live like this?'

The paint has come off the skirting boards. In places the bare wood is growing *bark*.

'Don't go in there!' he squeaks.

It's amazing, or would be if it wasn't growing in my bedroom.

'The fumes, they might be poisonous.'

The mycelia don't crush under my weight. It's like treading on thin electrical cables. Careful, mustn't overbalance, mustn't touch the fungus.

I crouch down next to the skirting board under my window for a closer look. The top of the skirting really does seem to be growing bark and there's the faint smell of resin. The wood itself is slick and apricot-pink, bulging like a stripped branch rather than a plank. This timber was cheap pine. It's damp enough in here for willow or poplar to sprout, but pine doesn't do that and no seasoned timber, planked and kiln dried and primed and painted could…

'Malcolm!'

I'm almost proud as I turn around. This is my plant. Look on and despair.

'Your phone's ringing. In the kitchen.'

We have to shuffle awkwardly close on the landing so that I can get past him and go down the stairs first.

It's Mel.

He knows.

Nothing for days and now this. She ends the call before I can think what to say.

My throat tightens, my scalp crawls. We should have burnt the stuff we took from Robin's house as soon as we got here.

'Jason, fetch those papers. Now!'

'Who was that?' He jogs down the stairs towards me still holding the paper. 'Was that him? Malcolm, was that him on the phone?'

I have to bundle Jason into the sitting room. It feels like there's no time to waste on words.

He flaps like a wet moth, spilling the newspaper clippings across the sitting room carpet.

'Never mind, pick them up. Pass them over here.'

There are so many, some nearly a whole page, articles several columns wide. My face, Mel's face. Uncle Jimmy's face. I can't light a proper fire, I can't give myself time because I'm panicking and I don't know how much time we have. The first clipping curls under a thin line of blue and orange flame, then extinguishes itself in a whiff of charcoal.

'Let me.' Jason shoves the rest of the cuttings on top of the ones I've failed to light. I strike a match but a downdraught from the chimney blows it out. I fumble the next match and drop it.

I don't let him take the match box from me.

'Jason, calm down,' I'm saying it to myself as much as to him, 'Go into the kitchen. Under the sink on the left hand side there's a bottle of white spirit.'

He scrabbles at the paper for a moment then pulls back and goes to fetch the accelerant. I keep on trying to get the paper to light but only succeed in making a litter of charred fragments, flaky but legible, faces traced in black on graphite.

Jason taps me on the shoulder with the bottle. I don't look up at him. I reach up for the white spirit and slosh a good amount over the evidence.

'Let it soak in.'

He's right. Five heartbeats. Six. My pulse hammers so loud he must hear it.

'Try lighting it now.'

I light a match like a smoker, cupped in my hand, nursing the flame until the match is close enough to drop onto the paper. A pale flame licks across the topmost layer which shrivels to black powder, then the next and the next. My history burns in front of me sheet by sheet. Where did Robin get all this? He can't have been collecting it for the last ten years? Why?

The flames take hold, hot on my face. Should we have looked through it more thoroughly, are we burning clues? Too late. Christopher's death certificate, too. I hope Jason didn't notice that.

Why did Robin collect this? What does he want with me?

Jason picks up the bottle of white spirit and puts the top back on. He's standing right behind me, as anxious as I am to see the papers burned.

'Jason? Do you know why he's doing this?'

'I know what he wants from me. He wants Radcliffe's heart.'

'It can't be that valuable, surely? Not enough to be worth all this fuss.'

'Why should I know what his reasons are?'

'So why didn't Robin take it himself? He had lots of opportunities.'

'He can't. That's all I know. He wanted me to wash it in the stream and bring it to him wrapped in a cloth.'

I can't imagine Jason crouching by the stream washing a lump of meat. 'But if Peter's taken the heart?'

'Then I wouldn't want to be in Peter's shoes.'

I get to my feet and rummaged in the ashes with the poker, tickling up tiny flames to consume the last pieces.

'Have you warned Peter?'

'And tell him what exactly? The bogeyman's coming?'

The mood Peter was in yesterday, Jason wouldn't get past accusing him of the theft anyway. 'You should go, Jason.'

He swallows hard. His feet jerk involuntarily. He wants to run, but it looks so cowardly. 'And you, Malcolm, what does he want from you?'

'I don't know.'

'Why did you want to burn the cuttings then?'

The grate is filled with soft black drifts of carbon. 'I…'

This archive he collected, documenting the end of my old life ten years ago – what if he was going to give them to someone. Is that why he kept them?

'I made a fresh start here. I've done it before, but something's always got in the way. I thought it was different this time, here, at the Castle. I couldn't bear it when I saw all that –'

Jason looks down his nose at me despite me standing taller than him. 'So he's threatening to expose you too. But what does he want in exchange for silence?'

I don't know. Robin's never asked me for anything but gossip and games of chess–

'– Jesus Christ, it's Friday. He's coming here.'

'Well I imagine he will, yes.'

'No, he comes here anyway, every Friday. It's our night for chess.' I need to sit down. 'All we've done is burn some bits of paper.' Am I criticising our lack of progress or practising my plea for leniency?

'You've seen his house; you know he's doing things with your mind. He won't like that. He won't want you contradicting him. Come on, Malcolm, he must have asked you for something.'

Have I forgotten? Have I missed something? Has he made me forget?

'Were you going to give him the heart if you'd found it?' I ask.

Jason stiffens. 'Probably.'

'Why?'

'Because I want him to leave me alone.'

'So we were looking in the wrong place this morning. If you want this to stop, you need to get the heart from Peter.'

'If Peter has the heart, then Christopher is perfectly capable of retrieving it himself.' Jason's scared, scared of everything, Robin, Peter, the task of finding the heart. Is Peter in danger?

'Do you think we should go to the Castle?' I ask.

'You saw the entrance. There's a police roadblock.'

'We could go along the river, up the old carriageway.'

'That would look good when the police found us.' He passes me the bottle of white spirit.

I'm not used to Jason challenging me like this. Usually he makes demands, and I point out why they are so unreasonable that I won't comply. I'm thrown by this practicality.

'We can't just not say anything to Peter. We have to warn him.'

'A thief?'

'He may not have taken the heart, you're only guessing.'

'If he hasn't, then Christopher won't bother him.'

'I want to know what's going on at the Castle, anyway.'

What a look.

He's read my history, he knows. Not everything, but enough. He's not stupid. 'What happened to the girl?' His voice is hoarse.

'I told you, I had nothing to do with that. I only knew her because she was forever hanging around the place.'

'The other girl, Mack. Ten years ago.'

'They never found her.'

'Would you know where to look?'

'She was alive last time I saw her.'

He'd better not try to go on with this. My fingers have clenched round the bottle so tightly it's hurting my hand. I wave it so he doesn't think I'm only running away and retreat to the kitchen. I won't answer his questions, but that doesn't stop each one from slapping me in the face.

It smells awful in here.

He follows me in. 'You could telephone Peter,' he suggests, talking while I put the white spirit back with my head under the sink.

'I could telephone Clara,' I suggest in a friendly manner as I stand up.

I pick up my phone from where I left it on the bench this morning. That's got him. Clara blames him for the Jacobites. He may not be scared of me anymore, but he sure as hell doesn't want to see her today. If anyone knows what's going on, Clara will, though.

He hovers in the doorway while I ring her. Her mobile's off.

'What now?' he asks.

'I'm not waiting here for Robin. Can you give me a lift to Clara's?'

He pulls a face.

'Don't worry, you can drop me off and go home. If you stay in your car she can't hurt you.'

❦

Clara is unloading her brats as we arrive. She scowls at Jason's vehicle. He drives off fast enough as soon as I slam the Land Rover door. The parking area is slippery with compacted mossy gravel. Overgrown shrubbery drips all around, hemming us in with sodden greenery.

'Good afternoon, Mack,' she says, straightening up. 'Go inside, Philippa.'

The girl gawps at me. She's got her mother's looks, poor little sod.

'Can I take Ariel out?' the child asks, still watching me.

'No!' The tone she uses. If it wasn't Clara, I'd have sworn that sounded like panic.

The girl transfers her stare to her mother.

'Everything alright, Mo?' the boy calls from the kitchen door.

The Bassets amble past his shins and waddle towards me. The boy asks again. His voice is beginning to break. He's outgrown the prep school blazer, soon he'll be outgrowing parental control.

'Go inside. It's fine. Now.' Clara grabs her daughter by the

187

shoulders and turns her round, giving her a shove towards her brother. 'Shoo.'

'It's Friday, why can't I go out for a ride?' the girl asks, walking to the door.

'Because the bridle paths are closed.'

'Why?' The child imitates the adenoidal whine I've heard on the few occasions Clara's husband has tried to say something. You learn to ignore it.

The fatter of the two dogs sniffs my knee.

'Because. Do as I tell you. Get down, Castor!'

It happens all at once. I see Clara's face, I try to ask what's happened and the bloody dog takes a chunk out of my leg. Christ it hurts. The kids yell as I try to kick it off me. The other dog is baying in a deep baritone. I make as much noise as it does. Clara grabs the first dog by the collar and hauls it away.

'Get in the house,' she barks at me over her shoulder. 'Ben, help me put them in the stables.'

I limp after the girl into the kitchen. She's silent, shocked.

The dog has ripped a flap in the denim. I lean against the big pine table and try to get a good angle to examine the back of my calf. Blood is pouring down my leg, trickling into my boot.

'He never bites people he likes,' she says. The shock didn't last long.

'Is that right?'

'You swore a lot.'

'Yes, well, it hurt a lot.' I can still hear the bastards howling from somewhere out in the yard.

'Uncle William swears a lot.' She passes me a hand towel, warm from the Aga.

'I had an uncle who used to swear a lot. I walled him up in a tunnel.'

She giggles. The towel is too grubby to use on the teeth marks. I cram it round the top of my boot to stop the blood dribbling down into my sock. I pull out a chair awkwardly, scraping it over the tiles and sit down opposite the mini-Clara. She has that deficiency of imagination that gives her complete self-confidence in any situation. It's quite relaxing.

'Why are the bridle paths closed?' she asks.

'That's what I was going to ask your mother.'

I can hear Clara arguing with her son outside. The side door slams. Clara is very red. The boy is at her heels.

'Go to the den. Both of you. Now.'

'I want to see the blood.' The boy ignores her and walks over to me. He favours his uncle, Lord Muck. Utter lack of humanity, tiny blank eyes, florid face, a few sandy whiskers. More spots.

It's quicker to let him look at my leg than for Clara to argue the point.

He bends down closer to examine the bite.

'It's nothing much,' he says.

The smell of children's sweat and stuffy classrooms takes me momentarily back to primary school. The taste of warm, full-fat milk floods my mouth. I concentrate on the back of his head, greasy, lank sandy hair. He won't be out of his teens when it starts to thin.

'It's not even gone through to the bone. You made an awful fuss. Can I have some bickies, Mummo?'

Even Clara has the grace to look embarrassed by the little bastard. 'You can go to the den or clean out the chickens.'

My leg throbs.

Clara waits until her offspring have left, checking the corridor to make sure.

'Have you heard about the Castle?' she asks.

I put my hand down to my calf, squeezing the muscle above the bite. It doesn't help. 'Have they found the girl?'

'No. Is that what you thought?' She thinks I sound guilty.

'So why is everything shut? Why the roadblock?'

'Juliet's been attacked.'

'Good grief.' I have an alibi. I was breaking into a friend's house at the time.

'It only happened a couple of hours ago. In broad daylight. One of the archaeologists found her down on the carriageway, halfway to the bridge.'

'Is she alright?'

'Frightened, humiliated, shocked. The usual, I would imagine. She's given a description, but it's not much help. The police reckon he can't have got very far. Everyone came running when they heard her scream.'

'But she's so old –' Damned stupid thing to say. My god, her face could curdle milk. 'Sorry, that came out wrong. It's unexpected, that's all.'

'I'm sure it was quite a surprise for Juliet, too.'

'Sick bastard.'

'Yes, so much more normal to go for little girls. Like the missing child.'

'That's not what I meant. Give me a break here, Clara.'

The sarcasm slides off her face. 'Anyway, no-one knows anything. It's not safe out there, anymore.'

'So there's another manhunt, then?'

'I presume so. I imagine they'll want to speak to you again. Oh don't get on your high horse, no-one thinks it was you. Juliet said the man was black. It's all she would say.'

'Where was Peter while this was happening?' They're rarely more than fifty yards apart during opening hours.

'They found Peter in the crypt.'

Something in the room shifts. I look up at her. 'Is he… OK?'

'They think he has had a stroke.' She's standing quite close, choosing her words carefully, using her horse-handling voice. 'He can't talk. They found him in the crypt, behind the wall

190

you were taking down, stuffed down a trapdoor. Now what do you suppose he was doing in there?'

'He'd definitely not been attacked?'

'I don't know. That's what the police say. They only found him when they were looking for whomever attacked Juliet. I had to come away to fetch Benedict and Philippa. I thought you might know what Peter was doing down there. You're as thick as thieves these days.'

My mind goes blank. The large, dusty case clock on the wall behind the table wheezes as it ticks. Somewhere deeper in the house, Clara's children squabble. The smell of the kitchen reminds me of the refectory at school, gravy browning and sponge cake and dogs. Well, the doggy smell's unique to this kitchen. I struggle to retrieve a relevant line of thought.

I am aware that the Chapel belongs to Clara's family; the Trust merely leases it. This is where she spent her childhood, scrambling through the brambles and saplings. I don't want to tell her about the heart. To her, I'm just another poacher, along with Peter. Peter wasn't meant to go back under the Chapel on his own. But the heart is no more her family's business than it is mine.

'I saw his face,' she says, 'Peter's face, when they brought him out on a stretcher. He looked like he'd been scared out of his wits.'

She's expecting me to say something…

'He went over the wall in the crypt yesterday. Jason and I were there. He told me he'd found a trapdoor. He wanted me to help. I never had a chance to say no. I thought it was all over. I thought that English Heritage would stop everything.'

'Did you really?' She leans on her knuckles on the table. Her knees are only a few inches from mine. She lowers her head so that I can smell her face-powder. Her face is so close I can't focus on it properly.

'*How's the bite*?'

It's like she stabbed it, hurts as bad as when the wretched dog sunk its teeth in.

I pull my head back and look her in the eyes.

'I didn't help Peter.' I swallow hard.

'You took the wall down.'

'It was my job. Ah. Your bloody dog.'

'He was protecting us.'

'What from? Me?'

'He thought so.'

She lunges across the table and snatches a pair of kitchen scissors.

Christ. The chair screams across the tiles as I push back from her. It clatters over onto the floor as I try to stand. Pain shoots up my leg when I put weight on my foot. I clutch the table to hold myself upright.

'Clara!'

She moves in fast, grabs my hair. What's she doing? I hear the scissor blades snack together but there's no pain. She pulls away and clacks across to a dresser, puts the scissors away in a drawer. It's done in moments.

Did she take some of my hair?

'Pick that chair up, would you.'

I do as I'm told. I can feel the wasted adrenaline draining the strength from my muscles.

'What the hell just happened? Did you cut my hair?'

'I beg your pardon?'

'Clara! For God's sake what's going on?'

She's standing there like nothing's the matter. I can't have... did it happen? There are no scissors. I want to check in the drawer, but she's standing in front of it.

'I don't think your leg will need a doctor, do you?'

The pain has died down, unless I stand on my right foot.

'I can clean it up,' she says. 'Have you had a tetanus jab recently? Of course, you'll have to with your job.'

I don't want Clara near my leg. The soreness might wear off as I walk home. I'm sitting back down on the chair before I realise it. My knees are shaking.

I can't decide if she's trying to freak me out or just being kind and I'm imagining, misinterpreting. It makes no sense; why would she do that?

I think I imagined it. My God. I'm so hungry I can't concentrate. Starving hungry, so that I suddenly feel sick with it. I think I whimpered out loud. Get a bloody grip.

She's watching.

'I haven't eaten today.'

'You'd better eat here, then.'

'No, no it's alright, thank you. I only came over to find out what was happening at the Castle.'

'As you wish. I'll drive you home.'

She could have tried harder to persuade me to the hospitality. I was ready to give in if she'd offered a second time.

It gets easier with each step as I follow her outside. Part of the pain was tensing my muscles. It hurts again when I climb up into the Range Rover. She's lucky I'm not suing. I hope I bleed on the upholstery.

'Ready?'

'Yes.' The seat belt clunks into place.

She glances at me, but there's nothing more to say. I look out over the hedgerows as she drives. It's all so familiar, but everything's changed.

♜

My phone's ringing. I'm reluctant to answer it. I can't deal with anything else.

'Hello?'

'*Mr. Macready?*'

It's the police. Not about Juliet, or Melissa. The man gives me a crime number for my bank card which I don't write down. Assures me they are looking into it. I check my hair in the mirror by the foot of the stairs. Can't see any missing, but my hair's too thick to be able to tell. I need a hair cut. And a shave. These bandages stink. More assurances, another number to write down, which I don't. I check my wallet as he rings off. I'm glad I have my wages, at least.

I take my clothes from the tumble drier and climb the squeaky stairs. There is no paint left on my bedroom door now. It has fallen off and formed a deep litter of sharp shards, like a draught excluder, along the bottom of the door. I'll leave the room undisturbed. I put my clean clothes on the bed in the spare bedroom.

Is Robin capable of frightening Peter that badly just to get what he wants?

I want to know exactly what happened to Peter. I'll ring the ring the hospital.

I get the number for the General from directory enquiries. There's the usual denial of his existence as a patient, then a chase around the wards to learn finally that he's 'poorly, but stable' – no visitors, ring back after rounds tomorrow.

No further forward. My stomach growls.

This bread is like a brick. I kept the cheese on the bench last night, didn't fancy opening the fridge let alone storing food in it.

I'd better eat something before Robin turns up, can't face him on an empty stomach.

He usually turns up about seven. That gives me an hour. He won't frighten me – my heart is stronger than Peter's.

All I have to wash down the bread and cheese is water. I don't like either tea or coffee without milk. I'm living like a bloody monk. Like a convict. There's a gulf opened up between me and mankind. I can't get a grip on what I'm expected to do, or not do. I've been this way before, but right now…

Oh, to hell with it. I'll light the fire and take a shower and set the board ready for the game. Whatever Robin's done to me, or intends to do, it can't be worse than what I'm doing to myself.

I

It's twenty past seven. Is he even coming?

My leg looks like some sort of Fuzzy Felt board, decorated with random plasters to stop the tooth-marks getting infected. This is my last pair of new jeans.

The bandages on my hands are frayed and matted so badly I can't get through them with the nail scissors in the bathroom. I tear at them off using my teeth, biting through each strand of cotton until I can rip them sufficiently to unravel them. The cuts are red and hot.

He's here.

I watch him park from behind the curtains in the spare bedroom. My heart is racing.

An elaborate knock. He usually just barges in, but then –

The stairs creak under my weight. My mouth's dry. Deep breath as I open the door. The door hinges screech. I brace myself for his advice on the regular greasing of ironmongery, but he just stands there, politely.

'May I come in?'

'Yes, of course.'

'I wasn't sure I'd be welcome.'

He catches my eye. His expression is indecipherable.

I stand back in the kitchen doorway so that I can close the front door once he has gone into the sitting room.

The fire is blazing up now. He spots the chess set and turns. I nearly flinch, but he's smiling. Forgive me my trespasses.

'Ah, good. I'm glad you still want to play.'

'I haven't cooked anything.'

'I brought wine. I have a little supper outside; I'll bring it in.'

He hands me two bottles. How much does he think we can get through?

I check the room as he goes to fetch the food. I tidied briefly. You can't tell I slept in here. It's warm. So warm the tendrils of mould in the corner seem to be wilting. They dangle down now like the long limp fingers of an empty glove instead of clinging to the wall. Maybe I just need to dry the place out.

He thumps against the front door, already on the return journey. I hold it open for him.

He has a tray covered with a red chequered tea towel. He balances the tray on one hand and pulls the tea towel off with a flourish like a magician with a tray of doves.

All I can think of is that kitchen, the dirt and decay. I choke on the rich, almost faecal smell of the roast chicken. It's still steaming. Far too plump and glossy to be anything other than home-roasted. It has a funeral wreath of thyme on its breast. He didn't buy this in a supermarket. I can't bear it if he cooked it at his house, in all that filth and chaos. Saliva fills my mouth.

Next to the chicken there are two little dishes of saffron rice and a bowl of dried apricots. I could cry.

He puts the tray down on the table next to the chess board.

'Shall I open the wine?' he asks.

I pass him the corkscrew and go to fetch two glasses and a small sharp knife from the kitchen.

My phone is ringing. No Mel 'til this is over. I end the call and go back to him.

He's sitting in his usual chair, on the same side of the hearth as the coal scuttle and the poker. He passes me a couple of sheets of kitchen towel as I sit down. He came prepared.

I wait while he pulls a leg off the carcass. My mouth waters. I become aware that I'm looming over the meat.

'Hungry, Mack? Help yourself.'

I don't mind where the food was cooked any more. I sink my fingers into the soft warm breast meat and tear a strip of flesh from the bird, cramming it into my mouth. I swallow and then shovel a handful of rice in using my fingers like he does.

This is amusing him. I don't care. I eat until the ravening pain inside has abated, swilling the meat and rice down with a full tumbler of headache-strength red wine.

'Oh, that is better.' I wipe my mouth with the paper towel. 'Thank you.'

'A little peace offering.' He picks up his glass and takes a sip.

'You know Jason and I went to your house today.'

He turns his gaze to the fire, his face bathed red in its glow. So red I can't tell if he flushes or if it's the heat of the flames.

I can hear the birds fussing in the hedge down the side of the house. It's dusk outside. My tongue feels thick and my throat constricts with sudden fear, and I realise that I am waiting for an explosion of anger. But he is calm when he speaks, like the peaceful room.

'It was only a matter of time, I suppose.'

He shifts forward suddenly, I jump involuntarily. He's on his feet, with the poker in his hand.

'I'm only mending the fire, Mack. Did you think I meant you some harm?' Robin looks down at the poker in his hand, smiling.

I shake my head.

He ratchets round in the grate, stirring the half-burned coals to make a flat bed, then shovels on half a bucket. It isn't particularly warm this evening, but that is a ridiculous amount, we'll be sweltering in a few minutes. The new coal covers the glow from the embers, making the room suddenly darker. I get up to plug in the standard lamp. As I turn around he holds up two fists towards me, knuckles uppermost. I glance down at the board, a white pawn is missing. I tap his left fist to find it. He opens his right hand to show me the piece.

I nod. 'Your move.'

He replaces the pawn.

Is that it? As easy as that? No recriminations, but no explanations either. Perfect acceptance that I broke into his house and know that he has researched my life and tricked me. I'm not sure I can be as sanguine about this as he appears to be.

I don't know what I want to know more: how he made me see things or why he made me see things.

We both sit down. My heart is thumping.

His first move is pawn to d4. He usually begins by moving the king's pawn, favouring a modern opening.

'Shall I draw the curtains?' I ask to give myself time to assimilate this deviation.

'If you wish. It makes no difference to me,' he says.

I don't get up. Outside it's already too dark to distinguish anything. All I see in the windowpanes when I look round is the reflection of two men bent over the game between them. My hand is shaking as I make my opening move, so that the little horse shivers on the wooden board as I put it down, knight to f6.

'Interesting. Have some more wine. Steady your nerves.'

'And get too fuddled to play well?'

He laughs. The new coal's already beginning to catch. Orange flames lick up the pile. I fill both our glasses. We have finished the first bottle already. His hand hovers over the board. He moves a pawn to c4. Careful. I need to be ready to castle as soon as he does. I move my king's pawn forward by one square.

'You're being very defensive tonight, Mack.' He brings his knight out to back up any attack.

I begin to clear the space on the back row so that I can castle. Robin just smiles and mirrors my moves on his own king's side. After we have tucked our kings safely out of harm's way, he pauses long enough for me to glance up. He is still smiling as he picks up his queen's knight. Without thinking I attack, bringing my own knight forward. Robin's smile broadens irritatingly as he slides his queen in for the kill. I have committed myself, my attack is too soon. I shall lose the piece, but I'll take Robin's knight with me. He knocks my own knight flying with his queen in reply. He knows I don't like it when he batters the chessmen. Dad passed them on to me when I left for university. He never used them, granddad taught me to play. The lead shows where seventy years of handling have rubbed through the enamel. It needs gentle treatment.

I prod the pawn in front of my queen forward a square. Damn. I can see from his face that I should have continued attacking. Robin slides his queen back, ready to a have a go at the defence around my king. We play on. He wants to exchange bishops. I'm not in the mood for doing what Robin wants. I move my queen to c8 to defend the piece.

Robin shrugs. 'Extraordinary. Best of three?'

'It's not over yet.'

'No. It's going to be long game if you keep on hiding like this.'

He brings another pawn forward so that he has a line of three pawns in front of his queen. I should have seen this coming. A strong line of infantry with the general's cohort behind.

I've made a shambles of my own pawns. My king is far too exposed. All I can do is bring my knight across. The new coal suddenly catches, and the flames rise as if they had been turned on. A uniform blaze spreads across the coals. I knew he'd put too much fuel on.

Robin glances at the fire, then moves his d4 pawn to d5. Why on earth has he broken the rank? I catch his eye and we both know he's made a mistake.

I refill our glasses. I lift my own glass and take one of his pawns left-handed, no more line of defence. I put it down next to the board with the other captured pieces. He smiles grimly as he retaliates, taking my pawn with his queen. I thought he might. I threaten his queen, knight to c5. He withdraws his queen as I creep forward, bishop to f6, so that there will be no advantage for Robin if he chooses to launch a central attack. No, he's going to attack anyway; he brings his bishop into the fray. There is a certain inevitability to Robin's aggression. I take a swig of wine.

That pawn on e6 is looking very flimsy. I bring my rook to e8 to defend it. Robin rubs his hands together and extends his fingers over the board like a hovering kestrel. Finally he swoops down and moves his bishop to e3, threatening my queen's side now, too. I shuffle my queen to d8. His bishop takes my knight. He expects me to retaliate. He gives a satisfying jolt as I take the pawn on d5 instead and threaten his miserable queen with my rook.

He recovers quickly, moves his bishop to e6. 'Check.'

I back my king into the corner.

'Always running away, Mack.'

He moves his rook, about to launch a full-on attack. The heat from the fire is uncomfortable. I stretch my arms up above my head, manufacture a huge yawn.

'I'm going to get a glass of water,' I say, standing up. 'Do you want anything from the kitchen?'

'Like what? What do you have in the kitchen that I might want?'

Arsehole.

'I'm sorry,' he says, 'that was uncalled for. No, I don't want anything, thank you.'

I bend down and swipe his bishop from the board, replacing it with my pawn.

♟

The cool dampness of the kitchen is lovely after being sat next to that fire. I don't bother to turn on the light but head straight for the sink. My left side feels scorched. I turn on the tap for a few moments to let the water run cold and drink two glassfuls in the dark. Maybe I can win this game.

My phone rings. I scrabble for the small blue screen in the dimness and notice that the crack of light coming from under the sitting room door widens just a little. I turn the phone to mute before I turn it off – that doesn't always stop her though. Is Robin standing there, listening behind the door? I wrap a tea towel round the phone and shove it a drawer.

'I will have a glass, thank you.'

Jesus! He's right behind me. How did I not see the light as he opened the door? How did I not hear him?

'What do you think you're doing, creeping up on me like that!'

'If you're this nervous, Mack, you should turn the light on.'

'You're closest to the switch.'

I need the light to find another glass, and it's harder to move round the room with him in it too.

He brushes past me. He's found a glass, the water splashes into it. I hear him drinking.

'I used your glass. I hope you don't mind.'

He's wrong, I do mind. I don't want to leave him in here with my phone, either. What light there is coming from the small gap round the sitting room door glints in the whites of his eyes as he watches me negotiate the table so that I can shepherd him back to the fireside.

♟

The heart of the fire is glowing white. It will burn through the bars of the grate. The heat is oppressive. He has poured more wine, topping my glass up to the brim. The pressure in my skull is going to turn into a headache if I have any more. I look down on the chessboard; I cannot help myself. He watches me check the positions.

'I didn't cheat, you know. All I did was move my knight to g2,' he says.

I sink down into my chair. The room is suffocating me. I move my pawn to d4. *Stupid, stupid, stupid.* I am threatening a knight he would gladly exchange for my bishop. I drink some more wine. A curly chestnut feather drifts down between us from nowhere.

Robin smiles at me.

His hand hovers over the game in that predatory manner. He does this so often I have stopped complaining. It is pure gamesmanship: I have less time to look at the board and it distracts me almost as much as it's meant to. It's hard not to follow his misdirection as his fingers flit like moths between the pieces. He would be disqualified in a tournament. This time he touches a pawn, accidentally, I think, nudging it, but it's enough. He has committed. He moves the king's bishop pawn to f4, clicking his tongue in annoyance at his own clumsiness. The heat and wine are affecting his dexterity but not as much as they are affecting my judgement.

With more irritation than thought I threaten his queen with a pawn. He laughs with pleasure as he takes it with his rook. I've picked up my queen before I can stop myself. No going back. He's lost his rook, and now he takes my queen.

We both sit back and contemplate the bloodbath on d3. He is the first to stir, raising his eyes. I look back at him.

'How did you do it?' I ask.

'It wasn't intentional; I had no idea you'd be willing to throw away your queen like that. Your move.'

'No, I'm not talking about the game.'

And suddenly we really aren't talking about the game because I have said so. And suddenly I'm not sure I want to know. His expression is bland, but I can't meet his eyes. I have committed too soon, just as I always do when I play against Robin.

I begin, 'You know what I saw when I went to your house.'

'I know what you saw today. Who can say what you saw the other times?'

'Yet you aren't angry?'

'Why should I be, Mack?'

Yes, it's me who has been duped, but we did break into his house.

I plough on, just as in the game. 'So what did you do to me? You made me see something different, didn't you?'

'We all see what we want to see, unless we see what we expect to see. Perception is a bitch.' The word sits uncomfortably on his tongue. It's more like something Peter would say.

'Did you hypnotise me?'

He nearly knocks the chess board as he flings himself back in his chair laughing.

I find nothing funny here, so I can't share any part of his mirth as he heaves and lurches with the effort of wailing with laughter. It turns to howls as I watch, howls of mockery and derision. The joke is on me, it always has been.

Of course! Of course he isn't angry at me going to his house today. He's been waiting for it, waiting to spring the joke, dying for me to find out how he has fooled me. I have seen two truths, touched, smelt, tasted two truths, one of which cannot be true.

He makes a valiant attempt to rally. It wasn't that bloody funny, he's pretending now. He leans across the arm of his chair towards me and tries to speak, but only rasps and splutters come out. His face is like a red plastic mask, the skin is drawn tight, and his eyes are wicked. I look away while the waves of humour gradually abate.

He gulps for air noisily, 'Oh, Mack...' he manages at last, but my face sets him off again.

I reach across and start to eat the apricots, concentrating on the board to avoid looking at his exaggerated recovery.

How did I get into this mess? Yet my defence is good. I want to tear through his army as it stands and pull down his king and stamp on it.

'How very *Freudian* of you,' he wheezes.

I did not say that aloud. I know I didn't.

He wants me to look up at him. I chew another apricot and keep my eyes on Granddad's chessmen.

'So, are you going to let me get away with taking your queen?'

I move my bishop to d4. 'Check.'

He blocks it with his remaining rook. I could take this, too, for the price of my bishop. I refuse Robin's exchange and nab his last bishop on e6 instead.

Robin pauses. The heat is making us both sweat. The ceiling creaks; the old house is drying out. He mops his face with a vast white cotton handkerchief. He flares his nostrils and narrows his eyes. Then he moves his king onto a white square, safe from the bishop I am playing on the black diagonals. This is the first time he has shown any need to defend himself. I find this encouraging and move my rook from a8 to e8 on the back row.

'I think I'm beginning to see things for what they are now.'

'Do you?' he asks, sounding suddenly very weary.

He pushes his pawn forward with a fingertip to f5. My rook nudges forward to e5. His pawn presses on to f6. I can take him, or he will take my king's knight's pawn, either way my defence is suddenly nonexistent. At the same time I can see the opportunity to go for his queen. The thought is barely formed when he moves his rook to defend her.

It's like trying to play against myself.

I switch diagonals, moving my bishop to c8. This clearly unsettles him. He moves his remaining knight. Idiot, that knight was all that stopped me launching the attack against his queen with my rook. He moves his queen back to b1, and I realise how close I was to getting checkmate there.

I pick up my rook. Robin sits very still, not wanting to help me figure out what to do next, but I've already seen where to put it. 'If you won't tell me how, at least tell me why, Robin. Check.'

'Why? Because I could.' He slides his king to g2. This is it.

'Why me, though?' I ask as I capture his knight.

'Because I am here for you.' His hand hovers over the pawn next to my rook.

'Take that and you'll leave yourself wide open.'

'Maybe it's time.' He takes the rook with the last pawn between his king and my army.

I move my remaining rook to g8. 'Check.'

We are so evenly matched, yet I have the whip hand for now. He pulled his queen back when he should have sacrificed, gone down shooting.

Still he does not resign but moves his king to f3.

I cool my aching palms on the wine glass. 'Tenacious.'

His eyes are black, unreadable. 'You have *no* idea.' His voice makes me shiver despite the fire.

I move my bishop to g4. I keep my finger on top and consider his moves. It's not mate, but so close I almost say it. '...Check. You have an odd way of showing you're here for me.'

'Once again, Mack, you misunderstand.' He moves his king to e4.

I move my rook to e8. 'Check. Again. When I've won you can explain.'

He rests his fingers round the neck of his king. 'A bargain?'

I can't lose. But there's something. The fire has died down, the room is silent but for the soft hiss of the glowing cinders. Something that nags at me. If I could only—

He suddenly breaks into the quiet. 'If I play king to d3, you'll have me mate next move with your bishop.' He only discusses a game like this when he's trying to distract me. He moves his king to d5.

'Can you win from this position?' I ask.

'Not against infallible opposition. Are you infallible, Mack?'

I'll use my bishop, rather than moving my rook. 'Check... mate. Isn't it?' I keep my finger on top of the piece while he thinks for a moment.

'Not mate. I can intercept with my queen.'

'It buys you one move. I'll take her, and then it will be checkmate.'

He picks up his king and lays it on its side. 'I made a mistake mid-game. This was luck.'

'You are a sore loser.'

'I'm not used to it, it doesn't happen very often.'

'Is that what you need me for, Robin? Someone who always loses, someone to feel superior to?'

'Well, that helps of course.'

'Oh, go to hell.' I drain the second bottle into my glass.

I didn't mean to offend, not beyond the usual post-game banter, but his face changes. The temperature in the room drops so fast I feel the hair on my forearms rise up into goose bumps. He throws the table over as he stands up.

'Do you think I'd hang round here for *this*?'

Christ.

I stand up too, but he's as tall as I am.

'You're right, Robin. I don't understand. Why the hell are you doing this to me?'

'I'm here to watch your back, and all you do is fight me.'

'You're some sort of guardian angel now?'

He throws his head back and laughs. It should be ludicrous, the way it sounds, the evil laugh of some dubbed Chinese horror movie, but not now, not right in front of me.

'*Stop it.*'

He drops his chin onto his chest and looks up at me from under his brow. He's not laughing now.

Of course he's shorter than me. My heart is hammering behind my sternum. Is this what he did to Peter?

He stoops to right the table in silence. He has to get down on his knees to pick up the chessmen.

It's bloody freezing in here.

'Why, Robin? Why do you hang around? It's not as though you even like me.'

'You sound like a schoolgirl with a crush.'

I could kick him, grovelling on the rug in front of me.

He reaches up and clunks a handful of lead pieces onto the table. 'Of course I like you,' he says. 'In fact I came here tonight to stop you making the biggest mistake of your life.'

'What mistake?' I've made so many mistakes I really don't know what he's talking about.

'You're thinking of turning yourself in, aren't you?'

'*What?*'

'Oh, Mack. Come on. Let's stop pretending, shall we.'

'What's it to you if I do? It's not like you'd miss the chess.'

'Sit down, Mack.'

He carries the table to the side of the room and puts more coal on the fire.

I don't feel so cold once I'm back in the armchair. There is a muffled cracking sound right above us. I must get Clara to do something about my bedroom.

I wait for him to sit down again.

'What good would it do?' he asks.

'I can't get on with my life with this hanging over me. I killed my uncle.'

'You did not.'

'I left him to die.'

'Circumstances.'

'He died because of me, Robin.'

'And what about your girl? Did he not deserve to die for that?' His face is serene, he does not smile or glare – it's all the same to him.

I can't speak. I picture the anger inside, even after ten years, rising like the molten magma in the throat of a volcano. Let it cool, watch it subside. Breathe.

My voice is not my own – it is too high, too whiny. 'But I don't know what he did to her, what really happened. Where she is, even.' I know I am shaking all over, as though I've been dragged out of an icy winter pond.

Robin seems agitated, concerned, maybe. He sits forwards to drink in my words.

'I never will know now, and I'll never have any peace for not knowing.'

His nostrils flare, he could snort up the whole room. His eyes are glowing with satisfaction. This is pleasing him. Christ, he's enjoying it.

I rub my hands over my face. 'Do you not understand? I can't bear feeling this way any longer.'

'So you want to be punished for killing your uncle when it wasn't your fault?'

'If I could live my life over, go back, explain everything at the time –'

'Weakness. This is weakness, Mack. You need to stay strong. It won't bring your girl back, or the last ten years. You will loose everything and achieve nothing.'

'If the police knew exactly what happened, they might at least be able to trace her, find out what he did with her.'

He makes a scoffing noise, 'I fear you are overestimating the ability of the police service. Perhaps if, as you say, they'd known at the time...'

My gut twists. 'I can't live with all this guilt.'

'Oh, Mack, you can.' His voice melts into my ears like dripping honey.

'Do you not understand what I'm saying?' He listens to the words I say but it makes no difference.

'I'll help you to live with the guilt.' He slides onto the floor. He's on his knees in front of me in the firelight, taking hold of my wrists with both hands before I realise what he's doing, gazing into my face with disgusting eagerness.

That's enough.

'Get away from me!' I have to push him backwards to stand up. I feel grimy. These two years, I didn't know. 'I'm not –'

'Oh lord, Mack, you've got hold of the wrong end of the stick as usual.'

'What are you trying to do?' I'm almost shouting, but I can't help it.

He's sitting back on his heels, staring at me. My shirt is sticking to the cold sweat on my back.

'Calm down.'

'I'm not homophobic. But this –'

'Of course you are, but that's beside the point. I'm celibate. And anyway, I'm not that way inclined.' He looks hurt.

'So what just happened here, then?'

'Do you really not know what I am?' he asks.

Some sort of emotional leech, continually upsetting me and enjoying the results.

The floor above us creaks, a prolonged noise, like someone testing the floorboards.

He scrambles to his feet. 'What have you got up there, Mack?'

'It's just the house drying out. I think you'd better go.'

At the door he lifts his head and sniffs. I can't smell the fungus down here. He pauses with his hand on the latch. The floor groans this time, wood protesting at an unfair load. Dust sifts down the wall in the corner where the mould has eaten a hole through.

He comes back, grabs my elbow, steers me to the door. 'We need to get out of here.'

Soot patters down onto the hearth. The whole house shudders and the lights go out.

He wrenches open the front door. I really don't care if the house falls down. I follow him from the dark, moaning cottage into the still, quiet garden.

Halfway down the path I remember the only luggage I need from my past. My chess set and Melissa's box.

♟

The room is pitch black and filled with choking, sooty dust. A soot fall in the chimney must have put the fire out. This is too dangerous, it's not worth it. The smell of rot makes me gag. I'll give it a minute – if I don't find the chessmen by the time I count to a hundred I'll have to leave them. I grope my way to the place I think Robin put the table and find it with my knee. Random draughts through the damaged ceiling keep swirling dust into my eyes. I put my hand in something wet and slimy, the chicken carcass. I fumble sideways, find the cold metal figures, scrabble to collect as many as I can hold.

I can't count, can barely breathe, an animal panic overrides everything with the necessity of leaving before the cottage caves in top of me. The floor above thumps down on its joists, timbers scream. I throw the chessmen onto the tray next to the chicken. Have I found all sixteen? There is a soft ripping noise, and I feel plaster falling on my head like heavy snow. No time. I grab the tray and slide over the debris on the floor. I misjudge the door, banging my elbow. Did I lose any pieces there? No time, I must get out of here. A sudden current of rubbish pushes me out of the front door as the sitting room ceiling collapses in a muffled explosion behind me. I am still holding the tray as I stagger along the path. Wreckage scatters down all around me on the moonlit lawn.

The moon is full, huge, flooding my garden with unearthly light. Everything is surreal. I can hear my own heartbeat and the hollow sounds inside my head, but the garden is in silence all around me. Robin is by his car on the roadside. The neighbours are standing in their doorway like poorly painted plastic ornaments from the top of a wedding cake.

I have to force my feet to stop running. It's an old stone house; it won't come down like a brick structure. It's less predictable, but also stronger. There are no gas pipes out here to break and leak and explode.

Melissa's box… will the back of the house be alright? The stairs should have survived if the bedroom floor was all that collapsed.

How many chessmen did I abandon? I focus on the tray. The moonlight shines so brightly I can see it clearly. The remaining pieces are embedded in the chicken – all that remains of a dead chicken, its bones red in the tricky light, feathers all around. He brought me a raw chicken. I ate raw chicken. I drop the tray, scraping at the stickiness round my chin and cheeks. I will kill him, even if this is not real.

♜

I'm on my knees, trying to throw up.

'Mack?' She's next to me, I can barely hear her. I can see her husband's shoes. I've been here before.

Her husband is shouting something. He kicks the tray over. I scrabble for one last chess piece in the grass, a black rook. I clutch the little castle so tight it makes my hand hurt.

She puts her arm around my shoulder. Comfort.

'I don't know what's real.' I didn't mean to speak so loudly.

'I can see that, Macready! Look at the state of you.'

'Leave him alone, Gordon.'

I hadn't even got his name right. Gordon. The garish moonlight has softened. I look up for Robin's car, but it's not there. He must have driven off, left me to the irate neighbours.

I swallow and the hollowness has gone. I can hear again, at least.

'What the fuck have you done to my hen?'

I'm choking, not sure if I'm laughing too. He stands above me, scrawny, hairy legs, unfastened trainers on bare feet, a towelling bathrobe. What time is it? I bury my face into his wife's soft cotton nightshirt to smother the odd noises I'm making.

Gordon howls in fury and hauls me backwards by my shirt collar.

'I'm calling the police. And the RSPCA.'

I nearly topple over when he lets go of me, have to grab turfs of grass to pull myself up. On my knees, so much more dignified than sprawling on my side.

He sets off for the gate, 'Come on, Lisa. Leave him alone.'

She's still kneeling on the grass next to me.

'Was it some sort of black magic thing?' she asks.

'Lisa!' he calls from his own gate.

'Mack? The chicken and the chess pieces. Were you making some kind of spell?'

I shake my head. A feather floats out of my hair. There are smudges on the shoulder of her nightshirt where I laid my face.

'They were my granddad's.'

She nods as if that explains everything.

'I didn't know it was one of your chickens. I didn't know it was –.'

'Are you taking drugs?'

I shake my head again.

'Lisa!' he shouts from their doorstep.

'Oh God.' I wipe my mouth on my sleeve.

'Never mind him.'

Gordon slams his front door.

'What were you trying to do in there, Mack? What happened?'

'The ceiling came down.' I can't look at her.

'Come on. I'm freezing and you're shivering. We can wait inside while Gordon rings the police.'

I let her help me up. It's harder than getting up by myself because I have to be careful not to put any weight on her. She leads me to her house. Maybe it's my turn to faint on her doorstep.

Her husband is coming out of the sitting room. He glares as she pushes me up the steps into their warm clean home.

'Let's get you tidied up,' she says.

I walk past him, up the stairs ahead of her and into the tropical humidity of their bathroom. She runs a basin of water.

Her husband is fetching the police to have me arrested for theft and God knows what else, and she's making me nice and tidy.

She rings out a flannel and starts to dab my face with it. I'm glad the mirror is steamed up. I don't want to find a Morlock in the glass. Of all the things Robin has made me see, why did this have to be real?

'I'm fond of my hens, you know.'

'I've eaten raw chicken.'

She didn't hear me. She's scrubbing my mouth and chin with maternal vigour. I take the flannel from her fingers. I can feel her eyes on me.

'I can't tell you what happened tonight. I don't know myself. All I can say is that I'm really, really sorry. I'll buy you a replacement hen. A breeding pair if you like,' she's still watching me. 'I know they're probably pets but…'

'She was my last Rhode Island, her name was –'

'*Please*. I said I'm sorry.'

'Everything alright up there, Lisa?' he calls from the bottom of the stairs.

'Fine,' she snaps.

'I've called his bloody landlord. It's his responsibility, it's his house and his tenant. The police said they'd be ten minutes.'

'Oh good.' Her voice softens as she turns back to me. 'Have you got anywhere you can stay?'

'Yes, I'll be fine. Be out of your hair for a bit anyway.'

'Probably best. Would you like a shower?'

I would love a shower. And some pills to make me forget this dreadful night. And somewhere to sleep. Where will I go?

'I'm going to call a friend. A doctor. Just to check you're not concussed or anything.' She passes me a pink towel from the airing cupboard. 'Five minutes. OK?'

'Thank you.'

The hot water is like a blessing. There are still a few bedraggled feathers in my hair. Their shampoo smells of cough medicine.

♜

She meets me at the foot of the stairs.

'The police are in there. If you're not up to this I'll explain you're ill.'

'I'm not ill.'

'Here, take this.' She passes me a folded piece of paper. 'It's the number for my doctor. He's very good.'

She turns away and opens the door, ushers me through into the sitting room.

Both police men stand up. I don't recognise them, must be a different shift.

'Malcolm Macready?'

I nod.

'You understand you're under arrest?'

Do I? What happened to my right to remain silent? It's not like it is on the television. They're on either side of me. Lisa

214

flutters around, reminding them I'm ill. She'll get me sectioned at this rate.

'Do you need the bird?' asks Gordon. 'I have photographs.'

'No, we'll take your word for it. You're not denying it, are you, Macready?'

I shake my head. A stolen chicken and they're here in a few minutes. Bloody provincial Bobbies.

'You need to lock him up this time.'

'We'll deal with this, now, thank you.'

'He's not right –'

Gordon is still bellowing advice as I walk between them to their car.

✦

They put me in the back. It smells of vomit and orange juice. I need to see a doctor. Bacterial infection. Robin tried to poison me again.

The car is crawling along. The constable in the passenger seat is listening to a conversation on his radio that I can't quite hear. They are plainly looking for someone or something in the dark shadows of the gateways on either side.

A big dark figure seems to manifest in the lane in front of us. They are concentrating so hard on the moonlit fields they almost hit what they are searching for. He bangs his fists on the bonnet of the car as they slam it into an emergency stop. Both policemen yell but make no attempt to leap out and grab him.

A black man. That's what Juliet said. A black man. This man is black. Black from head to foot, no features visible in the headlights. Some sort of cloak, a mask. The embodiment of shadow. So much so that he seems two dimensional, without substance, only he's smashing his fists down on the bonnet in a very substantial way. Their reluctance to get out is understandable.

'Reverse you f– '

'I am, I am.'

I lean back out of the driver's way as he turns with his arm over the back seat and peers through the rear window, following the wobbling beam of his reversing light. A long time since he took his advanced driving course. The black man keeps pace with us. He slams into the passenger side door, making the whole car shudder. The strength and aggression is more like a bull than a man.

A few metres more. He is trying to break the – Jesus – the passenger door window bursts apart, showering us with tiny cubes of safety glass. My door is locked. The man is jogging now, managing to keep up as the car lurches backwards round a bend. He reaches in, the passenger screams.

I yell at the driver to go forwards, but he can't, he'd have to stop to change gear. The black man has the officer by the throat. He thrashes around but can't fend him off, just gets in the way of his colleague at the wheel.

The driver slows; it's hard to drive with someone's hand smacking into your face.

'Put your foot down!'

We shoot backwards and leave the tarmac. The car bounces and jerks, then crashes backwards down into a ditch, sending a fountain of muddy water sluicing over the roof. The airbags detonate in the front, smothering the policemen's faces when the impact was from behind. I hang onto the headrest in front of me to stop myself sliding backwards and wrench at my jammed seatbelt. I can't open my door.

'Take the child lock off,' I yell at the driver.

He takes no notice. I don't know if he's even conscious. The black man let go when we crashed, but he's coming round to the driver's side now. My belt finally clicks open. I haul myself up, pulling myself towards the driver's door. I have to wriggle my fingers between the seat and the door. Christ. The bastard starts to rock the car. I can hear him grunting above the noise of the engine. The smell of petrol surrounds me as if I summoned it by realising the motor was still running. I scrabble against the door for the unfamiliar locks. Shit. I press a switch and hear the locks click open around me. As soon as the door's unlocked he's got it open, battling with the airbag. I let go of the headrest and slide down into the rear passenger door. It won't open fully because it's caught in a hawthorn hedge. I don't know if the gap is wide enough. It feels like I'm holding up the weight of the car as I struggle. He's shaking it so much it shudders as though it's alive. My skin is pierced and torn as I squeeze out. I clamber under the hedge branches and crawl away from the car as fast as possible. I can hear him struggling, thumping and kicking metal and plastic. He's not coming after me, not yet. Are they dead?

Lights. Headlights. I scramble to my feet and run towards the oncoming vehicle waving my arms.

The car screeches to a stop. It's Clara.

'Get in,' she shouts, leaning out of her door.

I'm on the running board, not even inside before I start to gabble.

'Shut up. I know,' she says.

I swing myself into the seat. She has the floodlights on, shining right onto the crash fifty yards away. He's just a black shape, an absence of light, hell bent on destroying the lives inside the car.

'This is what you've done.' She sounds furious. There's enough moonlight out there for me to see her face in profile. A roman general.

'Clara –'

He's seen us.

'We'd better get out of here.'

She pulls out to avoid the front of the crashed car and then accelerates. He stands in the middle of the road. She keeps her foot down.

I expect the impact to feel like it did when I ran into the bus shelter, but it's more like a brick wall. He doesn't crumple and fly over the roof; he's still standing. The engine screams, the tyres spin.

What the fuck has he taken, some of Clara's bloody horse tranquilisers?

She's leaning right out of her window shouting at him.

'*Clara* –'

The Range Rover jolts forwards, he falls before us, we bump heavily over him. She pulls up.

'Don't stop!' I scream over the noise of the engine, but she's already in reverse.

We bump back over him and slump to a halt. She's going forwards again, for Christ's sake!

I yell at her, bracing myself for the impact of running over him for the third time, but it doesn't happen.

She mutters under her breath and accelerates, past the crashed police car, throwing the Range Rover round the bends in the road.

Then we hear the explosion. I can see the fireball in the door mirror, pouring upwards into the sky.

'Where did he go?'

'He'll be after us. I need to make sure the children are safe.'

'He's dead, Clara. You rolled two tons of metal over him. Twice.'

'Dead? He can't die, you idiot.'

'You killed him.' I feel sick. 'We need to call an ambulance… the men in the car –'

She makes a noise of disgust and slews the car so viciously into her drive that I bang the side of my head against the window. Gravel scatters as she brakes hard, pulling up at the side of the house in front of her kitchen door.

'You'd better come in.'

'Clara, the policemen in the car…'

She's already out, marching to the house.

I don't know what's still out here in the night. Clara is still scared; it's not over. We must have crashed only half a mile away. The dogs bay from the stables. I don't want to be out here on my own.

My legs can barely carry me.

I trample fresh greenery as I step over the threshold into the dark kitchen. It smells like Christmas. Bunches of leaves brush against my face, southernwood and rosemary, hung on the doorframe. Stupid place to dry things. I follow her across the echoing space, deeper into the house than I have been before. She pushes open a door into light and warmth. The room is large, but half the floor space is taken up by three hideous floral sofas hemming in the big stone fireplace and there are a lot of people milling around so it feels oppressively crowded. I recognise the barman from the Traveller's Rest, the one who served me herbs, and a couple of his regulars. Clara's husband and Lord Muck are sitting on the sofa, facing the door we came through. Clara's children are huddled up next to the fire on footstools with hoodies over their pyjamas. The three children I saw yesterday are here, still in their school uniforms. In the shadows I can see some of Robin's congregation.

'He's not bound by the Castle anymore,' Clara announces.

'I didn't think it would hold him long,' Lord Muck says. 'Why did you bring Macready here?'

'Found him on the road.'

I can't speak. My mouth is dry and their voices sound distant. I can feel my brain shutting itself away from this.

'Mack's cottage, that's how he got through, I think,' Clara says to her brother, 'I don't know why he chose to push through there or if Mack had anything to do with it.'

'The old park wall comes right up to his garden. Maybe it's just that. Are you sure that's where he broke through?'

'He's torn it apart,' the barman says.

'Mack mentioned something about mould?' Clara suggests.

The barman shrugs, 'it's possible.'

'Who? Who was in my cottage?'

Clara turns to me. 'What was that, Mack?'

I can only make a scratchy sound in the back of my throat. The old men shift in the corner, pressing forward.

The barman walks up to me, puts a hand on my shoulder and lifts my chin with his fingers, tilting my head back so that he can examine my face in the light. I would push him away, but it's me who would fall back.

'He can see something.'

The voices swim around me.

'He must have known.'

'I want to know what he can see in here.'

'Would he do, do you think?'

'Look at him, he's finished.'

'We don't have much time.'

'We're safe in here.'

'Nowhere is safe; we need a permanent solution.'

I grab at a chair and sit down. One of the small children begins to cry.

'It's alright. Don't be frightened.' My voice is a croak.

Philippa looks over her shoulder sharply. 'There's something behind me, Mummy. He's brought something in with him.'

The barman bends down and puts his hand on my shoulder again. This time he shakes me.

'What do you see?'

'A bunch of lunatics.' The old men are closing in all around us.

Clara steps forwards and slaps me hard. 'You're frightening my daughter. Now answer Archer's question.'

'*You're* frightening those children.'

She glances over at them. 'Which children?'

The ones that aren't there.

11. SATURDAY

It's better now they've gone. Christ knows what Clara gave me to drink. My tongue burns, and my eyes are stinging. I can feel the caustic tract all the way down to my stomach. But I can't see them anymore.

Clara killed a man tonight. Two men are burning in a car. I ate a raw chicken. My house has fallen down. I have a week's wages and a plait of rushes in my wallet and a lead chess piece in my pocket. I've even lost my phone. Who will Mel call now?

I am so thirsty.

The room is dark. The fire has burned out. The barman, Archer, has been left to guard me. I think they have decided that I am being used as some sort of conduit. At least that's what I heard, but my ears may be no more reliable than my eyes.

I'm on my side, it's not too uncomfortable, but I can't get my face away from the upholstery. It stinks of Clara's Bassets. Lord Muck used a dog lead to tie my wrists behind my back. Clara said my hair would be enough. At least, I think that's what she said. Funny how many of them aren't real. Clara's husband, I could have sworn…

Is this really happening?

'Mr. Archer?'

'What is it?'

'Can I have some water?'

'No.'

I close my eyes.

♟

It's lighter now. The room is ash grey and deep shadow, with no gradation in between, a half developed photograph. Jason's voice rouses me.

'Then how did he get in this state?'

'Ask him, he's awake.'

Jason hunkers down next to the sofa so that he's in my line of vision.

'Are you alright?'

'Thirsty.'

'I'll get him some water,' Clara says from behind me.

'It will all be over soon,' Jason says.

I nod. Everything comes to an end.

♟

Clara helps me to sit up. I am as stiff as a board. She holds the glass to my lips. I take care not to gulp. Small sips at first, then as much as she will tip into my mouth. I still end up coughing. She pulls the glass away from my lips before I've slaked my thirst.

I turn my face as far as I can and wipe my mouth on my shoulder. 'What did you give me last night?'

'Myrrh.'

'*What?*'

'It's a purgative.'

'It's a poison.'

'Green apples are poisonous if you eat enough of them. I know what I'm doing.'

Heavy footsteps come up behind the sofa. I'm too stiff to be bothered to look around.

'Get a move on, Clara. The sun is almost up.' Lord Muck – I'd recognise his voice anywhere.

222

'Are you sure about this?' The fear in Jason's voice brings the room into focus.

'You agreed an hour ago.'

I am witness to Clara's hit and run. What are they intending to do with me?

'Can you untie my hands, please? I won't say anything.'

Clara glances at her brother standing behind her. 'I think it's best not to, Mack.'

'What are you going to do? You know I wouldn't tell anyone, you're all upset –'

'You started something, Mack. I know it wasn't on purpose, but you're going to help us put it right.'

'Does Robin have the heart?' I ask Jason.

'He knows about that?' Clara sounds surprised.

'I told him.' Jason shrugs, 'I was starting to see his priest too. He'd read something about it, anyway, I found the book in his cottage.'

'Bloody amateurs.' She nods at her brother behind me, 'Yes, William, I know, time is pressing. Come on, Mack, the hour is upon you.'

I ignore her attempts to make me stand up.

I ask, 'What are you doing here, Jason?'

He twists his mouth into a lopsided smile, 'Same as you, just trying to put things right. I had to come to Clara for advice in the end.'

Archer passes Jason a neat canvas roll, like an oversized version of my school dissecting kit. Clara won't look at me. Muck and Archer come up on either side and lift me onto my feet. This feels less real than Robin's house did.

They march me down a dusty corridor and through a cluttered boot room, the scullery, a dilapidated porch.

Outside the air is soft and cool on my face. Mist drifts between the yew hedges. They are taking me down to the wicket gate that leads from the back of Clara's garden to the

Castle, a short cut rather than going round by the road. And this way they avoid the police cordon at the main entrance.

They are hurting my arms. What is it I'm supposed to have done? Is it the Chapel? I was only doing my job. No one will reply to my questions. I would stop if I could.

Is it my imagination, or can I smell burned rubber?

'What are you intending to do with me?'

They are taking me right past the back of the Hall. It's too early for the staff to be here. There is no light on in David's Portakabin.

'Help me. HELP – HELP!' The words ricochet round the gloomy yard, bouncing off the high back wall of the hall with its barred service windows and steel door.

'Shut up, Macready. There's no one here.'

I try to dig my heels into the concrete, but together they are too strong for me and too wily to let me go for a moment. Clara and Jason are trotting along behind.

Out of the yard and onto the sopping grass. I have even less traction here and need to concentrate to keep my footing. They drag me past the dripping lime tree. The sweet smell overrides their stale sweat for a moment.

The buildings loom in the half light. We crunch onto the gravel path. My feet plough into the little stones as they pull me round the corner of the Chapel. Is David here, or has he been relieved of his night watchman duties?

'David!'

'He's gone. There's no-one to hear you.'

I am out of breath when we reach the Family door of the Chapel, too blown to muster the strength to try to bolt when Archer is left to hold me. His Lordship rips down the notice that English Heritage has posted on the door and tears it to shreds.

Muck has his own key. Chill, damp air wafts into my face as he pushes the door open. He takes hold of my right arm again and they shove me inside. Archer stumbles on the uneven flags that I know so well. They push me into the nave. It's cold and dim. The dark stained glass of the window above the alter lets in very little of the approaching sunrise.

Muck takes hold of me by both shoulders and makes me turn round a full circle. Clara and Jason stand and watch.

'D'you see anything?' His breath is rancid on my face.

'The Chapel.'

He shakes me hard. 'Anything else?'

'He means spirits, Mack,' Clara says impatiently, 'can you still see ghosts?'

Ah. 'Not since you gave me that drink.'

She nods, satisfied.

'He's rational enough now,' Archer says.

I am? I truly hope not, because this nightmare has to stop soon.

I don't move when Muck prods me forward. He's a great wall of English flesh, but I am fitter, and Archer is little use. We shuffle around. It's all I can do with my hands tied. They start to swear at me.

Jason joins in, poking me with the canvas bundle. It has longish rods or something inside.

'You pathetic little runt,' I say to him.

I will beat him to a pulp if I get my chance over.

Jason jabs me in the stomach. I roar with frustration and stagger back. I lose my balance and sit down hard on the flags, jolting my spine and biting my tongue. Muck picks up my ankles and he and Archer start to drag me towards the stairs down to the crypt. It's only a matter of three or four yards; they manage eventually. At the top step, Archer takes my shoulders and Muck grabs me round the knees. They can't lift me up, so they bump me down the stairway, his Lordship grunting with the effort like a rootling pig.

'Watch his head,' Clara yelps.

It's not light enough to see well, but these steps were made for carrying an awkward deadweight down. I fight them all the way on the ragged decent, arching my back so that they have to take my full weight for the few seconds that I can manage it. They drop me at the foot of the stairs. The impact shudders through my hip and shoulder and grit gets into my eyes. I can't blink it out.

'Get up, Macready!' Muck says. He's leaning against the wall by my feet while he catches his breath.

They are both dripping with sweat; it runs in streaks down the dust that clings to their unshaven cheeks.

I can't open my left eye, tears pour out, but the grit hasn't dislodged. I squint up, bracing myself for a kick or a blow, but it doesn't come. We are all too tired to fight much.

Muck straightens up and nods to Archer. The barman bends down and helps me up with a fair imitation of humanity. As soon as he has set me on my feet, Muck turns me to face my wall.

There is a ladder propped against the hole I made. Are they going to bundle me through there and leave me there to die?

Don't think, must keep throwing my weight around – it's the only weapon I have.

Muck has let go. I slam into Archer and knock him off balance. I back away towards the steps. Jason presses himself against the wall to avoid having to touch me. The others stop shouting and come at me from either side. They both grab at once, hauling me back with both my feet planted firmly on the ground, so that my heels leave two deep furrows in the powdery rubble on the floor. The grit has come out of my eye, but I want to rub it.

I have to spit dust out before I can speak. 'Let me go.'

Muck knocks my feet out from under me. I sit heavily on the edge on one of the coffin benches behind me. He pushes me backwards. I twist onto my right side to avoid landing on my wrists. The stone is smooth. The cold and damp seep through my shirt.

Out there the sky is brightening. From this angle I can see it through the little window behind me. An inverted cruciform. Who would put a window like that into a Chapel? I tilt my head down onto my chest so that I can see what they are doing. Archer is unwrapping the canvas roll on the bench next to this one. It's a chef's knife roll. Tools of the trade.

Clara obscures my view. She grabs hold of my ankles.

'Please, please don't.'

'Come and hold his head down,' she says over her shoulder. I think she's speaking to Jason. I try to sit up. They mob me. Jason wrings his hands at the periphery of my vision. Archer sits on my ankles. It's Clara who comes and puts her hand under my chin and pulls my head back down onto the stone. I can barely swallow.

Archer is still holding the knife. A long knife, I believe it's called a boning knife. He butchers game in his kitchens. I can feel the chess piece digging into my hip. Game over. Robin wasn't so bad, not compared to this lot. The apricot sky is turning to pale yellow. Sunrise.

When I close my eyes I can see the window from outside, half hidden by grass. They can kill me, and I'll still be here. They can do what they want. It won't be as bad if I control the fear. A coward dies a thousands deaths, a brave man only one. Yes, my mother even had a homily to take me to my deathbed. It's going to hurt.

Muck starts to unbutton my shirt. The intimacy is appalling. His sweat stinks. He faffs with the second button, loses patience, rips my shirt open. Buttons patter onto the thick dust on the floor.

The fear swamps me, instantly and completely.

I throw myself sideways, slipping off the bench. I don't want to die. Pain shoots up from my kneecaps. Just this once I wish I wore kneepads. I brace myself for Archer to lunge with the knife, but he jerks to a stop. They all swivel round towards the stairs.

Someone is clapping. A slow hand clap. I wriggle so that I can see over the coffin bench.

'A heart for a heart. Is that it? Call the Earl back. Wall him up for another three centuries?'

It's Robin, though I can't see him clearly through the dust we've raised. I try to get to my feet but only manage to stagger and sit down on the bench.

Muck is as white as a sheet. 'Is this his priest?' he murmurs to Jason.

'All I see is my brother.'

A thin thread of sunshine slants down from the little window, falling in a pool of light at Robin's feet.

'It's too late. This had to be done by sunrise,' Clara says.

'Seriously, spells?' Robin asks.

'Not now you've interfered.'

'Well you know it wouldn't work, really. If you were sure, you'd have got on with cutting him up, never mind me.'

'You have no right to be in here,' Muck says. He sounds like he's being strangled. 'Can't you give Macready more myrrh, Clara?'

'Good grief,' Robin laughs, 'is that what you've given to him? Clairvoyance doesn't do it for me, you won't get rid of me like that. I'm no ghost. Nor, for that matter, is the Earl. That's why your exorcisms haven't worked. That and you looked up how to do it on the internet instead of asking a priest.'

He walks forward a couple of steps. The dust swirls around him, golden motes hang in a halo all around him. Of course he's not my guardian angel. People like me don't have angels. I don't have enough of a soul to interest an angel.

'I know what Jason sees,' Robin says, 'but I wonder what you are looking at right now, Clara?' His voice is like silk drifting on the cloud of dust, 'All those lives you helped to slip away before they'd even started?'

His shape flickers, I see the grotesque outline of a man-sized foetus, the red veins in the membrane pulsing over the soft skull, the unformed eyes just two black beads. Do the others see this?

Clara takes a step back onto her brother's foot. Muck swears at her.

Robin's face is in shadows again. 'You were all divine when you started off. It's the guilt that makes you human. I have come for Mack.'

I lever myself to my feet. I am shaking all over. The cold from the coffin bench still burns like frost up my side. I totter past Clara and her brother to take my chances with the priest. No-one tries to stop me.

I try not to look at Robin as I approach. I don't want to see his face clearly. I don't want it to keep changing. I turn round so he can untie me. He takes hold of the leash around my wrists. The knot has pulled tighter while I was fighting.

'How do they not know who you are?' I ask over my shoulder.

He pauses in his tussle with the dog lead. 'Oh, such blameless lives. They forget, though: lack of guilt is not lack of culpability.'

The stuff Clara gave me, it's confusing me.

'If you know about the Earl, can't you help us?' Clara asks. Her voice cracks so that she ends in a whisper.

'You want me to help you with the Earl?'

'You know how to get rid of him?'

'Not waking him in the first place would help. Once you had, you really should have taken better care not to let him take his heart back. So no, I can't help you. It's too late. You just have to let it run its course. Like measles.'

'That was the Earl? Last night?' I ask.

'Keep up, Mack,' says Robin.

'But Clara ran him over.'

'I doubt he felt it.'

He tugs the knot loose and drops the leash on the floor. I ease my shoulders.

'Clara, did you give me enough of that stuff to kill me?'

She shakes her head. All the same I prefer Robin's tricks to her witchery. I'll stay on this side. My feet remember the way up the stairs before I think to leave. The others hesitate, uncertain, afraid to follow too closely, probably. I hope so.

Robin pauses behind me. 'I don't know how you'll put the Earl back, but I shall keep Mack safe. You'll not use him. Oh, and a word from the wise, *gratis*,' Robin throws his voice like a stage actor, 'I wouldn't wait round here. Not with Himself out there. Run back to your house and your bunches of weeds, Clara, and pray he's read the same books you have, so he knows he's meant to be deterred.'

Robin follows me. They are too wary of him to come after us straight away.

The halfwits believe this stuff. They believe the black man is the revenant Earl, as though that solid, vicious brute could be an apparition. They would have killed me, gutted me like a traitor and given my heart to the Earl to trap him somehow. They think they can outwit that monster from last night.

...but I believed it too, down there in the crypt five minutes ago, with liquid fear vaporising and fogging my thoughts.

I hesitate at the Chapel door. Robin is silent for a moment next to me. Out in the cold dawn the sun is hidden now by glistening mackerel clouds. The river mist billows up to the Castle. Behind us the building waits, helpless. Over there, through the mist, on the other side of the Tyne, sirens sound, distort, retune and multiply.

I take a deep breath and step across the threshold of the Chapel. I feel I shall not set foot in here again.

I set off down the path to the Castle. The priest keeps pace with me.

'Robin, will you drive me somewhere?'

'Anywhere but Selkirk police station.'

'How about to just outside Selkirk, then?'

He smiles. 'You are not subtle enough to negotiate, Mack. I'll drive you as far north as I want to. I left the car on the other side of the Lord's bridge, down on the road.'

We walk past the path which leads to the lock-up. I wonder if my tools have been put back in there.

'Do you want to get them?' he asks as though I had spoken aloud.

'Won't need them where I'm going.' I keep walking.

He smiles at me as he holds the gate open for me under the sycamore tree. The padlock and chain are missing.

I leave his side to cross the cobbles in front of the Castle door. My key is on the bedside table in the spare bedroom. Or under forty tonnes of rubble, if the whole cottage came down. I touch the door. The wood feels smooth, familiar but altered. It glistens wet in the slanting light. Next to my hand a knot has sprouted a short sturdy twig with an oak leaf on it. The timber has come back to life. I look over my shoulder at Robin.

He holds his hands up, 'Not me this time. The Earl is back.'

I pat the door. I won't say my farewell out loud, but *Goodbye, Castle*. I would have liked to have gone up the pepper-pot tower one last time, stood where I stood for all those months when I thought I could be happy, but it's not to be.

I can hear Clara arguing two hundred yards away outside the Chapel.

'Better keep moving,' Robin says.

We step down into the mist and follow the narrow, slippery carriageway through the heavy green smell of the Indian Balsam and the deep shadows. Halfway down there is a square roped off with police tape. That must be where Juliet was attacked.

The stream flows loudly over the stones below the Lord's bridge. Farewell. At each small landmark I think, *this is the last time*.

My heart aches as I take my leave.

The only place to park down here is on the flat field by the Scouts' hut. I can't see Robin's car. He walks up to a rusty yellow Triumph Stag. I haven't been in one of these since I was little. Dad had one.

'What happened to your car?' Trust Robin to turn up in this old rust bucket when I need a decent set of wheels for the trip.

'Eh. Oh. Not sure.' He stares at it as though he's only just noticed it.

'How far will this thing get us?'

'It'll go as far as you want.'

'I'll pay for the fuel. These things are greedy.'

'Mack, when have you ever known me need to fill up?'

It's cold down here in the mist. It feels like being in a giant fishbowl. There is noise all around us at some distance. The emergency vehicles keep coming. Could I have helped if I'd stayed? They cannot really have been about to kill me. Surely?

'Come on,' he says. He gets in and reaches across to unlock my door.

It's very cramped. I have to push the passenger seat right back. He can't have had it more than a few hours and there are already three empty cans of Fanta in my footwell.

The engine sounds throaty. Is this all my imagination, too? The suspension makes my teeth rattle as we ride over the corrugations in the turf. The soft top is as draughty as I remember. He bumps the car onto the main road without looking for oncoming vehicles.

'Was that real, in the Chapel?'

'Why are you asking me? Would you trust my answer?'

'Please, Robin?'

He reaches down and takes hold of my wrist with his left hand. He brings it up until it is in front of nose. I have to move my head back, further away from my wrist, so my eyes can focus on the welt the dog leash cut into my skin.

'That man, last night. The black man. They all lost their senses. What sort of madness is that, some sort of group hysteria? I know these people. What's happened to them, Robin?'

'Who knows? As if they could be rid of him that easily, anyway.'

'But he was only a man. Insane, deranged, high on something, maybe. But a man.'

'You believe whatever comforts you, Mack. Most people do.'

'I want the truth. I nearly lost my life over this.'

'I would tell you, but you wouldn't believe me. You aren't ready for it.'

He can make me believe most things. 'Extraterrestrial?'

Robin snorts. 'He's been here as long as the human race.'

'For god's sake, you're as bad as they are.' I wish I hadn't flounced into the seat like that, it kicks back. Something digs into my ribs. I wriggle to get comfortable.

'Do you know who he is? The black man?'

'Of course.' Robin sounds smug.

'But you're not going to the police?'

'They would not be receptive to my insights.'

'He was extraordinarily strong. The way he bashed into the police car.'

'True. You experienced that much for yourself.'

'Do you know what's wrong with him?'

'He's hungry, that's all. He has specialist needs.'

'He murdered those men. You're not suggesting he's a cannibal?'

'The Earl eats souls. Extracting them, it's difficult. Like a piggy bank, you can rattle it a bit, but in the end you have to smash it to get the pennies out.'

I shut out the pictures of the frantic men last night. 'You really think I'll swallow anything, don't you?'

'Not convinced? It's a good story, though, isn't it?'

'He's killed two people.'

'Oh, a few more than that by now.'

The lights are green on the bridge, but we have to wait to let an ambulance overtake us. Some poor sod being rushed down to one of the big hospitals in Newcastle. There is a lot of police activity on the other side of the bridge. The footpath is closed and a police Land Rover is parked on the pavement. The mist swirls round figures in white plastic overalls.

'They've found that girl,' Robin remarks.

'What happened to her?'

'I thought you saw her. She was drowned, wasn't she?'

'That wasn't...'

He shrugs. 'You're the expert.'

The whole village is in chaos. We join a line of cars filing along the one way system. All the parking spaces have been taped off in the market place. People are gathered in small groups on the pavements. It's that sort of place.

What the hell?

'That's right, a small preview of Hell.'

'Will they be OK?'

'Who? Your friends at the Castle?' he asks.

'Yes.'

'The ones who were happily sacrificing you when I came along. You're welcome, by the way. For me saving your life.'

'I'm sure you had your reasons.'

'You're learning, Mack. I can't tell you if they'll be alright. It depends how long the Earl wants to go on for.' He blasts the horn at a car which has slowed to a stop in front of us while the driver speaks to someone on the pavement.

'What did you want with the heart?'

'Jason told you? Oh come on!' He slaps the steering wheel with frustration at the jam in front of us. Blue exhaust fumes fill the air behind us.

'Why were you so anxious to get hold of it?'

'Actually getting hold of it was the one thing I couldn't do. Much too potent for me to handle. Jason does have his uses. I wanted to look after it to stop all this happening. I intended to wall it up again and put Himself back to bed. I was looking after you.'

'Huh.'

'And why not? We're friends. But it will come to an end, this business with the Earl. He will have his fill, and all this will stop, and you can go back to mending the Castle. Providing you haven't antagonised everyone to the point they won't have you back.'

'I would report what they tried to do to me if I thought anyone would believe me.'

'True, no-one would believe you. Besides, no point making life more difficult than it already is. I thought you might like to visit your father until all this has blown over, seeing as my house isn't quite what you expected.'

'Robin, you know why I asked you to drive me to Scotland.'

'Kill two birds with one stone. Nothing wrong with visiting your father on the way. No need to rush into things.'

'Dad wouldn't see me.'

'There are police ahead. They're checking every car.'

'I was under arrest when that *thing* attacked the police car.'

'No-one's going to fret about that now.'

'Are they looking for me?'

'The men who arrested you are dead. Shush.' He winds his window down. 'Good morning, madam.'

The constable bends down to scope the interior. Her eyes rest on my torn shirt. She hands Robin a sheet with contact numbers on. She straightens up and pats the top of the canvas. 'Move on.'

Robin passes me the paper. 'See, you're small beer.'

'An incident…this is at the Castle. Yesterday. What else happened?'

'Yes. Well, like I said, we could do with letting things die down for a while.'

♖

The motor wails as we climb up Stagshaw bank, the cars spacing themselves out, mostly leaving us behind. Robin's missing the power of his Lexus. The exhaust pipe sounds like it's coming loose. Will it hold on 'til Scotland?

An hour and a half and we'll be there. This will be over soon. There are so many things he ought to explain I'm not sure where to begin. I don't suppose it matters.

'Why did you bugger off like that at the cottage and leave me to face the music?'

'Why are you handing yourself in?'

'It's not the same thing at all. You left me to deal with –'

'You know you won't see me again if you hand yourself in.'

'You can visit. We can play correspondence chess.'

'It's just so… I don't know, Mack, after all the trouble I've gone to.'

'You think I'm being *selfish*?'

'And ungrateful.'

'You tricked me.'

'It's the same principal as hypnotism, I couldn't do it if you didn't want me to. You are a willing subject.'

'Where the hell have you been living, anyway?'

'Here and there,' he says.

'You've been living rough? Why didn't you tell me? Why is this always one way? I tell you everything.'

We have risen out of the mist. The sun is pale through high clouds. The morning is fresh and clean.

I have more grievances.

'And why did you make me eat that sodding chicken?'

'You were hungry– it was all I could find there and then. I wanted to please you.'

'It was *raw*.'

'And I knew you couldn't eat it like that. I don't carry an oven with me. It was easier to let you see what you wanted.'

'I could die from salmonella.'

'Not since Clara's given you myrrh, surely. It's every bit as antiseptic as mercury.'

'You're unbelievable.'

'I do hope not.'

Actually I don't feel ill. Stiff and sore but not sick. It must be… it's eight now, nearly twelve hours. How long does it take?

♜

We are out of the Tyne valley. The top of Northumberland spreads in front of us. The wind whistles through the badly fitting roof. In the far north the sun touches the tops of the Southern Uplands. I am going home.

Robin fumbles around in his jacket pocket. 'I found this at the cottage, by the way. Thought you might want it.' He passes me my mobile.

'Thanks.' I sound sulky even to myself.

'I don't know if you'll be able to hear her any more.'

I won't rise to the bait. I watch the distant hills sink behind the nearer hillside as we motor down to the Rede valley. I close my eyes and feign sleep for a few minutes. It's not convincing. The car is too uncomfortable.

'Will it wear off?'

'Oh, I though you were asleep. I would have woken you for the Border.'

'Clara's potion. Will it stop me…' I really was about to say 'seeing ghosts'.

'I don't know if it's permanent. Does it bother you?'

I shrug and look out of the window. 'I'm not sure what's changed.'

'They've cauterised your psychic connection.'

'My what?'

'They've taken a chemical cosh to your psychic ability, your clairvoyance. A herbal castration –'

'I get the picture. I didn't even know I was clairvoyant.'

'Yes you did. You just didn't want to admit it.'

I

White clouds pour over Carter Bar towards us as we climb out of Northumberland. The car is too old to make the hill at the speed Robin wants. We scream along in fourth gear.

I close my eyes. Mum's voice says when I open them we'll be back in Scotland.

'Do you want me to pull over at the top?'

I open my eyes and we have left England grey and grim behind us. Scotland lies in front, in brilliant spring sunshine. Robin takes the turning for Hawick and we follow the road around the hillside down to little valleys where the cottages are all scaled to men, not lords. Two front windows on either side of the door with two dormers above in the little attic bedrooms, like the house I lived in until ten years ago. When I was little, I used to think that was the only way a house should be: how would you fit a family into anything else?

The soil here is a rich brown, almost purple in some lights when it lies ploughed. Now a velvet green spreads over the curves that I know like my own hand. I drink in the landscape of fields and volcanoes as he drives us through this dream.

'Some people can manage, of course. Being cooped up, never missing what they don't know.'

'Give it a rest, Robin.'

'Just saying.'

'Well don't.'

He's right. How will I cope with being locked up?

'And you really won't see me again,' he says.

'Not much of a friend, then are you?'

'It's the way things are.'

I have the feeling in the pit of my stomach that I always got on Monday mornings on the way to school. The yoke of guilt I took up ten years ago seems quite light compared to what's ahead. I don't know where to begin. I need to turn myself in, but I don't even know what words to use so that I won't be misunderstood.

'Are you going to tell them that you killed your uncle?'

'It's close enough to the truth.'

'So is, "I had nothing to do with his death." Putting yourself behind another wall doesn't unbuild the one you made.'

All he says is true, in a way, and it's making me feel worse. I can't dwell on it, or he'll work harder at persuading me. I can't be sure I'm even feeling this the way it really is; Robin might be controlling what I experience again. How do I know this panic is real?

'How do you know that anything is real, Mack? You just have to trust your senses.'

'Stop doing that.'

'Stop thinking so loudly, then.'

'I'm apprehensive, that's all. I need to get this right. And if I'm punished for an approximation of what happened, it will still be closer to the truth than the way I left it ten years ago. Everyone thinks I'm guilty. My own father…'

What's the point? He already knows.

♟

We drive out of Hawick, past the headquarters for the Lothian and Borders police.

'I could drop you off here. They are probably better equipped to deal with your... confession... No?'

He smiles broadly and takes us off towards Selkirk.

'It's not weakness, Mack. Truth is a majority decision, paradigms shift, perceptions alter. Your truth is different to the rest of the world's, and frankly the rest of world doesn't care. It was ten years ago. Memories are short. The truth only exists when it's put into words, and you can chose any words you like so long as no-one disagrees.'

I have nothing to say to him. I look out of the window. I love this stretch of countryside. I allowed myself to be banished. Maybe they would have come round if I'd stayed. Maybe I should have tried harder to see Mum. Too late now.

'The past doesn't exist, you see, Mack. You can say what you like about it. It's like trying to slander a dead man.'

'You're wrong. What happens happened, even if there's no-one to remember it.'

'So you keep it behind a glass wall and gaze at it everyday and let it rule your life?'

I suppose that is what I've done.

We drive in silence. I am trying to keep my mind blank, not let a chink show that he can weasel into and crack wide open. We have come to Hillside Terrace. Past Dad's golf club. Past my old tennis courts. Almost there.

'Which house does your dad live in? This one?'

'Number fourteen.'

He pulls up at the roadside.

'Why not go in?'

He's probably at work by now. I wonder if he still works for the same company. 'I've told you, he won't want to see me. I disgraced the family. I drove my mother to an early grave. He blames me for everything. He thought I was a murderer.'

The pain of my father's disgust and anger squeezes my heart. I don't want to see him either. He has as much to be forgiven for as I do.

'You've already served your time for manslaughter, Mack, these last ten years.' His voice is soft, compelling, so sincere.

I will need my wits about me at the police station. What if they try to make me confess to hurting Mel? Think about something else, something better. 'That was my room, on the right.'

'Nice view.'

'It was.'

Dad hasn't changed the curtains.

'Forgive yourself.'

I can't. I let my chin rest on my chest. I could go to sleep right now.

And wake up a couple of hours later a hundred miles from here. I glance round at Robin. He seems to be nodding off too.

I release the seatbelt catch. 'I can walk from here.'

'There's no need,' he says quickly, sitting up and starting the engine.

He pulls out into the quiet road.

'Take the next right, then right again at the bottom.'

It takes less than two minutes. We are here. Really here. He parks on the roadside rather than down by the doors.

'Do you want me to come in with you?'

Actually I do. 'I'll be fine.'

The police station is seems even smaller than I remember it. There's not a lot of crime in Selkirk.

'You're sure, Mack?'

I nod. Maybe it's best. He can drive off without a backward glance.

I turn in my seat to face him one last time. He is staring straight out of the windscreen. Yesterday I was frightened of him. Now he's just a sad old man.

'Thank you. It's been very *interesting* knowing you. I wish you weren't doing this ultimatum thing; I'd be happy to stay in contact… Anyway, thanks for the lift.'

'Mack–'

I should just go, get the pain over with like pulling off a plaster.

'– I need you.'

'And I need a friend, too, right now. It's you who has decided this will mean you can't see me anymore.'

'You don't understand. I'm the same as the Earl.'

'Oh, forget it. I've had enough bullshit from you to last me a lifetime. Goodbye, Robin.'

The indignation helps. I nurture it as I get out of the car and slam the door behind me. I stride down to the doors of the police station without looking back. The palms of my hands are wet as I push open the door. I go up the hatch and press the buzzer.

♜

I was expecting more of a fuss – it's Saturday, though. I've been in here for three quarters of an hour. The interview room is smaller than I remember, too, less formal. Nothing like the windowless cube where they took me after I saw that poor girl jump off the Castle.

I didn't explain what I am here for very well. I was expecting Rafferty, not some kid younger than me. They'd not heard about Melissa or Uncle Jimmy. I can't remember exactly what I said. I gabbled. I think I may have a bit of a fever; my eyes are burning, and I feel very light-headed. I hope it's not the chicken.

The sun has crept across the lino to the edge of the table.

♜

The door opens. I must have nodded off.

Shit. 'What are you doing here?'

'The lad on the front desk said I could come in and talk

to you.' Robin sits down opposite me. He looks gaunt, and his skin resembles a wrung-out dishcloth.

'You are free to go, you know. They haven't even interviewed you,' he says.

He's right. How much easier it would be to leave.

He lifts his head, seems to be savouring the air.

'Whatever you're about to say, Robin, please don't.'

'You're afraid. Afraid to confess.'

'I was fine before you came in. You're like some sort of demon, egging me on to do the wrong thing –'

The stuffy little room is suddenly icy. My mouth is dry.

I see him, really see him, for a moment. His eyes are black, fathomless slits opening onto a dark inhuman void.

'No!'

'I knew you'd work it out in the end.'

There isn't even an emergency buzzer in here. He's between me and the door. He's sucking the air out of the room.

He smiles.

It's the most terrible thing I have ever seen.

I knew it all along, I must have. Ice water runs down my back. Christ, he even told me so in the car. I can hear my teeth chattering. It's me who dressed him as a priest, me and my infernal craving to confess.

'It's alright, Mack. You're having a panic attack.'

I can't breathe. I can hear the racket I'm making, but I can't stop. My chest is convulsing. The chair is on the floor. I put my back to the wall and try to creep round him, but it's been so long since I drew breath that I'm losing my peripheral vision.

I'm on the wiry carpet – did I fall? He is standing over me, taller than the room. His description of the Earl comes into my mind, smashing bodies to get at the soul. Help me.

He's beside me on the floor before I can crawl away, his arm pinning me round my shoulders, singing the song my mother used to sing to me long before I understood the words.

Help me!

'Cat got your tongue?'

'*Our Father, who art in…*'

'What was that, Mack?'

I struggle to fling his arm off my shoulders, but it weighs me down.

'Let me go!'

'You know, I thought I would. I've grown fond of you… well, as fond of my host as I can be. But in the end, I just couldn't let you go, Mack. You have the most wonderful dichotomy I have ever experienced. Your guilt is so profound it's matched only by your ability to do wrong. A perpetual source of nourishment. And you wonder why I look after you.' He hugs me to him like I'm a rag doll.

I am here to do the right thing. 'Please don't stop me.'

'I have no intention of stopping you. I drool with expectation. And you have no more true intention of giving yourself up than you have of flying.'

Someone will come in here soon.

'Jason, too?'

'What was that?'

'And my neighbours. You can't be doing this to all of us.'

'That's right, Mack. You do it to yourselves. You and your guilt.'

He's going to break my ribs he's hugging me so close. He has no heart beat, but he seems to pulse as he squeezes me.

'Jason? Why? And what did my neighbours ever do to be guilty about?'

'Jason has his brother's blood on his hands, never lifted a finger to save him when he needed the sludge form his bones to get well. And your neighbours…' He's squeezing me to death.

'Ah –'

'What's that, Mack? I was telling you about your neighbours. That is *delicious*. They are guilty about the day some drunk crashed into their car and mashed their children. That is something to be savoured. No repentance, no possible absolution, because it *wasn't their fault!*'

A shudder passes through him. He makes me part of it, clamped against him.

'Delectable. Nom nom nom.'

My whole body revolts; I want to wash off my own skin.

'What's the matter, Mack? You wanted to know all about me. It's in my nature to enjoy my food.'

My chin is resting on his arm, his bones pressing into my Adam's apple. Original sin.

'Yes, Mack. Sin.'

The phone rings.

My phone.

Robin drops me. I land on all fours and scrabble for my pocket.

The room is very still. I can't look up.

He is shaking, sending shock waves across the intervening inches. My fingers are too numb to find the buttons on my phone.

It doesn't matter.

She's here.

Here in front of me.

Robin makes a noise like an injured dog, half growl, half whine. I avert my eyes from the shape that is too bulky and too tall for the image I call Robin. It nags at the corner of my eye.

I turn to face her.

Whatever Mel was, she's not that any more. She has been such a gentle companion, these past ten years, a thing of light and shadow, but now...

'Are you in there?' I stare into the hollow sockets, but there is nothing. This corpse, this trailing body… it can't be all that's left of her.

'*I waited for you to find me, but you have chosen him.*' It's her voice, but I hear it in my head.

She reaches out for me. Robins growls louder.

'*I am lost.*'

I bump into the table when I take a step back.

I… I… I…

Her hands are cold and dry, and the withered skin gives a little as she grips my fingers. The cuts on my hands flare into a throbbing mass of putrid tissue as she pokes her fingers inside my skin.

No.

She won't let go. I cannot get away. The stinking, rotting flesh wraps around me. I try to hide inside, to shut myself away, but she's crawled inside my skull, foetid whispers sucking at my brain, pressing into my eardrums until they split and she can dribble the poison into them.

'*You will suffer like I suffer, Mack.*'

There are other voices, fast and loud, shrieking round me. The cacophony makes my ears bleed. The pain in my head is not possible. Someone please help me.

♜

They found me on the cobbles by the Castle door, but it was too late, the septicaemia had spread too far. I have lost my hands, I cannot speak. The damage to my spinal cord is irreversible.

They have moved me out of the intensive care ward into this side ward. Pastel green walls, thin curtains, clear sunlight. Wires and a monitor screen. On the cabinet next to the bed, they have laid a shrivelled plait of rushes and a black chess piece, a little lead castle.

They play that bloody tune every day because it makes my ECG leap and my blood pressure soar. I think he told them about it. Most of the doctors can see him. They don't know what he is. There's more than enough guilt in this place to keep him satisfied; he doesn't need me. He will tell them one day soon that I am ready to die, and they will let me.

And Melissa will be waiting for me in Hell.

ACKNOWLEDGEMENTS

I am deeply grateful to the members of the real Trust. Special thanks to Chris Clennell, who has offered so much information, help and advice, not to mention ghost hunts. Also thanks to Frank Giecco for giving me access to the crypt and to Robert Dodds, the stonemason.

I would to thank the lecturers at Northumbria University, especially Steve Chambers, without whom this manuscript would never have been submitted. Thanks, as always, to my supervisor, Tony Williams.

Apologies to the third Earl of Derwentwater; may he rest in peace.

In memoriam Paul Beniams: you shouldn't be here.

✗

Mack's last chess game was taken from the commentary on the 1939 game between Max Euwe and Paul Keres in Burgess G., Nunn J. and Emms J., (2010), *The Mammoth Book of the World's Greatest Chess Games*, London: Robinson, pp 170-175.